Taphophilia

– TRAK E SUMISU –

An environmentally friendly book printed and bound in England by
www.printondemand-worldwide.com

This book is made entirely of chain-of-custody materials

www.fast-print.net/store.php

TAPHOPHILIA
Copyright © Trak E Sumisu 2014

A catalogue record for this book is available from the British Library

ISBN 978-178456-002-7

First published 2014 by
FASTPRINT PUBLISHING
Peterborough, England.

Acknowledgements

I would like to thank everyone involved in enabling me to write this book. The list is long but there are a few who deserve special mention: the strangely permissive friends of my youth, who either shared my peculiar and sometimes macabre interests or were too frightened to resist (great times, long remembered) and those whose invaluable assistance was given after the ink had dried.

So my thanks go to Phil, who put up with most of my darker inclinations; Nick (wherever you are now) and the other members of the graveyard crew; Franz, who regularly and patiently listens to me murder his mother tongue; Angie, who diligently corrects the few (Ha!) grammatical errors I make in my own tongue; my beta-readers; my preliminary proofreaders; and Matthew, my fiercest critic. Taphophilia could not exist without you!

I would also like to thank Sophie, who kindly allowed me to use one of my favourite photographs of her from one of our more interesting photo shoots. She is the kind of girl you might hope to meet one day in a graveyard; if you are lucky enough, you will.

TAPHOPHILIA
TRAK E SUMISU

"The will to work must dominate, for art is long
and time is brief"

　　　　　　　　　　　- Charles Baudelaire

Prologue

By Way Of Explanation

I have always underestimated women.

When I was sixteen years old, a group of school friends and I borrowed a Ouija board from a girl I was seeing. I was only seeing her. We had not engaged in anything even close to resembling sex and, as my memory serves me, I think I had perhaps only touched her tits twice. To be honest, I cannot even remember her name, but I remember her Ouija board.

It was one of those lame, boxed Ouija boards, sometimes referred to as a 'talking board' – allegedly invented way back in the 1890s by William Fuld – although the one we used was made by the family games manufacturer John Waddington of Leeds in the 1960s. We bit the bullet one dark evening in October (as close as we could get to Hallowe'en) and plunged ourselves into the 'world of the occult'.

We had been warned about the dark powers of the Ouija by various people. Some of my school friends (who hadn't been invited to the 'séance') were especially damning. They told tales of possession by dangerous entities, mysterious occurrences and reports of some 'dabblers' who had been driven insane by information gleaned from the 'other side'. To my friends and me, it sounded exactly the sort of thing we should experience and there was a great deal of both fearful excitement and anxious anticipation involved.

The use of the Ouija board in the 1973 William Friedkin film of William Peter Blatty's *The Exorcist* is shown to be directly responsible for the demonic possession of the character Regan MacNeil, played by the fourteen-year-old actress Linda Blair. In the film, Regan encounters a character called Captain Howdy via the Ouija board and suddenly undergoes dramatic and violent changes to her personality.

Having not seen the film back then, most of us thought it would be a bit of fun.

The events of that night remain firmly ingrained in my memory for a number of reasons.

The board itself is a simple thing constructed from a rectangle of thick card on which the letters of the alphabet, the numbers zero through to nine and the words YES, NO and GOODBYE are printed. I seem to recall the board we used also depicted a smiley sun and a more seriously pensive crescent moon. The plastic planchette that usually comes with these boards was missing, so we used a glass tumbler instead.

We had arranged to meet at my friend Kevin Turton's house, principally because his parents – unlike those of the rest of us – went out religiously every Thursday evening, leaving the house adult-free. Kev had already cleared it with his folks for a few of his friends to visit that particular evening. He had, though, been economical with the truth.

In total, fourteen of us turned up. If I include our host, Kev, this resulted in fifteen loud, brash and hormonally unbalanced teenagers crammed into the less-than-spacious kitchen of a three-bedroom semi, clustered around a guttering candle and a Ouija board on a rickety table designed to seat four people.

I personally believe that had we stuck to our original

decision that girls *would not* be allowed to take part that evening, it would not have ended as disastrously as it did. Once again, though, the machinations of the masculine towards the possibility of pleasurable penetrative action afterwards swayed the vote.

There were eleven boys and four girls, including my girlfriend, the custodian of the board. We rolled down the blind at the kitchen window, turned off the light and, with a degree of nervous anticipation, lit a single, solitary, long, white tapered candle, stolen specially for the occasion from the local Methodist church. We were in high spirits, an unfortunate turn of phrase under the circumstances, but it described our outlook that evening exactly.

Nothing happened at first. Yes, there was the usual horseplay as someone or other pushed the glass so forcibly that it was patently obvious it was human, rather than spiritual, intervention. Someone else, Nick I believe, let out a blood-curdling scream that resulted in most of the girls becoming agitated and threatening to leave, but that was about the extent of the action initially. We were just having a laugh at the expense of the dead.

Things changed, I believe, when we began to get bored. Steve was becoming more interested in taking one of the girls upstairs to Kev's bedroom than he was in any messages from the hereafter. It was he, though, who first noticed how cold the room suddenly became.

Now, looking back with my rational head on my shoulders, I dare say I could come up with half a dozen scenarios as to how or why the temperature might have dipped so dramatically, and they wouldn't even have included the possibility of group hysteria and/or suggestibility. However, at the time it was, we all believed, a 'supernatural phenomenon' and the catalyst for the events that followed, imagined or otherwise.

The glass moved.

Only Matt and I were physically touching it at the time. It moved to GOODBYE. Steve spoke first.

"Fucking hell, look at me breath. Look how cold it is in here!"

The glass moved again and more fingers jumped onto its upturned base, testing whether the movement was as a result of kinetic force or something altogether otherworldly. We did not have to wait long to find out.

Emily, the one girl whose name I can categorically remember, shouted out each letter as the glass slid over it.

"S... H... E... K... N... O... W... I... T...."

We all wanted to ask the same questions: "Who knows it? What does she know?" The glass began to move again.

"S... H... E... K... N... O... W... A... L... L...."

The message was too vague. It alluded to something and yet, at the same time, fuck all.

We were getting into the swing of the process, regardless of how bogus it seemed.

"Who knows?" shouted Watty, the youngest member at our gathering.

The glass moved to the word YES.

It made little sense. We pushed the board for more answers.

"Who are you?"

"J... A... K...." It stopped but then started again.

"J... A... K... E...."

I must admit I thought *that* was fucking spooky. To pick out a random part name was one thing, but to have the same letters pointed out again and for it to actually make more sense was uncanny and certainly too elaborate for any of us around the table to have attempted. We were, however, none the wiser.

"Who is Jake?" I asked.

"M... A... N...."

The answer was met with derision and nervous laughter. The glass began moving again, unprompted.

"G... O... N... E... D... E... A... D...."

That was when one of the other girls started freaking out. She didn't like it, apparently. It was unnatural, it was scaring her and she was convinced that we should stop before something terrible happened. We were messing with unholy powers. Yeah, yeah, yeah, we all thought – in hindsight, we should have listened to her.

Watty ignored her, keen to continue.

"Jake, is it you who is gone? Are you gone? Are you dead?"

"Y... O... U...." Emily gasped as she read out the letters, her face ashen in the flickering candlelight.

"This isn't very funny anymore."

"Who?" I asked, beginning to feel very creeped out by the whole situation myself. The response was similar to the one given at the very beginning.

"S... H... E... K... N... O... W... S...."

We demanded to know the name of the person, the 'she' that knew. The playfulness had left the kitchen; we all were deadly serious. We were not prepared for the response, and neither was Emily.

"E... M...."

There was no way for certain that we could know that the board was referring to Emily, not from just the first two letters of her name. Emily herself needed less convincing.

"Oh, my God! It's talking about me! It's talking about me! Fuck this! I'm out of here!"

We tried to calm her down, to make her consider that perhaps the two letters were not the beginning of her name but someone's initials. That only made matters worse: her surname was Madeley.

"My grandma used to call me Em. I don't like this! It's fucking scaring me!"

Once she started panicking, the other girls in the group became lairy, threatening to leave if we didn't turn the lights on and stop messing around. It was obvious that our evening was not going to end according to a number of very carefully laid plans, which included me getting my fingers wet with whatever her name was.

Emily started hyperventilating, her eyes wide. The glass started to move again.

This time Kev shouted out the letters as, one by one, they were methodically indicated. Emily was in no fit state to do anything.

"W... I... L... L... D... I... E...."

We should have stopped at that point. We should have heeded the warnings of our peers, but the board was intoxicatingly provocative. It dared us – most of us – to press on in the pursuit of the randomly delivered, often-indecipherable knowledge. I cannot state with confidence who asked the last question, but in the years that have passed since that night twenty-two years ago I have convinced myself it was our host, Kevin Turton.

"Who?" The questioner sounded exasperated, as were most of us. "Who will die?"

The answer did not come from the board but from somewhere deep inside Emily. It was an old, guttural, filth-flecked voice that belonged in the throat of a chain-smoking harridan, not a fifteen-year-old terrified schoolgirl. She uttered one word. A name.

"Watty."

After that the evening descended in chaos. All of the girls, including Emily, who was in floods of tears, were inconsolable and we had to arrange for the parents of one of them to collect her from Kev's house. Later, Emily just vanished. Nobody saw her leave and she certainly didn't tell anyone she was going. Nick wanted to burn the board, much to the annoyance of my girlfriend, whose name, annoyingly, still eludes me. Kev just begged for everything to be returned to normal before his parents came home. Only Watty appeared to be calm, which, under the circumstances, was quite unbelievable.

I would have taken it much worse, I think.

He died three weeks later.

I watched my friend die in the gutter by the side of the road, his blood running into a dark, greedy, nearby drain. It was an accident. His fault. He had foolishly run, without looking, after getting off a number 48 bus, straight into the path of an oncoming car. It threw him about fifteen feet in the air; this was perhaps a convulsive reaction, a result of massive trauma to his nervous system.

They tried to save him, but his injuries (internal injuries) were too severe.

It was a peculiar experience watching him die. I felt strangely detached; I felt separated from the scene being played out in front of me, even though he was a friend and as a friend we had shared many childhood adventures together. None of it mattered as his life ebbed away. Each tattered, laboured breath, each exhalation was an expulsion of crimson fluid, getting darker and darker.

I remember the voice of a woman standing behind me; she was just another in the throng of onlookers watching the last moments of a young boy's life. She said to someone (I'm unsure whom): "Once they start bleeding from the mouth they are as good as dead." That was how I knew Watty was going to die. I believed her, even though I had no fucking idea who she was.

His eyes were open, although I am certain he could no longer see anything. He couldn't see me or Steve, who was just a few feet away on the kerb. He could not see the expression of absolute horror on the face of the man cradling him, a man who would have Watty's death on his conscience for years to come because he was the driver of the car that hit him. He could no longer see the sky, a cloudless, deep azure blue canopy above him or the lazy late autumn sun threatening to sink towards the horizon.

I never blamed Emily for what happened to Watty anymore than I blamed the Ouija board or the girl who lent it to us or even ourselves for seeking communion with the dead in the first place. I didn't even blame the dead, who received Watty with open arms, there, by the roadside, once his last breath had rattled in his throat.

But Emily knew. We had all underestimated her. I sometimes wonder if that was where my life really began.

I certainly know when it ended.

Chapter 1

Grey. Grey. Grey.

The monotonous sound of the clock above the fireplace served to remind me of my own inevitable, relentless, slow trudge towards oblivion.

Sigh.

Sighing had replaced what few words we ever exchanged. Beyond that there was only the silence.

Silence.

That and the clock.

Tick - tick -

tick - tick - tick - tick - tick - tick - tick - tick - tick - tick -
tick - tick - tick - tick - tick - tick - tick - tick - tick - tick -
tick - tick - tick - tick - tick - tick - tick - tick - tick - tick -
tick - tick - tick - tick - tick - tick - tick - tick - tick - tick -
tick - tick - tick - tick - tick - tick - tick - tick - tick - tick -
tick - tick - tick - tick - tick - tick - tick - tick - tick - tick -
tick - tick - tick - tick - tick - tick - tick - tick - tick - tick -
tick - tick - tick - tick - tick - tick - tick - tick - tick - tick -
tick - tick - tick - tick - tick - tick - tick - tick - tick - tick -
tick - tick - tick - tick - tick - tick - tick - tick - tick - tick -
tick - tick - tick - tick - tick - tick - tick - tick - tick - tick -
tick - tick - tick - tick - tick - tick - tick - tick - tick - tick -
tick - tick - tick - tick - tick - tick - tick - tick - tick - tick -
tick - tick - tick - tick - tick - tick - tick - tick - tick - tick -
tick - tick - tick - tick - tick - tick - tick - tick - tick - tick -
tick - tick - tick - tick - tick - tick - tick - tick - tick - tick -
tick - tick - tick - tick - tick - tick - tick - tick - tick - tick -
tick - tick - tick - tick - tick - tick - tick - tick - tick - tick -
tick - tick - tick - tick - tick - tick - tick - tick - tick - tick -
tick - tick - tick - tick - tick - tick - tick - tick - tick - tick -
tick - tick - tick - tick - tick - tick - tick - tick - tick - tick -
tick - tick - tick - tick - tick - tick - tick - tick - tick - tick -
tick - tick - tick - tick - tick - tick - tick - tick - tick - tick -
tick - tick - tick - tick - tick - tick - tick - tick - tick - tick -
tick - tick - tick - tick - tick - tick - tick - tick - tick - tick -
tick - tick - tick - tick - tick - tick - tick - tick - tick - tick -
tick - tick - tick - tick - tick - tick - tick - tick - tick - tick -
tick - tick - tick - tick - tick - tick - tick - tick - tick - tick -
tick - tick - tick - tick - tick - tick - tick - tick - tick - tick -
tick - tick - tick - tick - tick - tick - tick - tick - tick - tick -
tick - tick - tick - tick - tick - tick - tick - tick - tick - tick -
tick - tick - tick - tick - tick - tick - tick - tick - tick - tick -
tick - tick - tick - tick - tick - tick - tick - tick - tick - tick -
tick - tick - tick - tick - tick - tick - tick - tick - tick - tick -
tick - tick - tick - tick - tick - tick - tick - tick - tick - tick -
tick - tick - tick - tick - tick - tick - tick - tick - tick - tick -

tick - tick - tick - tick - tick - tick - tick - tick - tick - tick -
tick - tick - tick - tick - tick - tick - tick - tick - tick - tick -
tick - tick - tick - tick - tick - tick - tick - tick - tick - tick -
tick - tick - tick - tick - tick - tick - tick - tick - tick - tick -
tick - tick - tick - tick - tick - tick - tick - tick - tick - tick -
tick - tick - tick - tick - tick - tick - tick - tick - tick - tick -
tick - tick - tick - tick - tick - tick - tick - tick - tick - tick -
tick - tick - tick - tick - tick - tick - tick - tick - tick - tick -
tick - tick - tick - tick - tick - tick - tick - tick - tick - tick -
tick - tick - tick - tick - tick - tick - tick - tick - tick - tick -
tick - tick - tick - tick - tick - tick - tick - tick - tick - tick -
tick - tick - tick - tick - tick - tick - tick - tick - tick - tick -
tick - tick - tick - tick - tick - tick - tick - tick - tick - tick -
tick - tick - tick - tick - tick - tick - tick - tick - tick - tick -
tick - tick - tick - tick - tick - tick - tick - tick - tick - tick -
tick - tick - tick - tick - tick - tick - tick - tick - tick - tick -
tick - tick - tick - tick - tick - tick - tick - tick - tick - tick -
tick - tick - tick - tick - tick - tick - tick - tick - tick - tick -
tick - tick - tick - tick.

We used to read on those evenings when we found ourselves together in the same room. Sometimes I would read and she'd surf the internet; sometimes she'd read and I surfed the internet. I never knew what websites she visited and, frankly, I had long since passed caring. I didn't care if she knew which websites I visited either. We didn't have many secrets that either of us was that interested in anymore.

We hardly ever went out – together.

We rarely did anything together; even watching television together occasionally was actually more of a novelty than we could both usually cope with.

Sex was also occasional, perfunctory, dutiful, dull. Often I struggled to remember the last time I'd seen her fully naked or the last time I'd ejaculated inside her. I think in the end we both pretended to climax. To get it out of the way. To get it over with.

I had been married for nineteen years, three months, one week, two days, fifteen hours, four minutes, thirty-six seconds – and counting.

Pointless.

It had got to the stage where I could see nothing for us beyond the next day, marked out in the fabric of time by the ticking of that fucking clock.

She used to think that my late nights and evenings away were connected with my occupation. Understandable. It was perfectly feasible. To be fair, sometimes they were, but more often than not they were excursions to experiences that I desperately needed in order to halt the decay, to impede the slow mental and physical putrefaction, to stop the atrophy.

According to the various membership cards in my wallet I was – and, strangely, still am – a member of a chess club, a photography club, a ramblers' association, a cinema club, a public speakers' group and a literary society. The truth was that while I was a fully paid-up member of each I hardly attended any of the meetings. I used them only as excuses to escape the mind-numbing boredom of living with a woman I had begun to regularly disregard.

Chess is a Machiavellian extravagance that I have never had the patience to learn. Rambling is a pointless exercise that attracts people with so little imagination that they cannot visualise the countryside unless its stench is shoved forcibly up their hairy nostrils. I despise cinema (apart from classic film noir). The thought of addressing an audience would at one time have thrilled me, but after years standing up in front of successive generations of indifferent, noisy, lousy brats I really could no longer be bothered.

I do like photography, though, as can be seen from the selection of images I have chosen to accompany this narrative, and I've always enjoyed literature. Specifically, I like poetry. When I am in the mood for nothing else I read Baudelaire; *The Flowers of Evil* is my favourite collection. There is something about his poetry that has always resonated within my soul. (Shortly after the publication of *Les Fleurs du Mal* par Charles Baudelaire on 25 June 1857 [Poulet-Malassis Et De Broise, Libraires-éditeurs, 4 Rue de Buci, Paris 1857] *Le Figaro* published a vitriolic review denouncing the poet and his 'obscene' work. In July of the same year Baudelaire and his publisher, Auguste Poulet-Malassis, were prosecuted for their 'insult to public decency' and fined; they were ordered to remove six poems from the edition, a prohibition that lasted until 1949.)

My job, like my life, was fairly ordinary; one might even say it was boring. The only real challenges came from battering down the ambitious endeavours of the newly qualified over-enthusiastic female teachers that sadly proliferated my profession. They thought – they *believed* – that they wanted my job. They imagined that I was jealously guarding my position against the inevitability of their professional advancement. Actually, as they eventually discovered, they were welcome to it.

Newly Qualified Teachers: it had all changed since my first appointment.

Now they swarm out of university, proudly clutching their PGCEs to their breasts, imagining that they will be the ones that will make a difference – just like the NQTs that they have replaced and the ones that will replace them. They will not make one iota of difference. They will teach, they will get married, they will give birth to the next generation of children to be fed into the education machine; and many years from now they will watch joyfully as their daughters graduate from university, proudly clutching the equivalent of a PGCE to *their* breasts.

So it goes on.

Actually, it wasn't always pointless. Very occasionally my mundane existence would be illuminated by the achievements of a pupil (or ex-pupil) or brought, just as quickly, into sharper focus by one who, for no discernible reason, had suddenly gone off the rails. We all get to that juncture in our lives at some point, I think.

Intervention used to be commonplace in my school. In the last year there were eleven permanent exclusions. That wasn't good. The school had already been highlighted as one that was failing, so merely removing the shit didn't improve the situation. It didn't work like that. Sadly, it's never that simple.

For every ignorant, violent, belligerent cunt the school excluded they had to admit a similarly ignorant, violent, belligerent cunt who had been excluded from another failing school. The process was futile. It was like a huge recycling programme, where the crap spat out by the worst sections of society was passed around like an explosive parcel with a short fuse while someone tried to figure out what to do with them. Invariably, they exploded and took countless other innocent lives with them.

Questions always arose, like how *best* to educate them, how *best* to turn them into worthwhile members of society, or how *best* to prevent them ruining the lives of everyone they came into contact with. Much like doctors tired of treating contagious, repulsive diseases, we chose to believe that prevention was better than cure and we tried to integrate and teach; we failed at that and so adopted new strategies, reluctantly turned to intervention and finally exclusion – until the threat had passed or been passed on.

One day, someone will figure out a different way to deal with the shit. By then, though, the state schools will have closed down and been replaced by Pay-As-You-Learn academies, and the private owners will have to deal with it.

Teaching wasn't how I wanted to spend the rest of my time: drifting from one day to the next, ticking off dates on the calendar until that inevitable time came when it would no longer matter anymore. I always knew there had to be more to life.

Most days I felt like I was already dead, drifting in and out on the periphery of everyone else's vision, like a phantom.

Perhaps that's why I spent so much time in graveyards.

Here's a word to the wary about that which prevents most from exploring the darker places that man's vanity has constructed to carry forward the message that he once existed. Ghosts, those so-called ethereal spirits of the dead, do not haunt graveyards or cemeteries. Those places serve only as a repository for the mortal remains of the dead, for the dry, rotten, mouldering bones that lie shattered in the ground, beneath the earth and stone.

The spirit – if indeed that is what a ghost is – exits the body at the *point of death,* wherever that might be; it does not hang around in the corners near the lifeless husk until the remains are buried before deciding to materialise. How do I know this? I don't – for certain – but having spent far too many hours in these 'places of dread' I can confirm that I have never heard or seen anything that would make me believe – or even consider the possibility – that ghosts would choose cemeteries over other locations to wander around and haunt.

That means of course (and you have my word on this) that you are free to explore these bone yards, free of expectation and anticipation or fear and dread. You may take your time wandering around the headstones, reading the ancient and modern inscriptions – perhaps wondering who Justice T. Lennon might have been in life (and how he died) or whether he was married and had children, and how they fared after his demise – without looking over your shoulder in preparation for the materialisation of some ghastly spectre. Musings like this are liberating and grounding. They remind us of our place in the world and of the inevitability that, for each of us, there will come a day when there will be no tomorrow.

Why I chose such places to frequent is therefore not that complex. *Requiescat in Pace* the inscriptions read. Perfect peace. Solitude. Such places of subtle tranquillity rarely exist within the metropolitan structure of our modern towns and cities. The sensitive amongst us are no longer catered for. While libraries once offered such rarefied solemnity, they are seldom now places of serenity, given over as they are to new readers, new browsers and banks of PCs that enable users to access more exciting worlds beyond the printed page.

To be able to think, uninterrupted, is important to me. Graveyards allow me the space and freedom to think, to wander, to imagine, to dream. Cemeteries are artefacts of a past when respect for the dead went hand-in-hand with the accepted expectations imposed upon society by the church and state. Modern burial grounds are pale substitutes in comparison; they are nothing more than turf-covered ash beds. How can you pay your respects to someone whose mortal remains are subject to the vagaries of our unpredictable weather, in danger of being borne away by a gust of wind before their embers have even cooled?

They are also places of wonder. I find the monumental folly exhibited by the sometimes-crass erections that mark each life that has ceased incredibly egotistical. Such celebrations of a person's self-importance are decorative but ultimately wasteful; they are fit only for us that remain to gaze on and to reflect on the processes that could have permitted someone to imagine such a marker would be a fitting tribute to a pile of rotting bones. Those memorials serve egos beyond the death of those whose lives they mark. After all, self dies with the body. Identity corrupts along with the flesh. Nothing exists beyond the now, except memories held by others who knew us. There is no I in death.

These deathly meadows are also refuges for those who choose to understand about living. The graveyards I generally visit are shunned by those who have better things to do, or rather those who have pushed such thoughts to the periphery of their being. 'Time enough for that later', they say deliberately, avoiding the notion that the shadows waiting to claim us all are with us every second of the day, never more than a hair's breadth away.

For me, each of the cemeteries I visit becomes a life-affirming destination; some days, it is only when I walk amongst the dead that I truly feel alive.

Chapter 2

There is a tree in my local graveyard that looks like a cock: a huge, erect phallus jutting triumphantly out of the earth, ready to spurt its seed into the welcoming sky. Sometimes in the spring, when it has not been cut back sufficiently, the shooting branches erupt from the glans-like top, creating an impression of ejaculation. It is a sight to behold.

I am not sure exactly when I first spotted this marvel because the route through the cemetery was one I'd taken twice every day five times a week, and I had done so for the previous nine years. So, on reflection, it could have been any one of the three thousand, five hundred and ten journeys I had made since I first started my job in the College Street Secondary School & Sixth Form College.

Seeing that giant prick standing sentinel amongst the headstones would remind me of another (less inspiring) prick I would see every school day. Apart from me, he was the only other male teacher in the entire CSSS&SFC. He'd somehow escaped the mind-numbing monotony of continuous lesson planning and replaced it with something much more tedious by becoming vice principal to Mrs Heather Mallory; in doing so, he joined six other quarrelsome, back-stabbing bitches in senior leadership.

How on earth a school like ours, boasting a total of some forty or so teachers, had managed to have so few male teachers had always baffled me. I realised that there were more female teachers than male teachers being spewed out of universities, but our male/female teacher ratio was still seriously fucked up. The answer definitely lay with the Human Resources Department, or rather with those who conducted the interviews and decided who would fill certain positions.

Perhaps, I used to think, fewer men went for the jobs. I mean, surely there had to be fewer men than women *wanting* to work in a failing school. After all, men are naturally more ambitious than their female counterparts. Most female NQTs are happy to get *any* job just to justify the amount of time they believe they had sacrificed out of their busy social lives in order to qualify for their teaching degree. They also needed a job in order to pay off the ludicrous credit card bills that they'd run up over three years on clothes and jewellery and accessories and makeup and other essentials, like holidays and meals out every evening.

The chances were, though, that the female interviewers, attempting to fulfil some fucked up feminist agenda or other, decided that *their own* positions would be safer by giving the job to some sycophantic, fawning, ever-so-grateful female NQT who would be more than content to toe the political line in return for a monthly wage and to resist rocking the queen bee's boatload of apple carts. As a result, school discipline in the CSSS&SFC was out of the window and our exclusion rate was the highest in the county.

Got a problem? Get rid of it. Got another problem? Get rid of that too. More problems? Keep sticking your head up your arse until the problem goes away. Simple. That was how it was done.

The school was dominated by women who ineffectively influenced every decision made on a daily basis, from uniform (or the lack of it) to behaviour and school meals. They were a kind of Femfresh Mafia, and I knew that the day when I could I finally turn my back on them would be one of the happiest of my life.

Sitting in briefing every morning, feeling my testosterone draining away from me because of the army of back-biting, squabbling bitches who were unable to exist in the same room without putting another of their colleagues down, was debilitating.

Is it any wonder that I, and many others like me, did nothing more than I was contractually obliged to? My contractual obligation for each scholastic year was 39 weeks, or 195 days, or 1265 hours, and I really did ensure that I did nothing more than I had to. I never volunteered to go on any school trips; I never ran any after-school clubs; I never did any sports coaching. I didn't do anything extra, period. Fuck them. Not literally, obviously. I wouldn't have touched any of them with a dog's dick, let alone mine.

Apologies for the digression; back to the pricks, or rather prick.

His name was Andrew Thompson; he was originally head of science until his 'meteoric' rise to senior leadership. I doubt if he'd ever taught a decent lesson in all the years he'd worked as a teacher. His classes were rumoured to be the most unruly because of his inability to take charge of most situations. He had been put into 'capability' measures twice since I'd started working there, which was something of a record.

His 'promotion' had been just another example of the Principal's failure to tackle problems head on. The truth was that he was simply a crap teacher, but instead of getting rid of him – permanently excluding him like they would a pupil – they kept shuffling him sideways into positions where responsibility could be deferred to someone more senior than he was and then finally into

SLG, where (it was assumed) he could do less harm.

He still hadn't been safe in that role, however. There was talk once that he used to pay one Year 11 girl he was teaching a little more attention than was considered healthy. That was back in the day, when such shit wasn't treated as seriously as it is now. Nothing could be proved, though, and his 'reputation' escaped permanent damage, although there were still whispers from time to time. Bad smells linger the longest.

Personally, I never believed the speculation surrounding him, not just because it was obvious it was a political slur being perpetuated by one of the up-and-coming bitches snapping at his heels but because I don't think he's had a good fuck in him. He looked how I used to feel most of the time, and I knew that one day I would end up looking like him too – unless something changed drastically.

Sadly, I feared a role more ignominious than being invited to join the SLG lay in wait for me, such as becoming a SENCO (Special Educational Needs Coordinator), which would allow me to spend the remainder of my days teaching those cursed with ADHD, the behaviourally subnormal, assorted retards and pupils affected by any number of other mental and physical afflictions how to sit on a chair without falling off it.

Andrew would meet me at the school gate every morning. He'd walk the short distance up the path towards the main entrance with me, go through reception (still at my side) and take the elevator up to the staff room; then, together, we would enter.

I know why he used to do it. To a solitary male entering a staff room full of garrulous, gossiping, squawking female teachers, it could have seemed a tad daunting, perhaps even intimidating.

His behaviour had become so routine, so ingrained, I was positive it had crossed the border from being purely an annoying, but essentially harmless, habit to one that was an obsessive compulsion.

What did we discuss on our daily walks from the gates to the staff room? Nothing. He never had anything of any importance to say. Occasionally he would utter some inanity about a football match he'd watched the previous evening on TV; even less occasionally he would ask how I was. I was always 'fine'. Andrew used to stay with me (seated right beside me) all the way through morning briefing and did not leave my side until the first period bell sounded, indicating, for most of us at least, that the school day proper had begun.

I believe he used to spend the rest of the day hiding in his office, avoiding contact with any of the staff unless it was absolutely necessary. Mind you, knowing most of the teachers in the school as I do, I can understand why. Not one of them had a solitary redeeming feature. They represented the most barren educational landscape imaginable.

Educationalists state that there are benefits to having balanced gender role models within schools; they maintain that some pupils respond more positively to a more feminine, caring approach, but others require something that might traditionally be considered more masculine and/or authoritarian.

Both of those boxes were ticked at the CSSS&SFC, the only difference being that both roles were delivered by the same gender. Some of our teachers were so masculine that I sometimes wondered if it was healthy for the long-term psychological wellbeing of the pupils to be taught by them. Was it any wonder I used to feel so redundant and Andrew felt so emasculated? The games teachers had more muscle than both of us combined for fuck's sake.

Those were not the *only* boxes the mistresses of our school ticked. There were lesbians – almost exclusively connected with PE in one form or another – misandrists, bisexuals, single mothers, black single mothers, black disabled single mothers, philogynists, heterosexuals, widows, divorcees, newly weds, fiancées, Muslims, Wiccans, Christian fundamentalists, anti-vivisectionists, pro-lifers, the profoundly deaf and, of course, the profoundly stupid.

I'd spend half the day sorting out behavioural problems caused by the teachers who'd had my classes immediately before me and had allowed the kids to do what the fuck they liked; the rest of my time was spent avoiding any kind of interaction with my colleagues at all. When I went home at the end of the day I would be both relieved and appalled in equal measure, my outrage directed mainly at myself for putting up with it all in the first place.

There is a little piece of Eastern philosophy that is appropriate to mention at this juncture; it goes something like 'Never moan to anyone about anything that you can change'. I never moaned.

Yeah, right.

I bided my time and waited for when the time was right to change things.

Most notably my life.

Even back then, when I was teaching, I wanted out. I wanted to do something else. I wanted to be a writer. It was always a dream I'd had. I somehow knew that one day I would quit my post and spend the rest of my life doing what I'd always wanted to do: writing classic horror stories. I had already penned fifty thousand or so words towards my first novel – and I had a working title.

I just didn't know when it would be. I knew it *would* happen and when it did I would walk out of that school, leaving Andy to be ripped to pieces by those vulture-like harridans – and I would not look back.

Until that time, though, I continued admiring the cock tree on my way to work and being escorted into the building by a spineless buffoon; and when I wasn't being interrupted by Heather Mallory, or her host of heartless harpies, I just got on with teaching as best as I could.

It was a shit job, but someone had to do it.

Chapter 3

Evening

I closed the front door behind me and put my shoulder against it, applying gentle pressure to ensure that it was locked. It was almost the final part of a ritual that I had carried out countless times before; what was new, though, was the introduction of a heartfelt sigh immediately afterwards. I was leaving the marital home once again and, once again, I was not particularly concerned when, or even if, I would return.

Fact: My marriage was dead.

Question: How best for me to chart the death of my marriage?

Answer: Where do I begin?

Actually, seriously, and more to the point, was it really necessary? Was there a requirement for me to analyse our sorry state of affairs for anyone other than the only two people it affected directly? Such were my musings of late and they, like the superfluous sigh that signalled the end of my house-securing ritual, were becoming more and more apparent.

To be honest, thinking about my problems realistically, who would have been interested in the whys and wherefores of yet another failed relationship? After all, the world is full of people like Janice and me. People who had originally been drawn together by instinct, desire and the need to celebrate our amazing ability to do what millions and millions of others had done before us since the dawn of time: fuck. Big deal. No wonder most marriages are doomed. Why should ours have been any different?

Our union was an insignificance, a mote in the eye of whatever benevolent deity had seen fit to put us together in the first place. Our existence was transitory, something to be forgotten as quickly as a breath on the wind the moment we ceased to draw breath ourselves. The living death I had to endure with Janice in the meantime was worse than anything I could imagine – or bear.

How had it happened? I wasn't sure.

Was there a way back? A way forward? A way out? Hmm….

Had I considered suicide? No! I was bored, not insane. Besides, I hadn't yet run out of other options.

Looming large in my personal calendar was an appointment with a psychotherapist (actually a counsellor): something I was secretly dreading for one reason or another but had been forced to consider, finally, out of necessity. I needed to know what the fuck was going on in my head, why I felt so low all of the time, so unfulfilled, so totally impotent. Not physically, you understand; there was nothing much wrong in that department. When my needs rose to a level that could not be satiated by a perfunctory tug in the shower, Janice could still be coerced by the requisite amount of pleading and begging. However, it was *because* of Janice's general disinterest in sex that I had been reduced to such onanistic behaviour.

There was, I knew, a distinct possibility that our current situation wasn't just down to Janice. I had to shoulder some of the responsibility. All too often it seems easier to blame someone else when things are going wrong than to look to oneself. Blaming someone with whom one is overly familiar and who loves you unconditionally is the easiest blame to apportion because you are already aware of what you can get away with; at the end of the day, you will always be forgiven, whatever the transgression. Within reason.

Where was I? Fast approaching middle age – or leaving it, depending upon your own personal point of view – with nothing more than the prospect of fewer years ahead of me than I had already lived. That and the distinctly distasteful probability that my body, that wondrous corporeal engine that had served me so well in my youth, would gradually begin to fall apart and get slower; eventually, one day, it would splutter, judder and conk out. I needed an overhaul, some serious maintenance, and I needed to use my dipstick more than I had been doing of late. There I go again.

Don't get me wrong; it wasn't just about the sex. Reading this back I realise it sounds as though it was a major preoccupation. Well, it *was* a preoccupation but not a major one. There was more to life than sex, wasn't there? Certainly. The problem was that everything somehow led back to that tiny three-letter word, without doubt the most important three-letter word in the history of mankind, and certainly bigger than God.

Sex. It had divided nations, forged empires and destroyed civilisations; it had been directly responsible for the deaths of millions of innocents as well as for singular acts of grievous, depraved, bloody murder; it had incited mutiny and inspired artists, musicians, poets and writers; it had been responsible for the spread of some of the most devastating diseases on the planet; it had been the foundation of science and scientific theory; and it had created philosophical debate. On top of all that, it had ensured the continuance of our species. So it wasn't all good.

Procreation and sex were – and still are, I realise – very different. Effect and cause. Cause and effect. Copulation is one of man's three primary drives and, as part of the human condition, inextricably the link between us all. I tried not to think about the effect *per se* but, honestly, I did think about sex quite a lot; this is when I wasn't indulging in other diverting occupations, such as photography. It did take my mind off sex, or rather my lack of it, and for that I was eternally grateful.

So, once more I stepped out into the evening air, leaving my insufferable life behind me. On my shoulder was my camera: a Pentax K20D. I had inserted new lithium batteries and a blank SD card. All I had to do was find somewhere, or something, to shoot.

In the past (in the early years of our marriage), when our feelings for each other were still fresh and everything was delicious and exciting, Janice would pose for me. I found – ahem, I *find* – the female form fascinating: all curves and hollows, shadows and soft undulation. Janice possessed an exceptionally beautiful, slender, supple body when she was younger. She would strip for me and I would spend hours composing shots, often introducing props to make the images more like visual narratives.

The experience excited her, made her more willing to experiment with more daring poses and ever more unusual scenarios. Back then there was no digital photography. Glamour photography therefore came with its own intrinsic problems. Taking a roll of exposed film that contained nude, or even semi-nude, shots to the local Boots was understandably out of the question. Those so inclined could use a Polaroid, although the square, poorly pigmented images had a nightmarish quality to them. Or they could send their 35mm films to one of the professional photo services, such as Steve Regan's in Birmingham, for developing and printing.

The developing and printing of photographs dealing with subjects of a more 'sensitive' nature was not cheap. The bespoke handling charge meant they cost approximately ten times more than having them done in a high-street chemist. However, it was worth it. As soon as they arrived, discreetly packaged in a plain manila envelope marked PRIVATE & CONFIDENTIAL, we would view the photographs together and Janice would become excited all over again. I recall we had a very healthy, active sex life once, but that now seemed such a long time ago.

The advent of the digital camera has meant much more freedom for those who want to concentrate on nude or glamour photography. There are no hidden costs involved. Even an absolute amateur can photograph someone (anyone) naked and print it on a home printer. All it costs is the price of photographic paper. It was the death knell for firms like Regan's and many others offering the same kind of service.

I wondered if I still had any of those old photographs of Janice. If I did, they were probably up in the attic, consigned to the darkness of an old shoebox, to be discovered in years to come by someone who would view them and imagine that the subject was once a decent-looking woman; a model, perhaps. She could have been too, once.

Time moves on and invariably leaves its mark.

I made my way across town towards the old cemetery. I reasoned that the sun, which was still high enough in the sky to cast brilliant shadows around the tombs and gravestones, would not sink out of sight for another forty-five minutes at the very least. My pace quickened; I wanted to be amongst those rows and rows of stones. I needed to be lost amongst the enduring markers of our ephemeral nature and hoped no one would be loitering there, basking in the mellow heat of what remained of our Indian summer, to spoil my photo opportunities.

Chapter 4

Nowadays, I hardly ever bother using a tripod. Sometimes when I am out photographing buildings or people, especially if I have a telephoto lens fitted, I will use a monopod. It allows me enough freedom to change positions if I need to, quickly and easily, while enabling me to maintain the requisite stability to prevent camera shake when using a slow shutter speed.

My current Manfrotto monopod is light and conveniently compact. It measures 1.4 metres when extended and just 26 centimetres when fully retracted; and it weighs less than a kilo. It is constructed from aluminium and nylon. I can generally fit it into my smaller rucksack, provided I am not otherwise overloaded with lenses.

There have been times in the past when my old tripod proved to be an invaluable accessory.

★ ★ ★

The nights had started to draw in. The shadows were longer and paler. Personally, I hated the encroaching early darkness. It signified not only the definitive end of summer but the end of warmth, the end of people and the onset of the endless cold, grey, miserable days that would stretch out interminably through the months ahead, like an incurable, disabling sickness.

I had decided to make the most of what remained of the light and headed over to the great northern cemetery on the outskirts of the city. It was a vast area, covering over one hundred and forty acres of monumental sculptures, memorials and headstones that stretched back over three hundred years, when the land had been originally annexed from the nearby Saint Nicholas's church.

There resided the illustrious, the infamous, the ordinary and the unknown, all occupants now of the same, undiscriminating cold, clammy earth; most of them were nothing more than dust and bones or pale sediment.

Outside, along the perimeter roads, is where prostitutes plied their trade; they waited, walked or huddled together with their fellow professionals in conspiratorial silence to have a smoke before being whisked off to who knew where for a £60 'trick' in the dark, blissfully ignorant of the names of the men who would pay for their services that evening. Paradoxically, they were equally oblivious to the names of those who had preceded them in previous lives; these were now only chisel marks on the gravestones a few short feet from where they stood. The Johns of today were as transitory as those silently resting in the ground.

Sometimes I turned my lens on those women, surreptitiously, hoping to catch a candid image that would reveal their true feelings about the profession that had taken over their lives. Most of the times they were closed books, with emotions carefully concealed behind a mask made as alluring as possible, given the raw materials.

The younger women, their hair scraped back into a tight knot at the crown, applied very little in the way of makeup; a little kohl, some blusher, a bit of lipstick, but that was it. The older, more experienced (or more seasoned) street veterans required greater care and more product just in order to compete with their younger counterparts. They favoured foundation, occasionally concealer, as well as the standard enhancers.

My best images of their world, taken in the half-light of dusk during the summer, favoured one girl in particular; she had piqued my interest. I had spotted her while setting up a shot at one of the red marble tombs close to the road. She stood at the kerbside, smoking, idly waiting for her next client to roll up. I thought she looked extraordinarily beautiful – certainly far too beautiful to be a prostitute. I imagined her age to be around twenty or twenty-two.

Unlike the others parading up and down the street, she was dressed well – not in one of those generic slutty, short Lycra bodycon dresses (easy to hitch up and down) that were readily available at Primark and those generic pop-up slaggy clothes shops, but in a classic, Grecian-style, belted white-and-gold dress with a plunging neckline. She wore matching gold, strappy kitten-heeled sandals, and over her shoulders was a short fake-fur coat. It was the coat that made me look twice. I wondered what would possess someone to wear such an excessive garment in what had been quite mild weather.

Her pale face was framed by a head of perfectly coiffured chocolate and blonde permed hair and accentuated with a little blusher. She had chosen a cerise lipstick that complemented the detail on her overly large spectacles. I thought she resembled a librarian or a secretary rather than a prostitute, and wondered what had caused her to consider such a soul-destroying profession.

She noticed me staring and smiled back at me self-consciously, glancing at her watch immediately afterwards. I had no idea how long she had been there or when she had started work or indeed when she would finish. Strangely, I felt an affinity with her, although I was unsure exactly why. Perhaps she, like me, was lost in a job that she could not escape from because of circumstances that were out of her control.

I held up my hand and waved, which made her smile again. That was how our very brief relationship began.

Over the next three weeks I would make my way to the same spot in the hope of seeing her again. Sometimes she was already in situ; other times she did not turn up at all. I began taking the odd photo when she wasn't looking, but they did not capture her essence. Her soul was visible only through her eyes.

One evening, she caught me photographing her. Rather than being annoyed, which I imagined she would have been, she smiled and pulled a face, sticking her tongue out so that it resembled a ripe, pink plum. After that she allowed me to click away, taking shot after shot of her through the railings.

It was a natural barrier. I never went beyond the perimeter, although I was sure that she would not have minded really. It formed a natural safety net that separated us both physically and, I guess, socially: a demarcation that we both understood and instinctively obeyed.

Would I have liked to have spoken to her... perhaps touched her hand to thank her for the opportunity of allowing me to photograph her... maybe even politely kissed her on the cheek?

Yes, but it was not to be. We both understood our roles in the relationship and I truly believe that had I attempted to transgress those unspoken rules then the images I captured of her would have been different. They would have illustrated another person, someone not quite so mysterious and definitely someone not quite as beautiful.

I ended up filling three SD cards with over six hundred and sixty images of the girl, whose name I never learned but decided to call Rose. Some captured the occasional perplexing paradox of her profession. There were times when she appeared to be almost angelic, pure and radiant. Other times she looked exactly what she was: a whore. I was able to document a whole range of expressions, most of which, I am sure, was her playing to the camera. Even so, I enjoyed our brief time together and still consider those shots to be amongst the best portraits I have taken.

Where she is now, or even if she is still around, I am uncertain. On the third week her absence from her normal spot became more pronounced; towards the end of the week she just didn't appear at all. It was as if she had vanished; another soul taken up into the ether, never to return. On the Saturday I waited all day, without success. I never went back again to look for her.

It is strange how our memory forces us to face that which we would rather forget.

I did not stay up near the road. I walked down towards the old limestone caves, where some of the older graves are situated. It's where the stone for some of the ancient, weathered monuments was excavated nearly two hundred years before. In some places you can still see where the panels were removed. It is a rough-hewn, isolated part of the cemetery and the darkness when it settles there fills the area more rapidly, making it seem eerily darker than it actually is.

I connected my monopod to the camera and sat against the railings that closed off the caves; my intention was to capture a broad sweeping panorama of the area and later to stitch it together to form a long continuous image. Retrospectively, it was fairly successful, despite the failing light. It provided me with more than I had intended, although, at the time, I was completely unaware.

Chapter 5

I was not looking forward to my session with the counsellor.

When I was younger, and still at school, there was a certain mindset that affected me and virtually every one of my peers. I grew up in a time and location where anyone with skin darker than everyone else's was something of a novelty. I cannot honestly remember seeing an Indian or an Asian face until I was around sixteen. There were certainly no East European accents, although there was the occasional East Anglian dialect. In my entire school there were only six black kids amongst three hundred and twenty students.

Now, some twenty-five years on, I am a teacher in a slightly smaller school, where the ethnic landscape has changed so dramatically that we have to employ interpreters in order to teach some of the pupils. My Year 10, set one cohort, for example, consists of twelve naturalised white/black/mixed race local children, three Poles, two Latvians, three Romanians, two Pakistanis, a Somalian, an Albanian, three Eritreans, one Russian and one I have no fucking idea where she's from. During debates it sometimes feels like I am heading up a junior United Nations conference.

I am all for racial integration, but having a class that consists of kids from such a diverse racial background makes my job extremely difficult at the best of times. No wonder our exam targets fall so lamentably short of the mark year after year. How can we possibly deliver the best lesson possible and achieve the results expected if half the pupils in the class don't even have English as a first language? Some don't even have it as a second language, which makes the proposition of maintaining excellence in the classroom untenable.

But I digress. The point I was trying to get to was that back then, when I sat on the other side of the desk, there really were racial minorities. We realised that these other kids were different (mainly because of the colour of their skin), that their values were probably not the same as ours, and that we almost certainly didn't share ethnic roots. It was divisive. It did set them apart but not so much that we could victimise them, because we were uncertain what they were capable of.

Unlike our fellows, whose families had spent generation after generation growing up in the same sort of area and with the same backgrounds and aspirations, these new interlopers were an enigma. Being no more than socially conditioned animals, but animals nonetheless, we behaved in a typically animalistic manner: we simply gave them a wide berth or avoided them altogether. Seriously, I cannot remember a single incidence of racial discrimination or bullying; in fact, it was more likely to have been meted out by the teachers than by us.

Besides, all our spite was reserved for the more traditional targets of playground cruelty. These were the ones we could abuse with relative impunity: the handicapped, the mentally subnormal and the obese. With typical malice, these targets were more acceptable for us to ridicule because they were like us – yet they were not. They were spastics, spazzers, cripples or flids (a bastardised term for a thalidomide victim), mongols or mongs, nutters, loonies or simply mental; then there were obviously porkers, pigs, lard arses, chubbies, chubsters or (unimaginatively) fat bastards.

Nowadays, as teachers, we are required to come down hard on anyone using such offensive language to describe a fellow student; back in the day, though, it was more or less accepted by everyone, including those who taught us. It amounted to institutionalised discrimination and everyone who was anyone – in other words, those who did not themselves want to be singled out for ridicule and persecution – joined in.

I myself was quite lucky. I was rake-thin, a result of natural, adolescent hyperactivity and poor eating habits, so I avoided the fat fucker jibes; I remember being referred to as a skoggy (skeleton) once, not that *that* really bothered me. Similarly, being able-bodied prevented me from falling victim to vicious barbs about any physical disability. That left only three other possible points of reference that could be used against me to cause me the maximum amount of discomfort.

My sexuality.

My personal hygiene.

My mental health (as already mentioned).

Being referred to as a bummer, a bum-bandit, a queer, a homo (or its derivative 'mo'), a turd-burglar, a shit-stabber or a poof stung only if it was carried out in front of people you actually cared about or if your sexual compass was so fucked up that it could be – alarmingly, possibly – correct. My addiction to purloined top-shelf porn magazines was proof positive that I was unlikely to bend for England, so that was out.

My hygiene was not a subject for serious consideration. There were many other filthier, poorly clothed and badly shod urchins to choose from: poor bastards that were so parasite-friendly that they sported continual crew cuts before they were ever fashionable and smelled so obnoxious that the suggestion they really did eat shit for tea every night seemed a very real possibility.

However, everyone, myself included, feared the lunacy slur. Mental illness was not understood; it differentiated those who suffered from it from those who evidently did not and it was not tolerated. It was a disease, a cancer that could be spread from person to person, and the symptom everyone feared most was the permanent isolation that appeared to accompany it.

We imagined that the virulence of mental illness and the possible cross-contamination was probably why all the nutters were kept in the same class away from the main school; that was the reason they were shunned by normal kids and why the best tool to keep them permanently at arm's length was continuous protracted derision and persecution. Everyone in my school categorically knew whom to avoid: Daniel (Schizoid) Fletcher, Charlie Thompson and Ebeneezer (Ebo) Shorrock. The trio were the epitome of arrested psychological development.

Being mentioned in the same breath or referred to as being related to one of those three amounted to condemnation worse than any insult connected with disability, obesity or sexuality. To be labelled a nutter was to be damned for the rest of whatever remained of your time in education. It was a label that persisted beyond school, however; it was one that followed you, wraith-like, to destroy fledgling romantic relationships and hinder employment in any of the local factory/workplace environments.

It was one of the reasons that I was unenthusiastic about my visit to the counsellor. The legacy of my teenage years, which I spent desperately avoiding, at all costs, any notion that I might be disturbed, unsettled or retarded, remained with me still; to be honest, it probably always would. It wasn't as strong or as repellent as it once was, but it was there all the same, with all the associations that accompanied any visit to see a 'shrink' to see if there was a 'screw loose'. It is fair to say it was one of the reasons that I could feel the anxious butterflies in my stomach as I approached the offices of the therapist.

My appointment was scheduled for 10am. It was five to, so there was still time to reconsider, to walk away and phone to apologise because something 'unavoidable' had 'cropped up'. I could always rearrange. After all, the counsellor had cancelled my first appointment himself. Shit happens. Besides, how could I be certain that a visit to a psychotherapist would actually help me anyway?

Outside on the wall was a highly polished rectangular brass plaque that read:

Matthew Stent
HypDip CPNLP CEFT-I
Integrative Therapist &
Person Centred Counsellor

I inhaled deeply, checked to ensure my entry would not be witnessed by anyone I knew, and quickly went inside. I closed the heavy door behind me and climbed the flight of stairs to the first floor, where I approached another door; this also bore the details I'd seen outside, but this time they were hand-painted in a green and gold script. I delayed entering until the exact moment of my appointment; then I knocked once, turned the handle and went through the door.

My first impressions were not good. There was no reception desk, and the space was bright and very stark, almost clinical – certainly not a place where anyone with a phobia about psychiatry or psychotherapy in general would feel comfortable. Above me a single metre-long fluorescent strip light buzzed. Beneath my feet was the rough tread of a brown utilitarian cord carpet, possibly the most hardwearing but cheapest-looking floor covering available to any business. I was standing in a small claustrophobic hallway with an unmarked door on each side of me; it was as if I was being challenged to choose the correct one in order to continue.

My choice was curtailed by the sudden appearance of the therapist from the room to my left. He was of medium height and medium build, and dressed in a smart, formal grey suit with an open-necked shirt (white); he did not wear a tie. His brogues (black and patent) were polished, as was his manner.

"Mr Tempest?" He smiled and extended his hand, which I took, hesitantly. "Matthew Stent. You found the place okay. That's good. Please come in."

He gestured towards a chair that was just inside the room and beneath a large wall clock. I sat and waited for him to join me, which he did after first locking the door.

"Now we won't be disturbed," he said by way of explanation. "There's nothing more unsettling than having someone barge in during a session. So, how are you this morning?"

We exchanged pleasantries; his inane enquiries were obviously intended to help me to feel less anxious than I had outside. To his credit, it appeared to be a successful strategy. I gave him a brief explanation of what I did for a living, my marital status and family – that sort of thing. He took absolutely no notes whatsoever but simply nodded from time to time and occasionally uttered a word to indicate he understood what I was saying.

Most of the time he sat, facing me, listening intently and studying me – certainly regarding me – with his piercing, almost hypnotic, blue eyes. His hands left his lap just once, to run his fingers through his dark wavy hair. He would have possibly been considered handsome by some, myself included, although not in the traditional sense. There was an underlying feral quality to him that might make certain men, and definitely some women, feel uneasy in his presence. I could not shake the notion that some men would not have trusted him alone with their wives, girlfriends or partners. I did not personally feel threatened by him, however, and found myself opening up fairly willingly.

He began explaining about the process (as he called it) and his obligations to me as a client concerning things like his qualifications and other credentials, the integrity expected of him as a counsellor, the notion of confidentiality, etcetera. It appeared as though he was reeling me in and I put up hardly any struggle. When he asked what it was I wanted to talk about, I was more than ready to tell him.

"I don't think I love my wife any more."

There. It was out.

For a moment he said absolutely nothing. I imagined he was thinking that I should have gone to a marriage guidance counsellor rather than to him. His eyes flicked backwards and forwards as he scanned my face for any trace of emotional expression, or perhaps he was waiting for me to elaborate. Eventually, he nodded and spoke.

"How do feel about that, Richard?"

How did I feel?

I had never really confronted the reality head on and spent even less time considering its implications on me as a person. Urging me to do so enabled me to touch on the underlying emotions I normally swept to one side.

"Sad, I guess. Sad and a little lost."

"Okay." He cocked his head slightly to one side as though he was thinking intently.

"You mentioned your wife's name is Janice? What is it exactly that makes you believe you don't love her anymore?"

Where should I begin? Our non-existent emotional and sexual interaction? Her apathy? My disinterest? The endless monotony of our existence?

I struggled to think how best to illustrate my feelings about our relationship in a manner that was both informative and constructive. In the end I just started talking.

"Things have changed between us... really changed... over the last couple of years. I know relationships do alter, naturally, over time and that as people become more accustomed to each other they sometimes can become complacent, but it's more than that. It seems that we are total strangers now... that we have somehow drifted apart. It might sound like a cliché, but the spark has gone."

I wondered how many times he had heard that expression.

He pursed his lips. "Uh-huh. It is interesting that you mention this so-called spark and that you've recognised that it's no longer present, which presumably means that at some time you must have been *very* aware of its existence. Was there a specific time or incident where you first noticed it was missing? Would you like to tell me about it?"

I tried. It was difficult to isolate when I first noticed things had changed, although I knew *where* it was most likely to have happened.

"In the bedroom, I guess. That's not to say that it hadn't already crept into other areas of our life."

"Such as where?"

I paused to reflect on his question.

"Mainly any areas of intimacy. We stopped holding hands, we stopped looking into each other's eyes, we just stopped being lovers and became friends... actually less than friends, I suppose. We just share the same space now."

He nodded understandingly.

"Just returning to the bedroom for a moment. Have there been any incidences of intimacy lately? Are you, for example, still having sex?"

His directness was refreshing; it was something I felt able to respond to.

"We have sex occasionally... infrequently... but it no longer has the same immediacy, if you know what I mean. It's just a *thing* we do... a functional thing that we engage in whenever our requirements coincide."

"Requirements?"

"When we are both in the mood."

"I see. And that doesn't happen often?"

I shook my head.

"How often would you say? Every couple of days? Every week? A couple of times a month? It doesn't have to be precise; it's just so I can build a more accurate picture of your relationship."

It was uncomfortable for me to say, and it was embarrassing.

"About once every two or three months. Maybe every four months."

After I had said it I realised just how far I had allowed that aspect of my marriage to slide. Three to four times a year! It was ridiculous. There was a time when I'd screw Janice two or three times a night, every night, if I could and she would have been equally eager to participate. What the hell *had* happened to us? What had we become?

"Do you have any children?"

No. It was something that we had decided, after years and years of fruitless endeavour, to give up on altogether. It had been a joint decision. We had both agreed it was probably for the best. In retrospect, considering the state of our marriage now, it had been the correct choice.

"Can I ask you, Richard, *when* you and Janice have sex – forgetting about its functionality for a moment – do you still find her sexually attractive? If not, can you pinpoint why or, if she has changed in some way, how?"

Contemplation: the enemy of time.

Seconds passed; moments followed. I tried to picture the last time I'd seen Janice naked. She still had a half-decent body, as I recalled. But her breasts were larger, a little heavier, a little less defined. Her belly too had suffered (as had mine) from years of unchecked eating, drinking and virtually no physical exercise, apart from the odd brisk walk around the supermarket. She had perhaps gained around ten kilograms or so over the years, most of it around her buttocks. However, she was still not what I would have called unattractive.

She always tried to keep herself presentable. She wore makeup more now than she did, now that the thin, spidery lines of age had begun to gather under and around her eyes. She painted her nails, I think; at least I seem to remember they were bright red (or perhaps pink) the last time she had passed me the shopping bags from the car. Her hair, which had once been wonderfully dark and lustrous, had become so streaked with grey in her thirties that she had been forced to resort to dyeing it ever since.

At the end of the day she was a middle-aged woman, complete with everything that encompassed. She was no longer the slender, wide-hipped, firm-breasted, cock-hungry temptress I had married; but, then again, I'd changed too. It was inevitable. We were both older. Was I still attracted to her? I decided that, under the correct circumstances, I was. Shit, there were a hell of a lot of worse-looking women out there, some of them half her age.

The therapist smiled.

"I see. That's good, isn't it? After so many years together there is *some* chemistry left. How many years did you say you've been married?"

"Nineteen," I replied. I suppose he had a point, despite the fact that he never actually stated it. It was only implied, more or less. The implication made me reconsider a number of actualities and the truth of how I felt about Janice. Perhaps my initial statement had been a bit hasty.

"Do you believe that Janice feels the same way, that she no longer loves you?"

I had absolutely no idea. I had never asked her. It was always my assumption that we coexisted in a state of matrimonial oblivion because that was the way we both wanted it. Neither of us had resisted the tide of complacency. Instead, we accepted the inevitability of it washing over us, gradually eroding us until the only thing that remained were shadows of what we had once been, reunited briefly during what fleeting moments of passion we allowed ourselves.

"I don't know. It's hard to tell. We don't talk about things like that."

"Do you and Janice talk much at all?"

"Not really." It was pitiful but true.

"Do you think Janice still loves *you*?"

It was a difficult question that forced me to consider my response very carefully.

"Yes, I do think that Janice loves me... but that...

perhaps she is no longer *in love* with me."

"Uh-huh." He cocked one eyebrow and waited.

My therapist, Matthew Stent, must have lived a charmed life. He appeared to be totally unaffected by what I was discussing with him. He wore no jewellery on his fingers, so presumably was not married himself. He had a face that bore none of the usual indications of the daily struggles and turmoil that are generally etched on the faces of others. He was well dressed and perfectly manicured. A bachelor, I guessed.

For him, love was probably something that happened only to other people. I may have been wrong about him, although he did seem particularly cold and detached when he commented on my reply, as though he was oblivious to my emotional predicament. It's true; sometimes we do give in to that preposterous notion of devoted affection we call love far too easily. He seemed too pragmatic to have *ever* allowed that to happen in his life, though.

"Surely that is just *your* perspective?" he said.

I think I laughed; I'm not really sure. I know I said something like "Well, that's all I've got, so if that's wrong then I'm even more confused than I thought I was."

He ran his fingers through his hair.

"I'm not saying you're wrong, I'm asking you to consider *if* you are. I'm challenging your belief in case *it is incorrect*. You may be right. Your wife *may* no longer *be in love* with you, although she *still loves you* because she has a highly developed sense of matrimonial obligation or duty. Have you contemplated the possibility that what you ascribe to her might actually be what *you* believe of yourself?"

I hadn't. He could be correct. I *was* confused.

"Is a relationship like that, where partners love each other but are no longer *in love* with each other, normal?"

"What *is* normal, Richard? Let's just say it's more common than a lot of people might imagine."

"Really?" I wasn't convinced. "I'm not sure… I'm not sure what I should do."

He sighed gently.

"Can I remind you that *you* have come here today to see *me*, perhaps to seek my help or advice. I'm afraid I don't normally give advice, but I am able to make a number of observations that might help simplify the situation for you. Firstly, the fact you are here at all means that you either value your marriage, and want to save it, or you require some form of vindication from me for a course of action you are considering taking or may have already decided upon. Why would you seek help otherwise? Do you understand what I've just said?"

I nodded.

"Secondly, from what you have told me, it's obvious you still find your wife sexually attractive, certainly attractive enough for you to continue having sex with her, albeit on an *ad hoc* basis, although it sounds as though you at least wish it were more frequent. While sexual attraction may not be the best basis for the continuance of a relationship that you feel is doomed, it is, if you will excuse the rather clumsy sexual connotations, an essential glue that binds lovers like you and Janice together. Yes?"

I nodded again.

"So where do you think you should go with this?"

Genuinely uncertain, I struggled to find an answer I felt confident with. I shrugged instead.

"The road forward is something only you can decide upon, Richard. It really is not for me to say what course would be best for you."

He glanced at something above and behind me, the clock most probably because of what he said immediately afterwards.

"So, with your session here today almost over, I just want to clarify something, which we could perhaps continue discussing during your next appointment, before I begin to summarise what we have spoken about today. Is that alright with you?"

I affirmed that it was.

"Okay. So, based on what we've discussed here, would you still say your original assessment of your marriage is *still* correct?"

I shook my head. "No, maybe not."

"And do you accept that *part* of you *still* loves Janice?"

He was very forthright. It seemed he was seeking a spontaneous response. I tried not to disappoint him or overanalyse.

"I guess so... but probably not in the conventional sense."

"Forget conventions. They are simply rules formulated by others to force us to identify with some designated status, according to *their* point of view. They don't actually exist." He paused. "Is there a possibility that you still love Janice?"

"Yes." It was an automatic, and so most probably a genuine, acknowledgement.

He nodded thoughtfully.

"Do you think you are *in love* with Janice?"

Again, I responded spontaneously, shaking my head forlornly. That was the simple truth. I loved her, but I was no longer in love with her. And that was that.

He closed the session after first recounting, in precise detail, *everything* we had discussed over the previous hour, a feat in itself considering it was all from memory. His recall, unlike my own, was remarkable. Mine had a habit of failing me from time to time: another by-product of advancing years.

We arranged a further appointment for two weeks' time and I thanked him, paid him his fee and stepped back into the miserable greyness of the day. Pulling up my collar, I headed back towards the city centre and tried to shake off the feeling that I'd achieved nothing more than waste £80 by visiting him.

I never went back again.

It was nothing to do with Mr Stent as a therapist; in fact, he helped me more than I would have thought possible in just the brief time I was with him in the therapy suite. It was me. Despite the ease with which he was able to draw information from me and despite how comfortable my first visit to a psychotherapist was (I must reiterate, it was my first visit) it wasn't something I wanted to repeat on a regular basis. There were just too many troublesome associations: legacies from my adolescence.

The main thing I took away from the session was that I needed to get my head together, to crystallise my thoughts and to be clearer and more honest about my true feelings. In respect of that, again, Matthew Stent assisted me enormously, as painful as it was.

My marriage was a sham, held together by a thread. I knew it would take very little to break it completely. All I could hold on to were the shadows of much happier times and the promise of sporadic coitus.

Now that I recognised that my life with Janice had no real direction worth mentioning anymore, I had to decide what to do with the rest of what remained of my life and whom I would spend it with.

Chapter 6

There are times in our lives when we become aware of things that quite possibly would ordinarily be impossible to perceive, aspects of reality that are not immediately obvious. It is where facets exist that are outside of our visual parameters; they are at the edges (the periphery) so that it is only in our mind that they register, rather than being something definitive within our ocular range.

That was how I first met Ligeia.

I had chosen to visit the great northern cemetery again, mainly because I had found that working amongst the labyrinth of stones and monuments had inspired me to create what I considered to be some of my best work. I was also beginning to fully appreciate the layout of the grounds and had discovered a number of areas that appeared to be hidden from the casual visitor. One spot in particular had fired my imagination, and it was to there that I made my way that particular evening.

Working alone makes me more conscious of what and who is around. I am sensitive to the feelings of those who wander the same paths as I through the landscape, to grieve or perhaps just to remember their loved ones. I stay clear of those who might be offended by my behaviour around the graves. I let them mourn in peace.

There was, I am certain, no one else around that evening, at least not in the area I was. It was well away from the main road and far enough from the parking area to dissuade any casual rambler. The path was lined with lime trees, all of which were about to lose their leaves. I remember studying the varying colours of the leaves, which were turning different shades of yellow as the chlorophyll was diluted by the short-lived sun, now weakening day by day. I saw no other person. I am quite sure I was alone.

At the crest of the pathway, just before it dipped down towards the more secluded part of the cemetery, I looked back, alerted by something. I was – I still am – unaware what it was that caused me to check my surroundings. I was wary that something wasn't quite right but was uncertain what or why. I have since considered that it was a noise, something auditory rather than visual, that first perturbed me. However, nothing was evident, except the wind gently rippling through the dying leaves on the trees.

Once I had convinced myself that I was mistaken, I started the walk down the sloping pathway to the more isolated section of the cemetery. Cautiously I glanced back occasionally, just to ensure I wasn't being followed. The prospect of being mugged, or worse, was enough to keep me on guard, but I saw nothing. I reached the bottom and stopped for a moment to take in the vista.

All of the internments, according to the information on the surrounding tombs and headstones, had been carried out around 1890, so it was not an ancient part of the graveyard; it was more difficult to gain access to than other sections, though, because of the gradient of the path leading down to it. I could tell it wasn't well used because the weeds and grass that poked out from between the flagstones had not been trodden down.

I took out my sketchpad and made a few notes, illustrating the general layout of the graves and markers for future reference; I then began clicking away at the final resting places of the long-dead residents, being careful to capture the names as they appeared on each memorial legend. Before too long, I became totally absorbed in the task, working as quickly as possible to complete it before the light quality dipped. There was a specific shot I required that evening. It was my reason for being there.

When I turned around, the sudden appearance of a girl, probably in her early twenties, no more than four metres away caused me to catch my breath. To be honest, it was so unexpected it scared the shit out of me. I hadn't heard her approach or seen her following me, which I assume she must have done. It would have been very easy to spot her too, considering what she was wearing. Maybe she had been there all along.

I tried not to look too rattled, but it was difficult, considering that I could feel the blood draining from my face at much the same speed as my heart was hammering in my chest. Rapidly. I was definitely spooked.

As I stood, camera in hand, carefully assessing the sudden arrival, I realised the girl who had apparently materialised out of thin air was the same one I had captured several times before, wandering amongst the tombs near the Forest Road. A thousand questions now raced through my head. The most prominent were 'Who is she?' and 'What is she doing creeping around a cemetery, scaring the shit out of people?'

She sat on the edge of a tomb, in a sublimely ethereal pose, her long strawberry-blonde hair caught in the breeze that had followed me down the long, steep track to where we now were.

"I've seen you here before," she said softly. For an opening line it was pretty lame, almost as lame as my response.

"I've seen you here before too." I had the photographs

to prove it. "You must spend a lot of time here."

What? My reply made me sound like some kind of pervert. She smiled, her pale-blue eyes sparkling.

"Sometimes."

I noticed she was barefoot and it drew my gaze towards her long, shapely legs. I wondered if she was simple.

"Are you a photographer?" she said, interrupting my thoughts. Her top lip was a perfectly formed Cupid's bow.

"A schoolteacher." The words sounded ridiculous as soon as I uttered them and instantly I wished I could have taken them back. I should have said I was anything rather than a boring schoolteacher.

"Do you teach photography?"

The curious blonde had given me another opportunity to embroider the truth, to be something more than a mere would-be educator of ungrateful little shits. Dare I take that opportunity? Could I become, in her eyes at least, more than I actually felt I was?

"No. I teach English. Well, English and English literature."

What a fucking idiot! It was all part of my training: honesty and idiocy.

"Oh. Cool."

I couldn't tell if she meant what she said or not. It was probably, I concluded, an automatic response, one of those insincere glib throwaway lines that the young were in a habit of using. She began swinging her right leg backwards and forwards. Once again her lower limbs had my attention. I noticed that her toenails were painted pale pink.

"What do you photograph?"

I was struck by how simple her questions were; they

were like a child's. She looked like a child too: shoeless in a knee-length white cotton shift dress, her long blonde hair falling in front of her face. She brushed a strand away as though it was an annoyance; she was staring straight at me, or through me, waiting.

"Anything. Everything. Whatever I feel like really; birds, trees, graves, people. Where are your shoes?"

She indicated with a lethargic, floppy motion of her left arm.

"Up there somewhere." I followed the gesture with my eyes but saw no evidence of footwear. There was, however, something I did notice.

The paler flesh of her inner arm was a mass of thin, raised pink welts or scars. I had seen that kind of self-mutilation before. Some of my students – generally, but not exclusively, sullen girls – went in for that kind of pointless, experimental, attention-seeking shit. It had never impressed me and now only reinforced my notion that the girl on the tomb was emotionally, possibly even intellectually, immature.

I decided to terminate our conversation, firmly but politely, before we both became too entrenched in inanity.

"Listen, it's lovely to talk to you, but I really have to get on before the light starts to fail."

"That's okay; I'll just sit here for a while and watch you. I promise I won't disturb what you're doing. I just like to watch. I find photography fascinating."

I smiled meekly and tried to ignore her, sitting there with her long, smooth, lissom leg swinging, swinging, swinging, swinging, backwards and forwards, pink nails catching the fading light.

Determined not to be distracted, I focused on capturing the trio of tall-spired temple-like memorials, starkly illuminated by the golden-yellow light of the waning sun. I allowed the image in the viewfinder to become imprinted in my mind and pressed the shutter button. It clicked mechanically. Digital point-and-shoot cameras are noiseless, but digital SLRs still emit the same shutter sound made by their fully mechanical predecessors. Some think this is no more than a reassuring sound effect, but this is not necessarily so. Keeping the button depressed I fired off twelve or thirteen shots before changing position and perspective.

The girl was still watching me, making me feel somewhat self-conscious as I moved slowly to my new vantage point. I wasn't used to an audience when I was out with my camera. I preferred to be alone with my thoughts and ideas. Nothing inspired me more than the self-imposed solitude and the all-encompassing notion that I was doing it only for myself. That was why my photography had been so successful. That was why my images continued to win competitions.

Click - whirr - click - click - click - click - click - click - click - click - click - click - click - click.

The second stream of captures was better. I could tell without even reviewing them. The light was better, stronger in colour, and the shadows deeper and more elongated. The whole scene was reminiscent of some vast granular cathedral bathed in resplendent celestial glory. I was pleased.

As if in confirmation that I had achieved the best possible photographs for the evening, the sun was suddenly obscured by a pale vaporous cloud and the fabulous light was gone.

I glanced back at the tomb where the girl had been sitting moments earlier and, just like the sunlight, she too had vanished as mysteriously and as silently as she had appeared. Like a wraith, I mused.

Unknown to me at the time, my unintentional romanticising was far closer to the truth than I could ever have imagined; and at that time I still did not know her name.

Chapter 7

My first meeting with Ligeia had posed more questions than provided answers. For example, I was uncertain how she had appeared without me seeing her. Yes, I recall being aware of something that evening before my descent, but it was nothing specific, nothing distinct. She *was* barefoot, so presumably I wouldn't have heard her approach, although I am certain I would have seen something, if only a movement out of the corner of my eye. Eventually I concluded she had been there before me, perhaps hidden by some monument or other. It was the most logical solution.

What was she doing there?

It seemed a little odd – perhaps even potentially hazardous – for an attractive young woman to be wandering around a cemetery on her own. It was a place frequented by all sorts of people, not just photographers and mourners but those whose purpose for being there may be somewhat less obvious, and more dubious. It was also a haven for drunks who sought solitude and temporary reprieve from the judgemental glares of city centre inhabitants to indulge in the consumption of Special Brew and White Lightning amongst the slabs and stones.

What if she had been attacked? What if she had been raped?

Her thin cotton dress would have hardly been a barrier to the lustful intentions of a dedicated sex attacker and she had no possessions that I can remember seeing.

No coat, no handbag; it made very little sense. Women always carried bags. Had she left it with her shoes?

She was certainly an enigma.

I was determined to solve part of the mystery, though. I accessed all the photographs I had taken in the cemetery (and safely stored on the external hard drive) and copied every image in which she appeared, or in which I thought she appeared, to a separate folder. In some of these images, she (or what I thought could be her) was no more than a vague shape in the background. I then sat back and reviewed every single one.

What was apparent was that she spent a lot of time amongst the dead.

In some images she was captured, mid-stride, walking along the paths and avenues that criss-crossed the cemetery. Sometimes she was so close to the lens I was amazed I had not noticed her. She was extraordinarily beautiful and immaculately turned out in an array of different dresses of varying styles, lengths and colours, although it became apparent she appeared to favour vintage fashions.

There were shots of her in the distance, slightly out of focus but unmistakably her; she would be kneeling by graves or just staring up at statuary and monuments. I had inadvertently captured her sitting on one of the green painted municipal benches while she drank a can of Pepsi through a straw. In another she was sitting on the edge of a tomb, with one leg gracefully entwined behind the other: this was very much as I had first noticed her, but this time I noted she was wearing shoes.

In total, there were sixty-eight pictures that featured her in one form or another. I labelled the folder MGIG: Mystery Girl In Graveyard, and placed it alongside the other photography folders on my laptop.

I did wonder if I would see her again. It was almost certainly highly likely and over the days that followed I convinced myself that it was not a case of if but of when.

* * *

My second random encounter with Ligeia occurred three days later. Not in a graveyard but in, of all things, a city centre coffee shop. I noticed her straight away; she was sitting away from the bulk of the tables in one corner, book in hand, demurely sipping what looked like a frappe latte through a black straw. She did not seem to be aware of me as I approached or look up as I sat down a few tables away.

Her hair had been scooped up and piled on top of her head in a bun. I noticed the glint of hairgrips holding the confection in place. Her lips were full and bright red. She had chosen a metallic gold shadow for her eyelids, and in each ear she wore a large gold and red glass cabochon stud. She looked very glamorous and also very beautiful.

I saw she was reading Yukio Mishima's *The Sailor Who Fell from Grace with the Sea*. The slim tome looked overly large in her delicate hands. It appeared that she was halfway through the novel. I wondered if she was enjoying it.

While I liked Mishima's writing, I did not feel that this was his best work. This is my personal view rather than with my teacher's hat on. It was representative, certainly, and the characterisation was excellent, but, for me, it did not work as well as *The Decay of the Angel* with its reassuringly similar, although greatly expanded-upon themes, and maritime setting.

Mishima, for my money, was undoubtedly a literary genius. His work as a writer, playwright, poet, actor, and author of many incredibly powerful novels should have enjoyed much greater popularity than it currently does in the West. The main reason he doesn't – apart from the fact he was Japanese, a fiercely conservative nationalist and committed suicide after an attempted military coup went disastrously wrong – was the fact he was a homosexual. Not just a homosexual but a closet homosexual.

The West can forgive most of the sins that man is capable of but not the sin of homosexuality, it seems. In our own country we may revere the works of past literary masters and mistresses but only up to a point. As soon as they are revealed as participants of same-sex love, their orientation becomes the overriding factor, as the homosexual dramatist Oscar Wilde would confirm wittily, were he still alive today.

She looked up and found me staring at her. I coloured slightly, embarrassed, although she appeared to be unperturbed by my conspicuous attention.

"Hello again," she said, putting her book down. "Did you manage to get the shots you were after?"

A voice in my head warned me to act normally.

I nodded. "Just. Another few minutes and I would have lost the opportunity. I need the right kind of light, you see. It was exceptional that evening."

"Yes, very yellow. Like bile."

Like what? Bile?

What a peculiar comparison, I thought. It could have been worse, of course; she might have said piss. I then wondered if that was the kind of language she would use, and whether I was doing her a disservice by imagining that she was as foul-mouthed as I am wont to be on occasions. Certainly, sitting in front of me looking like a glamorous 1950's model, it did seem that 'piss' was most likely a word that she would not normally use. I tried to push any thoughts of profanities out of my head and concentrated on her once again. A thought occurred that she would have made a wonderful model; her eyes were so… expressive.

"Are you okay?" she asked, jolting me out of my slowly drifting reverie.

"Yes, yes," I gabbled, attempting to cover up my embarrassment, no doubt with my mouth open like a drooling imbecile, and staring into the space she filled so perfectly. "Sorry, I was just thinking about my camera. I need to buy one of those portable floodlights. The weather was fortunate for me that night, but it can't last much longer."

"Oh." She appeared to be disappointed, although she disguised it with a generous smile. "Usually when I meet photographers they spend most of the time imagining me naked."

During the silence her statement had created, she stared across at me, into me, with those exceptionally beautiful eyes, daring me to deny what had obviously been written all over my face. Were my thoughts really that transparent? Like a rabbit caught in a snare, I knew it would be pointless to struggle; I was held fast and I realised any amount of verbal defence would probably only serve to have me skewered further in her gimlet gaze. I did what any man would do under the same circumstances; I changed the subject.

"You're reading Mishima, I see. Are you enjoying it?"

She nodded and slowly inserted the straw between her full, painted lips; her eyes never left mine. I became aware that I was staring again and was grateful when she finished drinking and spoke.

"His writing is so beautiful; it's like poetry. I try to imagine what emotions he must have felt when he was writing it. The theme is one of my favourites: dark fascination, obsession, sensuality, corruption and death." She gestured to empty chair opposite her. "Please join me."

I did not want to refuse and so only protested half-heartedly. "If you don't mind. Just for a moment then."

She smiled as I moved across to her and sat down.

"Do you like his work?" she asked.

I admitted that I was partial to Mishima's rather stilted view of post-war Japan and agreed that there was indeed an intense, albeit sometimes overtly dark, beauty in his work. It was echoed in some of the short stories of another of my favourite authors, Angela Carter, and I proposed that perhaps it was the country, the common denominator in both, that I enjoyed most.

She continued to tease me unintentionally with the straw, her eyes hooded. I decided to drink my coffee, as hot as it was, and try to ignore the intrusive sexualised thoughts that bombarded me. It was, however, difficult and I realised that the only way to halt them was to remove myself from her company altogether.

"Have you read *The Decay of the Angel*?"

"Yes! I absolutely loved it. I think that Honda was a beautifully drawn character throughout the series, but it's the absolute nihilism of the work that sets it apart."

I nodded. "You know he committed suicide immediately after he wrote it, don't you?"

"Yes," she frowned. "How fucked up is that?"

Hearing her swear shocked me a little, I must confess. I had imagined that nothing more offensive than the most basic and ineffective of profanities would be uttered by that perfect mouth, by those beautiful lips; perhaps a 'damn' or a 'bloody' at times of intense frustration. Although I use the word 'fuck' myself often and in various situations, it somehow seemed vulgar and ugly coming from her. I didn't know how to respond. Eventually I simply used a bland reaffirmation.

"Quite."

"Do you think he really believed he could wake Japan up with his actions?"

"No, not at all. I think he realised that Japan was spiritually dead. His work – his essays, poems, plays, novels – all accept the inevitability of death and how it is better to control, or rather own, that moment than leave it to chance or fate. Regardless of what happened that day at the barracks, I believe Mishima planned to die young. A young death is glorious."

She clearly disagreed. "He was hardly young!"

"He was forty-five when he died."

"Exactly," she said, smiling.

I felt a light go out inside me. I don't think she realised how much her comment wounded me. For as long as I can remember, I have believed that we have two ages: a physical age, which is reflected by our continuous passage around the sun, and an internal age, which we hold, fixed in our minds, as a reminder of ourselves at one precise point in our lives that we were the content with. I am eighteen.

Exactly.

That internalisation is only effective up to a point, however. When it comes up against the blinkered honesty of those younger than ourselves, the truth of our situation is savagely laid bare. All the pills, potions and self-belief count for nothing when dissected by the incorruptible objectivity of youth. Bastards! The only comfort is that, one day, they too will find themselves in the same space and suffer the same indignities that accompany the process of ageing in a world that exists for and because of the young.

Exactly.

My silence extended well beyond what was normal for a casual conversation. I sipped my latte and avoided eye contact. In truth I wanted to crawl off somewhere: anywhere populated by people who were more accepting of my repulsive decrepitude. Part of me wanted to challenge her preconceptions, but, in the end, I realised it was pretty pointless. I *was* old. There was no denying it. I'd told myself enough times that I was as good as dead. It didn't make it hurt any less, however.

Ligeia was oblivious to my discomfort. She diffused it instantly with a radiant smile and a simple request.

"Could I see some of your photographs?"

Despite myself, I smiled back. "Sure."

Although I wanted to, I stopped myself from answering too effusively. I needed to rein in any overt enthusiasm in case it became too apparent that people seldom asked to view my work, even though it had won competition after competition. Two of my pieces were actually shown on the late-night weather forecast on the BBC, one in 2008 and the other in 2011.

"You'll need to view them online."

"Oh." She sounded disappointed. "What's the web address?"

I scribbled it down on the back of a napkin and added my name underneath.

"Just in case. There are thousands of other photographers on the same site. I don't want you looking at them and imagining they are all mine, especially as some of them aren't very good."

She studied the napkin intently before turning her attention back to me, her smile now more confident.

"Richard Tempest. What a fantastic name. It reminds me of dark clouds crackling with static, racing across a summer landscape, or of cornfields speckled with the heads of blood-red poppies, or of luminous barbs of lightning striking towering wave crests as they swell during a violent storm at sea."

It was quite poetic. Romantic even.

"Not a secondary school teacher skulking around a cemetery then?"

"No," she laughed sweetly. "Unless you are waiting there in the pouring rain with a long-bladed knife under your coat, ready to plunge it into the heart of a lover who has betrayed you."

Huh?

For the second time since we had first met I wondered if she was retarded. The way she dressed and the way she presented herself to the world made me realise it was an absurd notion, but the weird shit she came out with did give me one or two causes for concern.

"No, that's definitely not me," I laughed.

I decided to ask her name. She told me without hesitation, eyes flashing brightly, perfect white teeth exposed, pale white hand extended towards me.

"Ligeia. My name is Ligeia Hennessy. Actually, Ligeia Middleton-Hennessy."

I took her hand in mine, immediately aware of the coolness of her flesh, and gave her the only smile I possessed.

"I'm pleased to meet you, Ligeia."

"That remains to be seen," she replied.

Chapter 8

It wasn't just the girl that was odd. So was her name.

I recognised it instantly of course, being both a teacher of English literature and a lover of darker poetry and the gothic novella since my childhood.

Ligeia was the name of the tragic and beautiful raven-haired beauty in Edgar Allen Poe's short story of the same name, first published in 1838. In the tale, she is described as being tall and slender and unconventionally beautiful. Later, she is described as 'emaciated' but possessing a 'strangeness' about her, and as one who 'came and departed as a shadow'.

I could certainly confirm that the Ligeia of my acquaintance shared a number of those attributes.

The name itself is derived from the Greek *Ligis*, meaning 'a shrill, piercing voice'; it was the name of one of the sirens who plagued both Jason and Odysseus in their respective quests. It was said that all men who heard their songs would be lured to their deaths.

From an academic perspective, I preferred the latter 1845 republication of *Ligeia*, in which Poe explains that the melancholic poem 'The Conqueror Worm' was composed by the ill-fated beauty in the days before her death throes and recited to her by her husband, whose name we never learn. The rhyme echoes sentiments found in Baudelaire's later Poe-inspired poetic imagery, which, as you know, I am also an admirer of.

Since early adulthood I have associated the image of Alphonse Munch's *Madonna* with the literary description of Poe's *Ligeia*. Could there be a more accurate depiction of forlorn beauty? Here is one that inspires all who view it to consider the wretched impossibility of eternal love, hopelessly embodied in the corporeal prison that inevitably must decay and fall into corruption, momentarily reclining in the repose of one deceased (though not yet dead), eyes half-open as though in ecstatic post-orgasmic bliss.

How dangerous the suggestion that Madonna, the mother of the son of God and elevated above all women, should be consigned to the same reality as all other women. Loved. Loved in life and irrevocably in death. Desired, yet set apart. Sacred, yet in sin. Creator and destroyer. Nurturer and seducer. Munch's depiction, a homage to the 'petit mort' that orders creation and yet has consumed her, reminds us all of our inevitable mortality.

Hmm….

I have a tendency to overanalyse everything (it is a failing of mine), so what I have just mentioned might be utter bollocks. Art is, after all, subject to personal perception *and* interpretation.

How did this fit in with the weird Ligeia? It didn't. Except it did. There was much about the girl that demanded more attention, more investigation, and certainly more discussion.

Where was she born, for example? In some 'old, decaying city by the Rhine'? Not with her accent. I guessed Oxford, or possibly one of the other central southern counties.

Were her parents aficionados of Poe? Academics perhaps, or simply stuck for a name and thought it sounded 'pretty'. My money was on the former. I made a note to ask her if I ever got the opportunity again.

There were aspects of her that were totally

incongruous with her appearance, and this made her seem all the more mysterious. It was enough that she spent time wandering barefoot in graveyards in a summer dress, like a simpleton pining for a lost relative or dead child or like a pathetic heroine from a dire Victorian penny-dreadful. However, it was obvious that she was educated and, what's more, she was intelligent. She could hold a perfectly sane conversation with me, despite my original misgivings, and favoured neo-classical Japanese literature.

I liked the paradox she presented; it intrigued me. I found her fascinating; I found her whole persona alluring. I could easily understand how, given the right circumstances, a person could become totally intoxicated with someone like Ligeia. Not me, obviously; she was far too young for someone like me.

How old was she? Twenty-two? Twenty-four?

Besides, what the hell could someone like me offer someone like her that she couldn't get from any other man: any other *younger* man? Experience? Shit, no. I was only married, not experienced. It doesn't naturally follow that marriage is a prerequisite for experience, only existence. Look at Lulu and Maurice Gibb as a case in point.

I wondered if she was seeing anyone, if she was engaged, or even if she was married. I must admit I cannot recall seeing any symbolic ownership jewellery on her fingers, but I wasn't really looking. I wouldn't have been surprised if she was; after all, she was a particularly stunning-looking young woman. There had to be someone special in her life, someone in the background, someone waiting in the wings.

Sigh.

When I got home I went through the images in the folder on the computer again. Many of them were indistinct or too far away, but a couple were close enough for me to check.

I enlarged the best of them, the one that made her look uncannily like the 1960's model Jean Shrimpton, and carefully checked her left hand. There was nothing on her fingers.

That presented me with a further, secondary, mystery. If she wasn't involved with anyone, why would this be? I mean, if someone *is* single, there is usually a pretty good reason for it and, if a very attractive woman like Ligeia is single, what does it say about her? Is she messed up in some way? Or is it simply that men just haven't had the confidence to ask her out? No, no, no, there are always *chancers* who will push their luck with beautiful women; they can't say no to everyone, can they?

Perhaps she was between relationships, or *had* been engaged or was divorced. Maybe she'd had a bad relationship, or was recovering from a traumatic engagement. Or was it something infinitely worse? Had her boyfriend/fiancé/husband been killed in a horrific accident? Had he died painfully and slowly from some crippling, incapacitating disease? Was that the real reason she wandered the cemetery alone? It made sense if that were true.

It was obvious she posed more questions than it was possible to answer without knowing more about her, without knowing her. The other thing that was obvious was that she was taking up rather more of my time and thoughts than most people did.

Chapter 9

The following week I was surprised to find an email from Ligeia in my inbox. There was just one word in the subject line: Fabulous.

> Richard,
> Love your photos! <3 They are really expressive.
> I particularly like the brooding ones taken in
> Leicester General Cemetery. Been there many
> times but never saw clouds like those! Do you
> always shoot in black-and-white? Do you sell
> your pictures? I think you have a great talent
> for capturing the monumental. Awesome! Fabulous!
> I hope to see you with your camera again soon.
> Ligeia H.

There was no mystery about *how* she had obtained my email address: there was a link from the website I had given her. Should I answer her? Would that be the right thing to do? She *had* mentioned that she hoped to see me again. Should I tell her when I next intended to go? Would it make me sound like a desperate eccentric?

It took me two days to summon the courage to reply.

> Hi Ligeia,
> Thanks for the comments. Really appreciate
> any/all feedback. I don't sell my pictures, but
> if there is one you particularly like, I could
> always send you a copy :-) I prefer B/W
> photography as it gives greater depth to the
> subject, whatever it is. I will be at the
> cemetery next week. Tuesday or Wednesday,
> weather permitting. If you are there, I might
> see you. :-)
> Take care.
> Richard

After I had sent it I wondered why the fuck I had included the smiley faces.

I needn't have been concerned. It did not prevent her from replying to me. Her email had come in late on the Saturday night (I was already asleep) and was waiting for me when I got up the following morning.

The time stamp was 23:49.

```
Hey you!
Wow! That's really kind of you. I will let you
know which is my favourite if you really are
sure. I've just come back from the cem. Had to
climb over the gate to get out. Was really dark
tonight. Quite disorientating. :-D
Will definitely be there Tues/Weds next week.
Could meet you at the place I saw you before if
you like. :-) Let me know which day.
Speak soon.
Ligeia x
```

Why x? I hadn't expected an x. It probably didn't mean anything. It was more than likely one of those habitual things that some people are wont to do when signing off electronic communications like emails and texts. I appreciated it, though, whether it was inconsequential or otherwise, and replied within a more realistic timescale.

```
Hi,
Thanks for last night's email. You are braver
than me. You wouldn't catch me in that cemetery
so late at night. Let's say Tuesday. Is that OK?
I'll be down where we met before. Around 6pm.
Looking forward to seeing you.
Richard x
```

Was I being forward? I doubted she would even notice my reciprocated x. Yeah, right!

```
Hello again you,
```

```
Tuesday. It's a date! Looking forward to it.
Thanks for the x. You're sweet.
Ligeia xxx
```

"You spend far too much time on that computer."

I never even heard Janice come into the office. I jabbed the minimise button in panic and watched with some relief as the mailbox disappeared. I turned to find her standing in the doorway, dressed in her leopard-spot dressing gown and brandishing a mug of steaming coffee. I relieved her of it and attempted to ignore her inquisitiveness.

"What are you up to?"

"Just boring school stuff," I lied. "You know how it is."

She nodded, uncertainly.

"Don't work too hard. You don't get paid enough to kill yourself."

I smiled, as disarmingly as I could manage.

"Sure. Thanks for the drink."

Janice moved back into the hall.

"And don't work all night. I'm off to bed."

I bade her goodnight and as soon as I was certain she was safely out of the way I restored the screen so that I was able to read Ligeia's message again.

I was sweet, apparently. Not as sweet as the coffee Janice had made for me, though. I pushed it to one side, grimacing at the unnecessary sweetness of the hot drink and pulled up Ligeia's file again.

Tuesday, 6pm.

It was a date.

She'd said as much.

Chapter 10

Tuesday: 17:50

I arrived early, and in a state of nervous anticipation, at the great northern cemetery; this was uncharacteristic of me and wholly due to the arranged rendezvous with Ligeia. I say uncharacteristic, but that in itself may be incorrect; it could have only *seemed* unusual because I had not found myself in a situation that would warrant such trepidation in many, many years. I felt like I was meeting a new girlfriend on a first serious date, which was absurd.

Butterflies? The last of the late-summer Lepidoptera were a memory now that the weather was changing, although my nervousness was recreating their flight patterns in my stomach. It was ridiculous, I know, yet at the same time I felt alive, as though my body was charged with electricity. The sensation in my gut served to reconfirm the immediacy of our impending assignation.

As I trod the steep path down towards our proposed meeting place my breathing became faster and shorter, and a feeling of excitement coursed through my body. There were hundreds of thoughts racing through my mind, all concerned with what I would say, what I should avoid saying, what questions it might be prudent to ask, and whether she would turn up at all.

She was waiting for me at the bottom of the slope; she was sitting on a kerbstone set back a little way towards the rocky limestone walls that enclosed that section. She stood up as I approached and I noticed that, once again, she was not wearing shoes.

"Hello!" She seemed genuinely pleased to see me.

I returned the greeting, attempting to mirror her enthusiasm, and we kissed each other perfunctorily on each cheek. When she stepped away, the heady scent of her perfume assailed my nostrils and I studied her carefully, taking in every inch of her.

She was even more beautiful than I remembered. She was wearing a sleeveless, voluminous, floaty, ankle-length, Paisley-patterned kaftan-style dress that did little to hide her curvaceous form, which was outlined flatteringly every time the cool evening breeze flattened the material against her body. She had chosen the subtler colours of the pattern as a key for her eye makeup. She stared at me expectantly with pale-blue eyes hooded by smoky-brown eyelids. I wanted to kiss her.

There was an embarrassing moment or two as we became accustomed to each other through our reacquaintance, which left me feeling clumsy and socially awkward. Although it was shamefully obvious to me, I think she hardly noticed.

"So, what are you thinking of photographing this evening?"

What indeed. I hadn't really given it much thought. My principal reason for being there was so I could see her.

"I though I would check the area out properly and see if there is anything of interest that takes my fancy."

"Is it alright if I tag along and keep you company?"

I confirmed that was acceptable (actually it was *more* than acceptable) and she clapped her hands together, childlike, in unmistakeable pleasure.

And so we began walking, moving slowly between the headstones and towering tombs that rose up like the petrified trunks of ancient trees, talking occasionally about the names and ages of those commemorated on the memorial plaques. She had a soft, quiet voice that from time to time I had difficulty hearing. It made for pleasant listening, even though I missed some of her words.

"Do you ever imagine them?" she asked earnestly. "Do you think about them and their lives? Do you wonder who they were, what they did, what they were like… who they loved?"

It was apparent whom she was referring to, but I still sought clarification. I had no intention of appearing ignorant.

"You mean the dead?"

She nodded.

"It's such an abrupt term, don't you think? The dead. It doesn't say anything about the person. It's more like an impenetrable brick wall that denies us any further progress and disallows us the space for further thought or imagination. I prefer 'the deceased' or 'the departed' because it alludes to the life before death."

To be honest, I had never really given it that much thought.

"I suppose. Do you think about all of them… the deceased… in that way?"

She stopped by a wall tomb and ran her fingers over the Welsh slate panel.

"Yes, I really do. Like this one."

Sacred to the memory of
Elizabeth Ann Bartles
Who died September 18th 1881
Aged 29 years
Blessed are the dead which die in The Lord
Rom 14 Chap. 13 Ver.

"This is possibly the only visual clue that Elizabeth Ann Bartles ever existed. It doesn't say very much about her or how she died, but there is a story here, most of which we can only guess. The clues to her life are all here, though.

"For example, here she is in the wall, not in the ground, which tells us that the surviving members of the Bartles family, who held her memory sacred, were not rich enough to have Elizabeth interred in a regular plot. If we look around, there are no other Bartles in the vicinity, at least not in the immediate vicinity, so that is another mystery. Why?

"The chances are she and any siblings she might have had survived their parents and that they are buried in another part of the country somewhere. Elizabeth then moved away, settled here and got married. She's 29, so it is reasonably safe to assume she was married. She may have had children, but as they are not buried with her, or around her, we cannot really know that for certain.

And there is no sign of her husband. That's because I believe her husband survived Elizabeth and had her commemorated in the only manner he could afford at the time. While his intention might have been that he and their children would eventually be buried close by, perhaps altogether in a more fitting grave, as was common in Victorian times, he remarried and is now buried with, or close to, their children and his new wife. That makes the most sense."

I was impressed.

"You got all that from a grave panel?"

"I might be massively wide of the mark," she smiled. "Though I'd like to think not too far. It's only conjecture, based on my understanding of funereal etiquette in the nineteenth century."

"Are you a historian?"

"No." She moved on and looked back over her shoulder, silently imploring me to follow her. "I read a lot. I find it all fascinating."

She hadn't given much away, except that she was interested in death, was an avid reader and possessed a very competent analytical mind and/or a very fertile imagination.

What did she do for a living?

"I'm an artist... and a poet," she explained.

I took it that she meant she was currently unemployed and either living on state benefits or had very supportive and accommodating parents. I was quite disappointed. I think it showed on my face because she suddenly felt the need to elaborate on her initial statement.

"I was a model in my teens. I worked for Selection, a London-based model agency. Have you heard of it?"

I shook my head.

"Anyway, it's very big and very influential. They have a stable of girls like me who they promote to magazines... fashion houses... that sort of thing. It is a bitch of a profession, and very cutthroat, but the money is good. I went on their books when I was sixteen and by the time I was nineteen I had enough money to pay off the remainder of my parents' mortgage and buy myself a decent flat up here while I went to university."

Fuck me, that was impressive! At least it sounded impressive.

I was interested to learn what she studied and if she still did any modelling work.

"Sometimes. It depends. If I want a really nice holiday, I'll put myself back on the books and do a couple of cover sessions or a fashion shoot or something. That usually pays me enough not to have to worry about cash until I get back. Then I dive back into my art, which is what I studied... art and design... or I write poetry. It really depends on my mood. It is what I want to concentrate on."

I could tell she had an artistic temperament and it was evident in the way she carried herself, the way she dressed, the way she spoke and the peculiar way she romanticised about the dead (sorry, the deceased). However, I was certain that she could make money much more easily by doing more modelling work, and told her so.

"You say that and, yes, it's true, but, intellectually, it's less rewarding. I had an exhibition of my work two years ago and found that much more exhilarating than any photo shoot, even one in a fabulous location; and, believe me, I have been to some incredible places! It's the same with my poetry. Now I'm published and appreciated for my work it is far more rewarding than being recognised as the cover girl for *Marie Claire*."

Wow! Marie Claire?

"I'm sorry," I said; I was slightly puzzled. "You write as Ligeia Middleton-Hennessy?"

"No, that's my real name. I have three names: my birth name, my model name, Jennifer Dane, and my pen name, which I also use for my art. Beatrice Waverley."

The last name was familiar. It took a little while for my recollection to fully kick in and then I realised I had not only seen a volume of Beatrice Waverley's poetry in my local Waterstones, I had picked it up and read one or two of the poems within it. She was actually quite good, if my memory could be relied upon.

"I think I've read some of your poems!" I exclaimed confidently.

"Really?" Her face indicated she disbelieved me.

"Seriously! I remember your name on the front cover, and there was an illustration of…" – I struggled to remember the cover at first, but then, by degrees, it returned until I could visualise it in all its profane glory.

"It was an engraving by Félicien Rops."

She smiled.

"That's right! Le Calvaire! Oh my God, you have seen it! What did you think?"

Ah, the ego of artists. So easily offered up where it could be made to sit in the palm of one's hand, there to be gently cradled or utterly crushed in a heartbeat. Would she recognise my words as mere flattery or accept them graciously as an honest critique. Dare I challenge her anxious, fragile state, which surely would only exist while I spoke positively about her work?

"I really liked your poetry!" I was ebullient in my response, causing her to sigh outwardly and beam effusively. I watched her breasts heave, causing a shudder of pleasure to ripple through my body. I held up one hand defensively. "But I must confess I didn't get a chance to read them all."

"Then you must! We must exchange our work. Fair exchange is no robbery, after all. If you let me have a copy of one of your photographs, I'll let you have a copy of my book. Signed, of course."

I agreed and a deal was struck. She appeared to be very happy with the arrangement, although I saw a shadow of something flit across her face, some emotion that indicated she was experiencing some inner turmoil. I checked my watch, which only seemed to make matters worse.

"I'm keeping you from your work, aren't I?"

Work? What work? I had come to see her.

"No, not at all! I'm enjoying your company."

She seemed uncertain. I had to reassure her. I felt there was a danger that she would leave, wander off and cause me to curse my miserable existence even more than I already did. She was the first ray of sunlight that had fallen across my weary soul in many years. I didn't want her to go.

"Honestly. Please. Stay."

Ligeia studied me carefully, and slowly I watched her body relax and any resolve to leave weaken and then disappear. Her smile was radiant.

"Okay."

Then she did the most peculiar thing. She placed her hand, which was as cool and as smooth as alabaster, in mine and urged me forward. We continued walking, hand-in-hand, through the stones of the cemetery. It felt strangely unfamiliar but sensual and comforting.

"I want to show you something," she said after a while. "There's a tomb a little way off that is really beautiful."

It was an unusual choice of words to describe a place that contained the bones of the departed: beautiful. However, I nodded and allowed her to guide me through the labyrinth of archaic structures and across the fat, lush grass towards a huge red-and-white marble construction that resembled a scaled-down Corinthian temple. It was big enough not to miss, so I wondered how the fuck it had evaded my camera all the previous times I had visited the cemetery.

Her hand slipped out of mine and she ran ahead, genuinely in rapture at being so close to the sepulchral structure. I watched her whirl around, as though dancing, eyes closed, arms outstretched. I put my camera to my eye and fired off a volley of hurried, candid shots. The noise captured her immediate attention,

"Yes!" she cried. "Please! That would be divine! I have always wanted to be photographed here, in the shadow of this monument to those who have passed this way before us... this edifice constructed to celebrate the lives of those whose mortal bodies have fallen into decline. Would you do that for me, please? Would you capture me in youthful bloom forever, in this place of solemn reverence to the flesh decayed?"

It was a very poetic request. How could I refuse?

"Sure." I turned the camera on. "I just need to check the AWB."

"Okay." She drew her dress effortlessly over her head and stood there, completely naked.

It was unexpected. I struggled with the situation at first, uncertain how to respond. My eyes were drawn to the perfection of her body, a glorious temple that demanded admiration and silent adoration, although guilt consumed me for my shameless need to devour the entrancing vision before me.

She was a pale-skinned Goddess, her flawlessness marred only by the raised lacerations on her inner arms, which were themselves inconsequential when compared with the whole. My body ached with an unfamiliar longing for her.

"What's wrong?" Her voice jolted me out of silent reverie, although I was uncertain if I could answer; my mouth was dry.

I lifted the camera and began to record the image of her, a flaxen-haired Hecate in a landscape of corporeal desolation.

She needed no direction, being used to the demands of the industry she had allowed herself to become part of. Her body moved effortlessly from pose to pose, an essay of movement and astonishing versatility; flesh stretched taut over firm, toned muscle as she changed position to accommodate my ravenous, insatiable desire to capture her entirely and so later create an enduring chromogenic impression of each sublime moment.

I allowed my camera to be an extension of my senses,

my lens examining every part of her, caressing the soft voluptuousness of her body, tasting the essence of her, breathing in the scent of her skin, of her hair, listening to the thrum of her blood rushing excitedly through her arteries and veins, and hearing the gentle sound of her breath as it escaped from her lips.

Captivated, I did not even stop to consider if we were alone. An audience may have assembled and I would not have realised; neither would Ligeia, I am sure.

She was consumed in the performance of an exhibitionistic display that had caused some part of me – a part that had seemingly lain dormant for far too long – to rise up and strain against its material constraints until, throbbing with an intensity that was impossible to ignore, it caused me to spontaneously discharge myself of its crippling embrace. I cried out, liberated from the burden of emotional and physical constriction.

Ligeia heard me, I am sure, and she moved towards me, smiling beguilingly. She took my hand and drew me closer to the doorway of the tomb where she let go so she could continue posing; she stretched languidly against the carved doors, arms above her head, ribs more evident beneath her firm, exceptional breasts. I closed in on her, the zoom magnifying those aspects that captivated me the most.

Lips moist and tinted, and parted slightly to reveal the pearl-white splendour of her teeth.

A roseate areola crowned by a stiff, taut nipple.

The swell of her bosom, peerless in spherical profile.

The soft, rounded mound of her mons pubis, devoid of hair; the swollen edge of her clitoral hood just evident in the cleft of Venus.

Hips, thighs, stomach, arms, shoulders, throat, eyes; I continued to commit all to digital memory until there was no longer any space remaining. Disappointingly, I had to bring our impromptu photo shoot to an end. I couldn't tell if Ligeia was as frustrated as I was – her face was hidden in the deepening shadows – although she thanked me and, shivering slightly, walked back to where she had unceremoniously cast off her clothing and pulled the dress back over her head.

I was still in shock.

"Will you let me see them?" she asked. "Once you've had a chance to review them, obviously."

"Yes, of course."

"It's just that I've always wanted to do that. I've written poem after poem about it, about the sensation of liberation that being naked in unconventional surroundings arouses in me; now I will be able to identify if the joy that I imagine I feel filling my body is just in my head or something that is actually discernible."

I found it hard to believe it was the first time she had cavorted naked in such a place. Her behaviour indicated that, like most photographic models, exhibitionism in one form or another was part of the way she was.

My heart, thankfully, was no longer hammering in my chest and my breathing was gradually returning to normal. The only physical evidence of what had occurred and how it had affected me was the uncomfortable dampness in my trousers. Was it obvious to her that I'd been overtaken by desire? I was grateful that the light was beginning to fade.

Ligeia took my hand again as we began to walk towards the path that would take us back up to the main part of the cemetery. Her hand was warmer, still smooth but noticeably softer. We didn't say very much, although there was an unspoken connection, accentuated by her occasionally gripping my hand more firmly. At the top of the slope she turned to me and kissed me gently on the lips.

"I'll see you again, I promise." She started to walk away. "I need to get my things."

I panicked.

"What things? When? Will you email me? Can I give you my mobile number?"

She put a finger to her lips, smiling.

"I'll contact you. Soon." With that she turned and I watched her walk down the avenue until, finally, she was lost from sight and my heart felt heavy once more.

★ ★ ★

Later that evening, I transferred the contents of the memory card onto my laptop. I spent an hour applying a black-and-white filter to each shot and another reviewing each individual image. I discarded none. My erection returned, but there was still too much to do before I could turn my attention to the satiating of my lust. I needed to safeguard the integrity of the images by duplicating them and saving them externally.

I set up the equipment. The process of pushing cables into sockets only confirmed my immediate preoccupation with sex. As soon as I had downloaded the images onto the external hard drive I went into the next room and fucked Janice as hard as my passion would allow. She was fairly surprised by my insistent ardour; it had been a while since we'd had sex, though, so was more than up for it. She was quite enthusiastic, more animated, or perhaps that was just my imagination.

As I thrust into her a final time and emptied myself in her I realised she wasn't exactly Ligeia, but, in the absence of anything even closely resembling her, she'd do.

My allomulcian indulgence aside, it was the best sex I'd had in years.

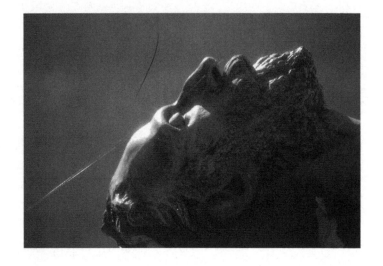

Chapter 11

My life felt different. Since meeting Ligeia I had become more unsettled. Paradoxically, my disposition was both disconcerting and, simultaneously, intoxicating. My creativity had returned. I started writing once more and my passion for photography was easily in danger of eclipsing all my other interests combined. I spent several hours each evening – that is when I was not out, camera in hand, searching for new photo opportunities – going through old anonymous folders of miscellaneous images, compiling them by theme into instantly identifiable, more cohesive groups. I deleted those that I felt were not representative of the work I was now doing, a distinct direction now solidified in my mind.

Ligeia had her own folder (previously entitled MGIG), comprising sixty-eight photographs in which she appeared as an incidental figure, taken before we knew each other properly. Then there were the others, almost four hundred and eighty high-speed, high-resolution captures of her dancing naked in front of the mausoleum. At times I was afraid to look at them, aware that my reaction to each frame had become almost habitual. Invariably, my weakness would get the better of me and I would sit transfixed as I viewed them all again, slowly, one at a time. It strengthened my resolve to ask her to pose for me again.

I intended to contact her to arrange a mutually convenient time when I could show her the pictures I'd taken that night. I was desperate for her to appreciate my work; indeed it was essential if I was going to work with her again, although the prospect made me anxious. For that reason I had yet to email her. What if she disliked what I'd done? She was a model, after all. I knew a lot of my work could not be compared to that of the professionals she'd previously worked with, most of whom no longer needed to even consider composition because it was second nature.

Shit.

I despised my destructive self-criticism. It made me doubt myself, even when I was positive, even when I possessed the courage of my convictions. It was a coping mechanism employed by my subconscious to keep the more instinctive part of me safe. I knew that. Safe from what, though? It wasn't as though I was going to try and form some kind of relationship with her. That notion was patently absurd. Wasn't it?

There was a degree of fixation creeping into my life. It was quite troubling, but it was nothing I couldn't keep under control. Or so I believed.

I glanced at the clock on the mantelpiece: it was 11:52pm.

Sitting alone in the darkness of the living room, aware of Janice – or, rather, aware she was there – only a few feet away, directly above me, no doubt sleeping soundly and oblivious to the turmoil I found myself in, provided me with no comfort whatsoever. Rational thought was inviting, intoxicatingly so, and definitely more desirable than the pointless, futile machinations that filled my head as I attempted to formulate some kind of emotional resolution to the predicament I increasingly found myself in.

It was a peculiar situation. One part of me embraced Ligeia and everything she was, everything she represented; this was the same part that celebrated the fact that I had found someone with whom I could communicate intellectually, and be fascinated by artistically. Yet there was another part that upbraided me, berating me even though I was only *contemplating* – rather than surrendering to – the idea of physical infidelity.

Guilt consumed me and I justified this feeling initially by announcing (internally) that it was because I actually did care about Janice. By degrees, the guilt dissipated, only to be replaced by the realisation that it was predominantly fear that assailed me and had laid siege to my mind and emotions.

I was afraid, understandably; after all, I had been in a marriage that spanned almost two decades and had survived despite every kind of problem that period of time could throw at us. We were established; we were a habit. We had been institutionalised by our own imagined expectations of the society we lived in, although 'lived' might be a bit strong.

After so many years of compliance, of course I was afraid. What if something did happen between Ligeia and me? What if, for some inexplicable reason, we did begin a torrid love affair? What would our families say? What would the other people who know us say? I was afraid of that possibility, certainly. I was also afraid of what Janice would say and how she might react; afraid of what could possibly happen to our home and our other financial arrangements – usually the first casualties in any marital dispute – notwithstanding all other eventualities. It was too horrible to contemplate the maelstrom that would occur during the inevitable disruption that all such marital disharmonies create.

Balancing the fear was easy. I justified my interest, my fascination, my (dare I admit it?) obsession with my enigmatic, beautiful new acquaintance with stroppy indignation. Did I not owe it to myself, I reasoned, to *have* a rewarding, satisfying, fulfilling life? To live a life that was emotionally, intellectually and sexually satisfying? I would be doing myself a huge disservice by *not* exploring our developing relationship further, merely because of outmoded marital obligation or duty. Nothing *untoward* had happened between us for fuck's sake, although I desired it and her more than anything. We were just....

What? Friends?

I realised that, unconsciously, I was stroking my cock through the material of my pyjama bottoms. I didn't stop. I allowed my arousal free rein and when I was certain that it could engorge no further, I pulled it free and began masturbating slowly, taking infinite care and time to savour the sensation of each stroke.

Friends? No, I wanted more than that. Friends didn't spend time fantasising about each other to the point where the only course of action left open to them to express their feelings for the other was onanistic self-gratification.

My penis was solid in my hand, warm and reassuringly familiar. I imagined Ligeia, dancing naked through the gravestones, her lissom body pale and exciting under a moonlit sky. Instinctively, my hand tightened around my shaft and I pulled back as far as I could physically manage, until my frenulum strained and my glans wept a silent tear of anticipation, but I did not alter the speed. I laboured methodically, allowing all of the emotions that my visualisation of Ligeia filled me with to take over. I ejaculated silently and felt the emission splash up my body.

My impromptu evening embrace by the five-fingered widow was halted by a sound above me. I stopped dead, my hand still wrapped around my member in mid-stroke, my spasms ebbing away. I opened my eyes slowly and waited as the noises grew closer. The landing light went on, creating a thin line of brilliant illumination around the edges of the door. I inhaled quickly, holding my breath, scarcely able to move. It was Janice, probably awakened by her bladder and the increasingly regular necessity to empty it in the middle of the night. I sat and listened, exhaling slowly, the sperm on my chest trickling slowly down towards my navel, growing cold and distinctly unpleasant.

After a short while I heard the muffled sound of the toilet flushing and the gentle padding of Janice's feet on the carpet as she made her way back to the bedroom. She stopped at the top of the stairs and sleepily called down to me.

"Richard? Are you coming to bed?"

"Yep, just give me a minute," I reassured her, trying to sound as natural as I could.

After that there was the grinding metallic sound of the door handle, the creak of the bedroom door, the peculiar sound of springs inside the mattress being compressed, and then nothing.

I waited a few minutes and then stood up to clean the cum off my upper torso and the end of my softening cock with a Kleenex. Then I pulled my pyjama bottoms up, sat down again and immersed myself in thought. Over the next few hours I studied the various grades of darkness in the room until the first rays of daylight began chasing it, and any remaining doubts about my future, away.

I didn't join Janice in bed. I doubt if she even realised.

★ ★ ★

The whole of the following day I waited in vain for Ligeia

to contact me. I was very disappointed when she did not; I actually found myself willing her to call, or text, or anything. I swear that every time my phone vibrated silently in my pocket, my heart began to hammer a little faster in my chest. The messages were not from my new, strange acquaintance, however; the only texts I received were alerts from the chess club, reminding me that my annual membership subscription was due, and from Janice, enquiring what I fancied for our meal that evening.

Ligeia did eventually get in touch, three days later, initially by text and then by phone; she asked how the photographs had turned out and if/when she would be allowed to see them. I tried to remain as calm as I could when I replied but, in truth, I was so eager to see her again that it must have been noticeable in my voice.

"We can look through them together. I'd really like that. You can come round to my flat this weekend if you like." Her suggestion caused me such psychosexual consternation that I couldn't answer her for at least a minute. I could not have hoped for a more promising invitation, although I felt it was important that I did not seem *too* eager.

"Great," I replied in as nonchalant a manner as I could manage. "Which day are you free?"

When she said that she had nothing on the following afternoon I have to admit the gap in her social calendar was not the first thing that went through my mind. I chastised myself inwardly, cursing my over-fertile imagination.

"That sounds great."

Great.

Great?

For fuck's sake!

I'd responded with 'great' twice in as many sentences:

a classic blunder, a nervous error. I hoped she hadn't noticed.

If she did, nothing was mentioned, apart from her address, which I hastily scribbled down and shoved in my back trouser pocket. It was done. I allowed myself a selfish, satisfied smile. I needn't have done, but at that point I was not to know what would transpire through knowing her or that the day that followed would alter my life irreversibly.

Chapter 12

Inevitable. Inevitably. Inevitability. Three words I particularly loathe.

The words themselves, in isolation, are fine. I have a problem with their use only when either or all of them are used by folk seeking to blame their own moral lassitude on something more abstract, like destiny or fate. Quite often the words are used by poor 'agonised' souls eager to bear the innermost workings of their heart to those hokey relationship 'experts' in the problem pages of tacky tabloids. You can often see one or more of those words used in connection with, or when describing, illicit, illegal or adulterous relationships: 'We'd been seeing each other for about a month before the inevitable happened' or 'Inevitably, we ended up sleeping together'.

It is as though they are declaring that, as human beings, we simply have no control over what we do or whom we do it with, that people are just thrown together according to some immense and bewildering preordained cosmic plan. The same people must imagine that if they submit to the notion that there is some indecipherable scheme that determines whom we fuck, they don't have to shoulder any responsibility for their actions. Bollocks. I personally believe there is nothing remotely inevitable about two sentient human beings coming together and deciding to have sex. It's called choice.

So it was not inevitable that I ended up sleeping with Ligeia. I chose to. Our sexual union came about from a conscious decision that we both made in respect of the other and which we carried out, knowing exactly what it would entail and what the possible consequences might be. Inevitability played *no* part in our first frenetic coupling at her flat that Saturday, during what was an unseasonably warm late-October afternoon.

Certainly there were other factors that did play a part. For example, we were drawn together, by either mutual need or physical (perhaps even emotional) attraction. I won't say lust at this point, even though it played a part later on. Initially, however, I was smitten. This quickly gave way to infatuation; eventually my interest in Ligeia bordered on obsessive. So when she invited me up to her flat for coffee I jumped at the opportunity. It was how our physical relationship began.

Many images of Ligeia are precious to me, and I hold them sacred over all others. The way she was dressed when she answered the door to me the afternoon we first made love is a particular favourite of mine. It was simple; in fact, it was understated. She wore nothing more elaborate than faded jeans and a t-shirt. The jeans *were* skin tight, admittedly, and the t-shirt fitted her perfectly, exaggerating the swell of her firm breasts beneath and the stiffness of her nipples; apart from that, it was fairly modest. She was also barefoot, her toenails painted in what I later learned was her favourite default-coloured nail varnish.

"Come in," she welcomed me.

With the door closed on the outside world, she embraced me and kissed me fully on the lips, which I was not expecting but did not protest about. I remember her perfume, a heady blend of scents that I imagined included rose oil, violets and liquorice. I could feel her body pressed against mine and I needed her to stay like that for as long as it was physically possible. The sensation was delicious and I felt my cock stir in approval.

"Thanks for coming over." She pulled away from me, her smile warm and alluring.

"Thanks for inviting me." I returned her smile and glanced around at my surroundings.

It wasn't particularly awkward; it was just part of the ritual, the next step in the getting-to-know-you ritual, that procession of perfunctory, polite phrases and carefully orchestrated movements. I was acknowledging her and simultaneously keen to illustrate that I recognised her personal space. It was her territory, and so I carefully began exploring it, taking in as much as was possible. As I did so, she began to move around the room effortlessly.

The flat was tastefully decorated and well furnished; I was pleased to note it was not remotely minimalist, the latest in what seemed to be a never-ending catalogue of fashionably banal home decor trends. She was definitely more Heals, or rather Hopewells, than IKEA. The only thing that looked out of place was a large picture that almost completely filled one wall, and which, uncharacteristically, I felt compelled to comment on.

"I'm used to it now. When I first put it up it felt so intrusive that I spent a lot of time in the bedroom, anywhere where I wouldn't have to look at it."

I laughed. "So why put it up at all?"

"It's a family piece. It has been in our family for about four generations; handed down from one of my eccentric great-great-great-aunts, who used to spend all her time lusting after young Parisian artists in the 1890s. She bought it from one of them, I think. Dad told me once she was the sitter, but I think it's impossible to say definitely because you can't see her face. Now it's a bequest that's handed down to the youngest female Hennessy on her eighteenth birthday. So now it's mine, for better or for worse, indefinitely."

I noticed her voice trail off slightly at the end of the sentence, as if there was something darker connected with the legacy. I decided against probing any further, despite my curiosity.

And thus the afternoon proceeded, politely, with me being more self-conscious than was healthy, and Ligeia being charming, honest and relaxed; she was a breath of fresh air. She was keen to view my photographs and so we sat side by side on the sofa, her laptop balanced between us while I inserted my memory stick.

The photographs were good but not great, by my own standards. Even so, they drew gasps and murmurs of approval from Ligeia and transported me back to the evening I'd taken them, watching her stunning naked performance in the near darkness. I could tell from the smile on her face she was very pleased with my efforts, but she confirmed it for me anyway.

"I love them, Richard. They're excellent! You're a very talented photographer."

The slideshow revealed every single shot I'd taken, one by one. She paused on one in particular; in it her pose gave her the appearance of a dancer caught mid-pirouette, one leg slightly raised and her arms stretched above her. She tapped the screen gently.

"That's my favourite."

I nodded in agreement.

"It does capture you very well."

"It makes me look very graceful. Which is your favourite?"

Which one indeed?

I couldn't tell her of course. How do you broach the subject of which one is a favourite and how it was chosen, except by telling the truth? Even though I had seen her naked I felt our friendship was still in its infancy, so I couldn't very well tell her it was the one that caused me to have a spontaneous erection every time I viewed it, or the one I had masturbated to every night since.

Instead, I waffled on about composition and light and other crap that I knew made very little sense in terms of photography but was technical enough for a layman to be drawn off the scent. I pointed to one random shot, stating that was my favourite, only to see it replaced by the actual one. I quickly looked away and out of the window.

I waited ten seconds for the next image to appear and resumed viewing. Ligeia was regarding me in a very strange manner, the faintest smile on her lips. I pretended not to notice; I could feel the warmth of her leg against mine and caught the merest hint of her perfume on the air. She leant in towards me, making me swallow nervously.

"Do you want to take me to bed?"

The question came out of nowhere and, foolishly, I was uncertain how to answer. In truth, my honest response would have been to have blurted out an unequivocal 'Yes!' – maybe even adding 'Please!' immediately afterwards. Instead, I begged her pardon, forcing her to repeat the question using more conspicuous terminology.

"Would you like to fuck me?"

I will not go into detail about how I answered her; suffice to say we ended up in bed together. I hold the memory of our first time together and everything it entailed – our first embrace, our first passionate kiss, the first time we made love – as sacred and I have allowed nothing that occurred between us afterwards to sully my recollection of what was, for me, an almost spiritual experience.

I'm not certain how Ligeia regarded it. I am certain that she had enjoyed other lovers who were most probably more adept, sexually, than I; and if my first endeavour was awkward, clumsy or brief, I feel certain that I more than rectified that with every act of coitus that followed.

Afterwards we lay together beneath the sheets, her body warm, soft and wrapped around mine, in silent, satisfied bliss. I could hear her carriage clock ticking away noisily in the living room. It had begun to mark time for us as a couple.

Chapter 13

Ligeia and I met often for sex after our first time in her flat, although there were times when she was inexplicably unavailable. She never said why she wasn't obtainable. Occasionally, she could not be reached by mobile at all, sometimes for days; in the beginning, I never asked. I assumed a great deal at the start of our affair. I convinced myself it was because of the demands of her craft, and pictured her torturing herself in the gloomy, cold spare bedroom of her flat while she wrestled with the acquisition of the correct word or phrase for her latest poem.

When she did reappear she was never apologetic and continued as though nothing had really occurred; that was just the way things were and so I never questioned it. Besides, it was not really my place to do so. Occasionally, though, I wondered about her life when she was not with me, or writing poetry, or painting or wandering around graveyards. She must have friends she met up with, I figured, but there was very little evidence, either from her directly or in her flat, to indicate such companions existed.

She was always pleased to reacquaint herself with me, and our reunions were always extremely physical. Sex at first would be frenetic, our coupling almost violent in its intensity; we gave in willingly to the *first* expression of our lust, after which we took up a more sporadic, leisurely exploration of carnal delights, which lasted several hours. It seemed her ingenuity, or perhaps inventiveness, if not her youthful curiosity, always ensured that we engaged in at least one example of complex erotic commixtion, at her insistence.

The last occasion that we met up at her place for sex, before things began to change, an opportunity arose for Ligeia to explain, or at least attempt to explain, why she felt it had been necessary to lacerate her once perfect skin so prolifically.

We had finished our first round of sexual gymnastics of the evening and were lying together, her legs entwined in mine. Reaching over, I tentatively stroked the lacerations on her forearm, tracing them with a fingernail. I still found it perverse that someone so beautiful could even consider taking a razor blade to herself. Perhaps she sensed my bewilderment because her eyes narrowed, prompting me to express my thoughts, although I erred on the side of caution.

"I suppose these make it difficult for you to do certain modelling jobs."

"Not really." She sat up suddenly and propped herself against the headboard. "You'd be surprised, to be honest; it's the attitude towards self-harm that is the most obstructive. Everything else is treatable. There's nothing these days that can't be hidden, airbrushed or touched up cosmetically. Pure photographs, those that haven't been manipulated in someway, represent less than ten percent of the total used by the industry or eventually seen by the public."

"These," she said, stroking her scar tissue, "have never prevented me from getting work. I can do just about everything: face shots, portraits, hand modelling, legs, swimwear; if they want to use you, they'll use you and simply airbrush out the parts they don't want anyone to see."

Having seen Joan Collins on the cover of magazines such as *Hello*, I knew exactly what she was referring to. There was no way that an imminent octogenarian could appear to be so well preserved in a photograph without the artistic application of an airbrush. It made sense, certainly more sense than why Ms Collins thought that it was prudent to fool her adoring fans into believing she looked younger than she was.

"Are you wondering why someone would go to such lengths to deface themselves in such a manner? Or what purpose it serves?"

"I haven't... I didn't... I'm not certain...." I stammered, uncertain *how* to answer. "No," I said.

"I guess it is difficult for a lot of men to understand why a woman would resort to something as extreme as self-harm, but other women appreciate it. They recognise that the scars are nothing more than the physical remnants of a mental struggle that we have had to endure and survived. It is very hard for a lot of women, growing up. It was certainly difficult for me. I spent my childhood protected from the harsher realities, cosseted by my parents. All I needed was provided for me in abundance: love, warmth, shelter. It was like being in a bubble, far removed from the everyday world. As much as I would have liked it to, it couldn't last forever. Everything has to end, including my lovely childhood.

"Everything changes. It is an essential part of life. We all have to grow up and the menarche was the signal for my life to change forever. I was expected just to throw away the dreams of enchantment and give up the belief in the fairy realms that I had been spoon-fed since I was old enough to understand them. I was expected to instinctively understand why my parents' attitudes towards me altered so drastically. I was no longer the pretty little girl I was originally told I was, that I believed I was, but now a young lady standing on the threshold of womanhood and all that entailed.

"All I really wanted was for that dreamlike existence to continue for just a little while longer. Instead, I was forced to accept new roles that I was ill-equipped to deal with. I was still young, remember. I imagined, incorrectly, that the cause of my increasing feeling of isolation from that unconditional love I once enjoyed was the blood that flowed from me every month; it was a symbol of my lost innocence, and it became something that I learned to hate. Each cut I inflicted on myself reminded me of that relationship with my body. The flow of blood was an affirmation of the end of all that I once loved, the pain of each cut a tangible expression of the agony of the loss of my innocence."

"Really?" Part of me wanted to believe her. I had seen such cuts on so many of my own pupils, although I doubted that they had the intelligence to think of such an elaborate coping mechanism, let alone construct such an eloquent defence of their actions. I wondered if part of it was simply the desire to belong and, being slaves to both their hormones and fashion, young girls just cut themselves because their peers do it, because it is trendy.

"You're over it now, right? You don't cut yourself anymore?"

"I don't need to." She stroked my stomach. "I've replaced it with other things. Like sex."

I laughed, but she wasn't even smiling. She was serious.

"It's the closest I can get to the ecstatic sensation that making myself bleed used to give me. It has to be the most sublime feeling in the world, simultaneously experiencing the ultimate physical manifestation of pleasure and pain. Don't you agree?"

Did I agree? Were we talking about the same thing?

I assumed she was describing the debilitating euphoria experienced during orgasm.

I was in a quandary. Was it necessary to inform her that the rapture she was describing and obviously enjoyed was not shared by everyone? Should I explain that it begins like that for everyone, even for me, but the continued gratification of our innate desires naturally culminates in the desensitisation of the nerve-endings that once served us so sensationally in our youth? Should I tell her that, gradually, over successive years it becomes less of an intense rhapsodic climax and more like a satisfying but dull throb? Would it be right to shatter her illusions?

It was at this point that I had one of those moments of epiphany, where I realised that despite my own orgasm now representing only a fraction of the joyous feeling it once had I still persisted in its pursuit, and now with renewed vigour with Ligeia. But to what end? I have already described it as no longer being the same, but I must confess my pleasure in pursuing it had not diminished. Was it the thrill of attainment that spurred me on?

No. The nerves in my glans might have been desensitised, but the other ends were still hard-wired into my brain's pleasure area, the nucleus accumbens, and that was far from numb. For me, it transpired that other aspects of sex resulted in the successful release of dopamine. They included the thrill of physical penetration, the impression of apparently causing significant sexual discomfort with my cock, and the subjugation of my sexual partners through sheer physical dominance.

In short, what floated my boat? The act of sex, not the

prize. It was inconsequential compared with the delight of watching Ligeia writhe beneath me, eyes wide open, as I held her down and rammed myself into her so hard that she moaned.

Her orgasm? Yes, that was spectacular. It was important to me that she was pleasured properly, so I worked hard to ensure she reached her own beautiful release every time we fucked. My own release was less important.

She was staring at me, expectantly, awaiting my answer.

"Absolutely," I said categorically and then manhandled her into position on all fours so that I could slide my erection into her warm wetness from behind. She guided it in with her hand, cupping my balls as I pushed it home; relentlessly I drove her towards a noisy, explosive conclusion with my rhythmic exertion. Afterwards she collapsed, contented, beneath me while my cock, still proudly rampant and far from satiation, glistened with her juice.

It was the first and only time we mentioned her scars. That was also the last time I felt I was totally in control of anything that happened between us in, on or out of bed.

Chapter 14

There were a few things that troubled me about Ligeia.

Actually, there were many; too many to mention here, that's for certain. Most of them I generally pushed away from me, as far away as possible. Ignorance was blissful, believe me. But there were certain things that returned to haunt me again and again, no matter how hard I tried to disregard them.

The most prevalent was her family, particularly her parents.

During the time I had known her there had been the odd reference to them, almost in passing. They had never been discussed in any great detail, only on a superficial level. Admittedly, I seldom mention my parents anymore, but that's because they're both dead. I had the strongest feeling hers were still very much alive and that, for reasons best known to herself, she simply avoided contact with them, which was odd for someone so young. Unless....

Because of the lack of anything resembling a realistic explanation, my mind had begun to provide me with peculiar, improbable possibilities that, in the absence of anything more concrete, I was wont to seriously consider. Ligeia was always very open, so I doubted if she would have kept abusive or sexual revelations about her past from me, regardless of how dark they might have been, as her later disclosures about the unsettlingly creepy Max proved. So I bypassed the more obvious abuse-laden scenarios in favour of almost Shakespearean family conflicts.

I wasn't that far of the mark, as it turned out, although the details provided me with another tantalising glimpse into her world and another possible reason for her unconventional behaviour.

You will not have heard of her father, but his brother (Ligeia's uncle) is still a household name in some quarters, depending upon where in the country you live. Even here in the Midlands I was acutely aware of the reputation of Gerald Middleton, the self-proclaimed lord of Bassingbury Grange and Institute.

Set in fifteen acres of prime Yorkshire woodland, Bassingbury Grange, constructed from Yorkstone in the 1860s and originally the residence of Sir George Bassingbury, the Leeds-based cotton importer and clothing manufacturer, was purchased by Gerald Middleton for £20,000 in 1969. The Bassingbury family had long since vacated their grand and imposing home.

Burdened by various scandals concerning government contracts during the First World War, tax problems and death duties, the Bassingbury industries were forced to close and the family abandoned the Grange in 1938. After that, it acquired the unfortunate title of Bad Luck Mansion locally. During the Second World War, it was acquisitioned by the War Office and became a division headquarters, quickly falling into disrepair once its wartime use had ended. It remained empty, overgrown and neglected until Gerald rediscovered it and set about turning his dream of creating an educational institute into a reality.

Where exactly Gerald obtained the money to purchase the Grange was, like so many other parts of his life, a mystery, although there was a rumour that he had caught a prominent member of Harold Wilson's cabinet in flagrante delicto with his wife, Eugenie, and that the Bassingbury purchase had been a 'loan' rather than a reward for Gerald's discretion, or rather silence. Gerald Middleton never said what the actual truth was, but he secured Bassingbury and moved in, cutting himself off immediately from his family and friends.

Ligeia's father had been eleven at the time and remembered very little about it, except that his parents had been outraged by their elder son's behaviour. However, that was inconsequential compared with what was to follow, all of which he, and most of England, were made aware of in the typical manner that the British gutter press were only too happy to resort to in the pursuit of ever-increasing circulation.

The cause of the scandal was Gerald's educational aspirations. He and Eugenie were not concerned with the numeracy and literacy of the nation. Their establishment was directed towards a singular aim or goal: the ascent of human spirituality through sexual emancipation.

Yes, *that* Gerald Middleton.

It was, of course, a movement born of the zeitgeist. It was specific to that particular period in time and was heralded by the licentious behaviour exhibited by the hippy movement two years previously during the 'summer of love' and a different form of 'freedom of expression' adopted by the *nouveau* intellectuals, the radicals and the politically aware.

'Sex is power!' Gerald announced to anyone who would listen. He maintained that 'sexual repression' was 'nothing more than an example of governmental attempts at social control'. He had a point, it seemed, as illustrated by the sudden influx of devotees who flocked to the Grange to join in with his kooky, avant-garde way of life. The institute was initially conceived as a retreat for like-minded libertines, but it soon became apparent that without enforcing controls it would quickly become overrun. After only four months Gerald reluctantly had to introduce a form of membership: paid membership, of course.

The press loved and loathed him in equal measure. The merest mention of his institute ensured a three-fold increase in sales; if the reports included photographs, circulation went through the roof. They saved the most salacious stories for the Sunday editions and tried to include heavily censored pictures and stories that served only to illustrate how depraved Gerald and his followers were.

Several reporters attempted to break in, climbing over the outer fence, originally erected only to prevent *casual* or accidental trespass. None succeeded in getting farther than the second perimeter enclosure, although it did not stop some journalists fabricating accounts of the 'wild orgies' they had witnessed or the 'vile degeneracy' of 'sex-crazed delinquents'.

Strangely, according to Ligeia's father, the reality couldn't have been further from the truth. It was true that the institute *did* encourage promiscuity, and actively endorsed and encouraged sexual experimentation between consenting members (or 'students') in whatever manner those participants saw fit. This was not merely for titillation. It served a very real purpose as far as Gerald was concerned. Open, honest sexual liaison between consenting adults was essential to the emotional health and spiritual wellbeing of all those who took part.

The tenets of the creator of the institute were based purely and simply on honesty; that and a firm rejection of *anything* that attempted to stifle free thought or expression. All religious books were banned from the site and any member found in possession of such reading material would be removed and disallowed from ever returning. All religious beliefs were required to be left at the gates, as were item of jewellery, such as rings, necklaces and wristwatches and/or any other symbol 'that might denote, or be used to denote, financial superiority or indicate inclusion in a specific social group, class or caste'.

Clothes could not be worn at any time. Full nudity was compulsory because both Gerald and Eugenie maintained 'it is impossible for someone who is naked to be false with another who is similarly unclothed'. Such was their charming naivety.

At any one time there were around seventy 'students' in attendance. They were enrolled on 'courses of enlightenment' that lasted 'anything from two to fourteen consecutive days'. They all had to be members and each member could reside there only if they brought along, or attended with, another member 'of the opposite sex'. This was to facilitate 'parity in integration'. Allegedly. However, David Markham, in his 1985 exposé of the institute, *Not With My Wife* (Borderline Press), suggested that it was 'to ensure no one was left at the bottom of the pile *sexually* and that the Middleton pile, which was secreted in various bank accounts across Europe, could continue to grow'.

I had to admit it was a shrewd move from a business point of view. From a purely hedonistic standpoint, I was certain that equal numbers of opposing sexes could only help to ensure widespread sexual equality. No one would be left wanting, so to speak, whatever their persuasion; for example, the Middletons considered bisexuality to be the highest form of sexual freedom.

You may have read accounts of the so-called Bassingbury educational debates. They can be found in various books, and sometimes still feature (although in edited form) in Sunday newspapers and magazines, especially when there is nothing of any consequence going on elsewhere in the world. Weirdly, Gerald never lost the monicker given to him by the press during those early, heady days of the institute's far-reaching influence and power: the 'sex guru'.

The following is from 'Stiff' by ex-NME hack Dominic Dennison (Bloomberg Publications 1998).

I was aware that shit was going on in other rooms too. There was a smell that reminded me of a brothel in Amsterdam. Sweat and juices, male and female. That and the stink of marijuana. It was fucking wild and so was most of what was going on around me. Fucking. Wild.

There was a big chandelier above us. I swear I could see every one of us reflected in the crystal. Beautiful. A sea of naked arses and tits. Sweaty bodies rising and falling together like sea waves. Some were moaning like the wind and every now and then a little spurt of white. Liquid. Like sea foam coming off the waves and falling between the rest of us lying there in that big fucking ballroom. We were all like mermen and mermaids.

At first I wondered why Jack had bothered to bring me. It was obvious. He always had two girls on his arm and I know he wanted to fuck them both. The rules said one guy, one girl. I was making up numbers. Assisting the rock royalty, Jack said. I went along with it. He was pile-driving Penny, and Amber was licking his arse, but I didn't feel out of it.

Everything was beautiful.

Some coy black chick was noshing on my bell-end while her boyfriend (I think it was her boyfriend) was giving her the old vinegar stroke with a face like a tortured pig. Thankfully, after he'd pulled out, he left the grave open, so I buried my old man in her slash and banged the fuck out of her. I tell you, spunk looks really good on smooth, chocolaty Negro skin. She was a fashion designer or something. I told her it didn't matter.

None of it mattered. It didn't matter who I was, or who any of us were. Even Jack, the fucking megastar with his triple platinum-selling albums and Rolls Royces and expensive coke habit and shit. He was just another John plugging away at a horny little bitch in a house full of Johns plugging other horny bitches and getting their rocks off. Fuck, it was the cream.

Not the most eloquent of descriptions, I'm sure you will agree – the guy was a rock journalist after all, with everything *that* entails – but it paints a fairly accurate picture (apparently) of a typical soirée at Bassingbury. Members included stars of TV, stage and screen, prominent politicians, several high-ranking police officers, musicians, footballers, rock stars and – as those appalling seasonal Ronco record adverts used to announce – many, many more.

Despite all of Gerald and Eugenie's higher moral posturing, most people realised fairly early on that the Bassingbury Institute was nothing more than an exclusive swingers' club. For example, there were no factory workers swelling the membership, no miners and definitely no one who was unemployed. Only three things could ensure automatic, unchallenged membership: money, power and fame. At the height of the institute's popularity it was said if you were permitted to join the 'fellowship' then you had already reached the pinnacle of all possible achievement.

Ligeia's father had hardly known Gerald. His elder brother was always remembered by him as being slightly 'mental' or 'eccentric' and 'the cause of more family altercations' than anything else. After he'd established Bassingbury, Francis met up with Gerald on only three occasions: the funerals of their parents and of their younger sister, Deborah, who died a few years after their mother. Deborah had overdosed on heroin. They were all difficult events that led, on the final occasion, to a horrific and much publicised family row.

Francis idolised Deborah and was devastated when she died. He believed her descent into drugs was directly attributable to Gerald's permissive influence. He adored her, but *she* only ever looked up to Gerald. To Deborah, Gerald was a beacon, a torch held aloft in a world that was slowly dying and becoming dimmer. She aspired to embrace Gerald's lofty ideals wholeheartedly, even joining him at the institute several times. Francis believed she was introduced to drugs during one of her visits.

She became involved with a series of celebrities, artists and rock stars, often being photographed on the arm of musicians like the blues guitarist Dave Ventiss and Pete O'Phile, the lead singer of the punk band Spasm! However, it became quickly apparent to Francis that Deborah was not cut out for such a high-profile life and the depression that set in after the death of their father was only exacerbated by the death of their mother four years later. When Francis saw his sister at the graveside he hardly recognised her. Pale, drawn and dangerously thin, she had to be supported throughout most of the ceremony by Gerald.

Ligeia said that was when Francis began hating his brother. All his life he had wanted only to be loved by his sister, the way he loved her, yet when it appeared she needed help she turned to Gerald instead of him, the one person who loved her unconditionally.

"Dad never forgave him. When Aunt Deborah died he just sat in the chair and cried and cried and cried. I had never ever seen him so upset before or since. Mum didn't want him to go to the funeral because she knew there would be a scene and, of course, there was. Uncle Gerald arrived as ostentatiously as he always did in this big gold Bentley, which was more ironic than anything else; I mean, there was this ageing hippy who had purportedly thrown away the trappings of materialism to start up his free love commune turning up like a megastar.

"It was all bullshit. The truth was Uncle Gerald was no different from anyone else. Dad saw it, Mum saw it, even I saw it, but Aunt Deborah saw only what she wanted to see. Her brother Gerald, the most liberated, enlightened man in the world! She died because of her addiction to the drugs. The drugs were how she coped with the fact that she could never be like him. She wanted to be, but it was impossible.

"I'd never heard Dad swear before the funeral. When the cameras had finished flashing and the paparazzi had taken enough photographs of 'Lord' Bassingbury, Uncle Gerald came over to talk to us. Dad just stared him in the eye and called him a cunt.

"After that all hell was let loose. It caused another media scrum as reporters jostled to take photographs of Dad and Uncle Gerald, who were trading blows with each other. The whole thing was an absolute disgrace."

I remember reading something about the incident at the time it happened. It was considered sensational, although I was too far removed from it all to be particularly bothered. After Ligeia's revelation, however, I found it unbelievable that there were now only two degrees of separation between media celebrity – and 'sex guru' – Gerald Middleton and me. It suddenly occurred to me that the world had somehow become so much smaller.

After the graveside fracas, any bonds that had existed between Francis and his brother were permanently and irreparably severed. The siblings never spoke to each other again. That rift affected everyone, and its legacy was the reason Ligeia eventually found herself ostracised by her own parents.

"I think fathers especially have problems when their daughters become sexually active. I know Dad did, even though I was what might be considered a late starter by today's standards. Mum was okay with my experimentation; she knew me well enough to realise that I wasn't going to do anything stupid. She'd say things like 'I was the same at your age' in regards to my inability to maintain any steady relationships."

It transpired that after her stifling affair with Max, Ligeia embarked on a series of 'liberating' short-term relationships; some were only one-night stands and most lasted less than a couple of months. Her father vehemently disapproved of her flighty behaviour.

"And that was Dad's problem too. He was using his own youthful behaviour as a frame of reference to judge the men I dated. Dad was hardly a saint before he met Mum, apparently. His reaction was less supportive than Mum's, though, and things got pretty heated at times. He would try to prevent me from going out and seeing certain men, making up preposterous stories about them.

"Finally I told him I was not a little girl anymore. That just made things worse; the more I retaliated, the more defensive and insulting he became. He would regularly call me a 'slut' or sometimes a 'slag' because of, in his words, my repulsive promiscuity. I knew it wasn't me he was angry with, though; it was Gerald. He blamed Gerald for everything: from the deaths of his parents and Aunt Deborah's overdose to the lax morals of modern society. The final straw was the fact that his daughter was expressing herself sexually in a manner he was not comfortable with; he said I was 'running with the pack like a bitch in heat'.

"Gerald had become the great corruptor in Dad's eyes. Despite the fact that I was not behaving in a manner that brought shame to the family door, he began pushing me away, becoming more distant with each new relationship I announced. Eventually he just stopped speaking to me altogether. I became a surrogate for the brother he hated, a symbol of everything he despised about Gerald and the lifestyle that Bassingbury promoted."

And that was that. It was fascinating. Ligeia had provided me with a glimpse into her family's past and, coincidentally, into the life of a notorious sexual luminary. It proved once again that even those we imagine we know well have a darkness to them that is rarely illuminated by our association with them, however well established or involved that might be. What skeletons do those we never get to know have locked away? It didn't bear thinking about!

It wasn't all darkness and despair for Ligeia, though. Apparently, her mother *was* still in contact with her on a fairly regular basis, but it had been many years since she had spoken to her father. *That* was why Ligeia hardly mentioned her parents. I asked her when was the last time that she had seen either her mother or her father. She flapped her hand rather dismissively, her lip curled in a nonchalant way, but I could tell that the enforced isolation, however long it had been, still hurt her.

Over the months that followed there were no other instances where her parents came up in conversation. It wasn't that we avoided the subject; it was simply that no occasion arose where it was deemed necessary to discuss them. I knew that one day, if our relationship continued to flourish, an opportunity to meet them, or at least Ligeia's mother, might present itself; however, I knew it was unlikely. Like so many other things, I imagined Ligeia would keep that aspect of her life particularly well guarded, at least until it suited her not to.

Chapter 15

"I want us to try something."

That was how the conversation began, and it seemed innocent enough. We had been seeing each other, on and off, for around three months and our passion was far from spent. So I did not imagine the suggestion would be in any way connected to our sex life. I thought that perhaps she wanted to visit a bar one evening or try out a new restaurant. There was so much left for us to explore as a couple and, although I was uncertain how long we would have together, I was convinced we would not spend the whole of our coin in the foreseeable future.

It turned out I was right, about part of it at least.

Ligeia specifically requested that I bring my camera and studio equipment the next time I visited, so the bar/restaurant option was definitely out.

The weather had turned miserable and cold again. It seemed the brief Indian summer was over, turning any chance of outdoor shooting as bleak as the forecast, so I was only too pleased at the prospect of photographing her in private, where it was also warm and dry. In retrospect, the entire year had consisted of a series of continuous downpours and deluges that had soaked the earth to saturation point. For a while I had almost forgotten what consecutive days of sunlight felt like.

When I arrived at her address she was deep in conversation with a young man at the door. He was holding what appeared to be the world's smallest briefcase. She waved as I approached and her companion glanced over his shoulder at me before bringing their conversation to an end.

She kissed me on the cheek.

"Go up. The door's open. I'll be with you in a minute."

I did as she instructed, sidestepping them both in order to get the bulkier of my cases through the door without banging into either of them. He nodded towards me and smiled disarmingly as I passed; it was apparent, even to a weary cynic like me, that he was an exceptionally handsome man.

He was possibly in his late twenties or early thirties; his skin colour, combined with a full head of wavy, jet-black hair, gave him a distinctly Mediterranean air. He was clean-shaven and well dressed, although possibly inappropriately for the time of year. I wondered idly if he had just arrived back in the country from Italy, Spain or Portugal. It looked like he was still in his holiday clothes. I found out later his name was Raphael.

"Raphael?" An image of the High Renaissance artist I'd once seen in the Uffizi gallery in Florence came to mind. "Is everything okay?"

"Yes," she reassured me with a kiss on the lips. "He's just someone I know."

I wanted to know *how* but was uncertain how far to pursue it in case it made me appear insecure. Were they just friends? Had they been lovers? I decided to leave the conversation for another time. I noticed she was now carrying the plastic case her friend had been holding downstairs. This also piqued my interest.

"So, what's all this about? What do you want to do?"

"I want you to photograph me in the throes of death."

And that was that: stated as matter-of-factly as someone expressing the desire to be captured for posterity in a new hat or a favourite pair of shoes. It was *not* an ordinary request, so I took my time to respond; I needed to be certain in my own mind that she was being serious. She disappeared into the kitchen and a minute later returned with two glasses of wine.

"Here." She passed me a drink, sat down next to me and opened the small plastic case on the coffee table. "You know what this is, right?"

She was correct; I knew what it was. The case housed a small plastic unit that resembled a digital radio surrounded by black foam. It measured about 10cm x 5cm. There were also two cut-outs, each with a silver rectangular 9-volt battery. A third recess contained several lengths of grey electrical wire attached to what appeared to be small squares of adhesive fabric plaster. I had seen another identical device being used by my mother to help alleviate the pain caused by acute arthritis. I nodded.

"It's a TENS machine, a Transcutaneous Electrical Nerve Stimulator. Why would you need that?"

"I don't *need* it, but I want to use it, and I want you to photograph me while I'm doing it. Watch this."

Expertly, she unravelled one of the wires, placed the two pads on her left hand and pushed the jack plug at the other end of the wire into the unit. Next she twisted one of the two dials on the top of the device to the left and turned it on.

"I can't feel anything at the moment, although there is current passing through my hand between the two sensors, but if I turn it up a fraction, I start to notice it pulsing." She turned the dial slightly and gently gasped.

It was mildly interesting, but, as I mentioned, I had seen one being used before. What was more intriguing to me was why Ligeia had one in the first place.

"Where did you get it?"

She turned the dial up another notch and gasped again, in surprise rather then in pain, a smile spreading across her face.

"I borrowed it from Raffi," she said. I learned that Raffi was her pet name for Raphael. "It really is *very* addictive. It has a number of different settings that are designed to either control pain or stimulate the production of endorphins. Do you want to try?"

I shook my head.

"No thanks. Why does Raffi... why does your friend... need a TENS?"

Ligeia deliberately ignored my question. She turned the machine off and removed the electrode pads. She held them out towards me.

"Try it. That way you'll understand better what I have in mind."

I resisted again, but she was persistent, pouting petulantly when I refused a second time.

"Please?"

I conceded, much to her delight, and positioned the pads side by side on my wrist. On reflection, I realise it was a stupid thing to do, but at the time I had no idea of the possible power that could be generated by such a small instrument.

"Ready?" she asked, and turned the dial.

I felt nothing initially. She turned the dial again and I began to feel something, the faintest tingling sensation, between the two pads. She was watching my face intently, smiling and nodding encouragement, as though asking if she should continue. I chose not to reply.

Another level up and the rhythmic throb she described became apparent. One more and I noticed an immediate physical change in my hand. The fingers that were originally relaxed began to straighten as the current altered the nerves that fed my hand, and the rigidity increased as she turned the dial still further. It was now an overwhelmingly intense feeling that was impossible to ignore, and I realised how something so physically and mentally disruptive could benefit those who were in pain. I found it incredibly uncomfortable.

Switching between looking at my arm, which was becoming increasingly useless, and Ligeia's face there is a possibility that I may have missed the signal that indicated that she was about to introduce me to its full potency. It was impossible not to react to it, however. The extreme pulsation caused me to convulse spontaneously and cry out in shock, as though afflicted by sudden cramp. It disorientated me to the point where I did not think about attempting to remove the cause of the agonising contractions but simply continue to jerk spasmodically.

Realising that I was becoming progressively more distressed, she turned the machine off abruptly. Immediately relieved and in control of my body once more, I ripped the adhesive pads off.

"Fuck!" I flexed the fingers of my hand to check that they still functioned. "That really hurt."

"Yes! And that was only one channel. I'm going to use both!"

My original notions about her sanity nudged themselves back into my thoughts.

"Why? Why would you put yourself through something like that? What kind of harm will it do to your body?"

"It's my body," she said softly but defensively. "It's up to me to choose what I do with it. No one else. I thought you would understand that. I thought you might be willing to help me. I am really struggling with a concept here and I need you to help me identify with it."

My wrist no longer hurt. My pride returned.

"Is this for a piece of art?"

"No, a poem. Can I read you what I've written so far?"

I agreed she could.

"I haven't got a title yet, but that's not really important at the moment."

I stood quietly while she recited it.

"Though that I am and have been a slave to love
In rusted chains not material but vicious still
I turn each night to seek the solace there
In darkness that my lovers share
The silence broken in those memories dear
A cry muffled by time rejoices with me still
A poison'd barb to burst those dreams again
Writ in ash are words spill't from his pen
Poured once into mine cup, filled, again refilled!
Ah, nectar sugar sweet and tree bark bitter still
Harsh tides that drown me though breathing still endures
Shall wash me up on death's barren shores
Dead eyes rolled back and sightless can witness none
Beating heart betray me not, be still, be still
Sluggish heart can pump only sluggish blood
To stain the earth where dark phantoms stood
Robbed of all, by all for all eternity
Not one of you shall hear although it echoes still
A broken dream held in a broken hand
All too close for me to understand."

I was impressed. It would not be to everyone's liking, but I thought it was excellent, certainly better than any of my efforts, but then some of my students could write better poetry than I could and I taught it, for Christ's sake. It did need a title, though; it seemed bereft without one. I failed to grasp the context that would make the TENS machine and the poem link in any way. I decided I would humour her, despite the obviously obscure connection.

"Excellent!" She smiled and kissed me quickly on the lips. "Take your stuff through to the bedroom. You can set it up wherever you think offers you the best vantage point. But I want to be photographed from above, as though the camera is the eye of God or an angel watching me in agony. I'll strip the bed."

Her bedroom was sumptuous. Over our time together I got to know the four walls of her sanctuary very well, but my overall impression was, and still is, that her bedroom represented a private, intimate, sensual space, reserved for her alone and whichever fortunate souls she invited to join her.

The bed, in the centre of the room, was a classic late Victorian or early Edwardian oversized cast-iron and brass framed affair that housed a deep, expensive branded supportive mattress. Directly above it was a circular mirror, perhaps a metre in diameter. Behind this a curtain of ivory voile hung from ceiling to floor, and encircled the bed, creating an almost ethereal space within.

The walls, painted in a subtle, pale yellow, reflected light from a number of squat scented candles around the room. The candlelight bathed everything in the room with a warm, golden hue. The wall facing the foot of the bed was filled with various framed pictures, irregular in shape, size and medium. They were images of exquisite nude female forms, naked male bodies and scenes of copulation. In the centre of these was one large black-and-white photographic portrait of Ligeia, appearing for all the world like the overseer of everything that was depicted there: the epicentre of carnality.

While I worked out the best angle to optimise what natural light trickled in through the long sash window without my presence casting unwanted shadows, Ligeia began removing her clothes. It was a distraction, one that I eventually gave in to totally; unashamedly, she removed the last vestiges of clothing, her lingerie, as provocatively as was perhaps possible. My heart hammered in my chest, and my body demanded to be pressed against her soft, pale nakedness. My cock strained against its confinement. My lips, dry with anticipation, ached to be pressed against hers.

"I'm just going to shower," she informed me. "You carry on. I should only be a few minutes."

I obeyed her and set my tripod up so that I could enjoy the full sweep of the bed and the surrounding semi-transparent drapes behind it. I chose a 70–300mm telephoto lens to allow me to zoom in on her face or other parts of her body, if and when required. Deliberately, I raised the tripod to its maximum height, having secured my camera to it. Next I positioned one of the chairs from the hall behind the tripod; I would need that to stand on in order to look through the viewfinder. I was virtually ready. The only remaining factor, absent from the room, was Ligeia herself, the intended object of my creative focus.

When she emerged, eyes alive, hair tousled, skin radiant from towelling herself dry, I wanted to take her right then. Only the task at hand prevented me from abandoning any professional ethics I still had. Professional ethics? Maybe just personal mores.

I spent the hour that followed in total conflict. I believe I learned more about the nature of self-harm and masochism in that one hour than I ever had previously. I could see in her face the paradoxical nature of agony, the ecstasy of pain. The weird thing was I was responsible for the delivery of that pain, which she had to endure from the moment I turned the machine on and climbed up to take my shots until I clambered back down from my lofty position and turned it off again. Her body was, for that duration, gripped by torturous spasms.

The truth was I enjoyed seeing her body contorted by the pulsating charge. It was a form of electrical BDSM, or voltage-bondage. Part of me did at least, the part that throbbed in my groin at seeing her prostrate on the bed, her back arched, eyes screwed shut, mouth frozen in a cry of torment. I tried to picture her in the throes of orgasm, realising that the look on her face was identical to the one she presented to me now, in the grip of distress. The duality was apparent. I understood what it was she wanted to achieve. I tried to capture that with every frame I took.

Without going into too much detail about the positioning of the conductive pads, I can honestly say she endured more than I would have been able to, or would have allowed myself to be subjected to. In the moments between taking photos, when the current was off, she kissed me hungrily, stroking my erection through my trousers. I reciprocated and found her eager to part her legs for my fingers to explore her. I could tell that the combination of physical pain and the situation had excited her beyond anything we had experimented with previously. There was the promise of consummation, hastily conducted, hanging in the air between us.

I killed her lust with each application of the TENS, and watched her writhe in agony and die. I captured her essence, her death, again and again and again, and I enjoyed it far more than I should have. Then, when she had all but expired for my lens, I revived her, turning off the cause of her discomfort, bringing her back to life with a kiss and, in doing so, resurrecting her burgeoning desire for me.

When we had finished – or rather when I had decided that I had taken enough images and my cock was moments away from bursting in spontaneous exhilaration – I ripped the electrodes from either side of her mons pubis, gently pushed her back and feasted on her hot, succulent, moist lips and clitoris. She was panting even before I began and I knew that her resistance to my probing tongue was intolerably reduced. I ran my hands over the satin flesh that covered the angular bones of her hips and pushed my mouth against her so that her juices saturated me.

I did not photograph her genuine petit mort, which came abruptly and violently; that was not the object of the exercise. I rubbed my face in her until I was wet from her sex and her orgasm had ebbed away to a pleasant plateau from which we were both reluctant to allow her to return. She allowed me to enter her then, but she was so well lubricated that I scarcely felt myself slide in; I was aware of my ingress only by the internal heat of her vagina. I came almost immediately and, with a sigh, collapsed on top of her, whereupon she tenderly kissed my face.

"Thank you," she whispered.

I replied in French, which made her hug me tightly.

"Mon plaisir," I said again.

We lay like that for a long time; we may have even dozed off together for a while. When I opened my eyes she was staring at me, a look of utter contentment on her face.

"You make me very happy," she said. "I want us to stay like this forever."

It was a pipe dream, a pleasant one but ultimately an

unachievable one. In reality we both understood that. We lay in bed all that afternoon, making love several more times beneath the dead eye of my camera, watched dispassionately by a two-dimensional representation of Ligeia just beyond the diaphanous material that enclosed us.

The photographs I'd taken were better than either of us could have hoped for.

Chapter 16

A week later, on the pretext of attending a photography exhibition and seminar, I collected Ligeia from her flat and drove her out towards a small, intimate public house that, strangely, was exactly equidistant from both the M1 motorway and what I would describe as the Leicestershire countryside. The journey took us along twisting, winding roads lined with trees, some of which retained some of their foliage, although that was now turning various shades of yellow, orange and brown.

The pub was called The Herdsman's Arms and boasted 'a fine selection of locally produced traditional ales' (although I would not be sampling them) and fine food. The signpost, visible from two hundred yards away on the road, depicted a grizzled looking, red-faced farmer leaning on a cattle-stick, staring wistfully at his livestock (seen milling around aimlessly in the background). As we pulled noisily into the sparsely gravelled car park Ligeia smiled in recognition and told me that she had been there before.

"Recently?"

"No, about a year ago. I was seeing a guy called Derek."

Derek? She hadn't mentioned anyone by that name previously.

"We used to come out here before we went out to the Spinney. It always used to excite me and so I would get a little nervous, which sounds unbelievable I know, but it's true. Anyway, I would have a couple of Southern

Comforts and I would feel better... more relaxed."

I wondered if the Spinney was a restaurant. She laughed.

"No, nothing like that. We can go there later if you like. It's not far."

I told her it sounded like a plan and she shivered involuntarily.

"Brilliant! You better get me a SoCo then; it's been a while and I know I'm going to need a couple to loosen me up."

She did not elucidate further on the Spinney. In my innocence, I truly believed we were going to visit another pub or, better still, park up and engage in open-air (but clandestine) sex in a shady glade. I was to discover that I was much closer to the mark with my second notion than I could have possibly imagined, although that was still an hour or so off and so I gave it no more than a passing thought.

We spent a very pleasant early evening watching the sun go down behind a broad expanse of woodland far off on the horizon, no doubt part of the ever-growing national forest. We held each other's hand and chatted about various subjects, one of which was Baudelaire. Ligeia was adamant that one day she would make the pilgrimage to his grave in Paris.

"Of all the dark romantic poets, Baudelaire is still my absolute favourite. He inspires me in so many ways: to write, to compose, to create. You only need to read a couple of lines of his poetry to see why he was considered so dangerous and why so many others tried desperately to be as original as he was."

"Really? I always believed he tried to emulate Poe," I ventured.

It was common knowledge that the demonic French

poet was in awe of Edgar Allen, providing the first translations of Poe's work into French, and that his poems in *Les Fleurs du Mal* were often direct responses to those dark gothic verses penned by the tortured American writer.

"I'm not talking about him; there were others, many others, who were swept up by his dark visions. That's why I *have* to visit his grave. It would be a fantastic opportunity to get as close as it is possible to the very essence of the man."

I nodded thoughtfully, in part humouring her, as there would be nothing, in my opinion, of his essence remaining. He died in 1867. She would get closer to the man and obtain more by reading his poetry than by standing in front of his final resting place, however grand it might be. It did make me realise, though, that despite my own admiration of the man as a poet I knew very little about his latter days, or indeed where he was buried, except that it was rumoured he'd died of syphilis.

"He's buried in Montparnasse Cemetery in Paris. I've read that authors and poets journey from all around the world to visit his grave and place small tributes, sometimes their own poetry, on his tomb. In the summer, apparently, it's awash with metro tickets and pieces of paper, books, pictures... presents to one of the greatest poets of all time. It's a bit like Jim Morrison's grave in Père Lachaise; Baudelaire was similarly a huge celebrity."

I have to admit she made it sound as though it was a trip that she had already planned in some detail, albeit in her head. I wondered if she had already written her own verses to leave as a tribute.

"We should go together!" She drained her drink and gripped my hand tightly as though unexpectedly struck by an epiphanal thought. "Yes! We should both go! It would be fantastic!"

It was the first time she mentioned going to France and I am certain now that had I been more forceful initially then we would not have ended up in Paris, tirelessly hunting through the tombs, monuments and markers that scarred the surface of the great cemeteries of the vast city. And we would definitely not have met the strange and alarming African fortune-teller, Cheikh Calipha. However, fate is a weird thing and I like to think that part of my reluctance to be more resistant was driven by the destiny that had been laid out for us both.

"Sounds great, we'll have to see," I said, rather ineffectually.

It was one of the stock phrases I often uttered to dissuade, deflect or detract any suggestion that might require more consideration by me than I was prepared to commit to it. It was the root of several of my other associated sayings, such as 'We'll see' and the more ambiguous 'Let me think about it'. Basically, the answer was a less direct way of saying 'I'm not sure it's a good idea, so let's leave it a while and maybe (hopefully) you will have forgotten all about it'.

She accepted my woolly response as a positive reaction to her idea, however, and immediately began to plan schedules for places we could visit and things we could do, and she grabbed willingly at the idea of the creative processes such a trip could unleash with almost feverish enthusiasm. I decided to get more drinks from the bar; it enabled me to escape temporarily from the verbal onslaught started by her single catalytic thought but not indefinitely.

After the third SoCo and coke her boundless, excitable ardour began to wane, assisted (I'm certain) by my naturally Laodicean attitude. We would return to the subject of Paris again – of that I was also certain – but for the time being it was no longer the main topic of conversation, for which I was especially grateful. Things turned altogether more carnal in nature.

She leaned forward amorously, affording me a revealing view of her cleavage, and kissed me on the lips. She tasted of fiery bourbon and ice-cold sweetness. Her eyes were dark and the look I saw in them was the same as when we made love. It was desire, tinged with lust, forged by arousal. I licked my lips, savouring her alcoholic kiss, and she tried to bite my tongue. I was quick to retract it to prevent possible pain, leaving Ligeia having to content herself by sinking her teeth into my bottom lip. That also fucking hurt; it made me flinch. I resisted the urge to whimper.

Seeking a different kind of satiation, her hand slid up my leg until she found my groin; tenderly she began to knead my balls, encouraging me to stiffen. My reaction was understandable and instantaneous, causing her to murmur appreciatively and move her head closer to mine so that she could nibble my earlobe.

"Why don't we go now? You can drive me to the Spinney and fuck me," she whispered seductively in my ear.

I greedily gulped down what was left of my orange juice and grabbed the car keys from the table. I didn't need to be asked twice. As we left, her hand still toying with my cock, we were the subject of a number of severe glances from others in the bar; they clearly disapproved of Ligeia's display of wanton sexuality, but no one said anything. The comments about our shameful and inappropriate behaviour would wait until we were out of earshot.

She had stepped out of her knickers before we reached

the car, a graceful, fluid motion that I doubted few other women could have performed without tripping themselves up or falling over in ignominious disarray.

Once in the car, it was apparent that she was in a state of extreme sexual agitation, and her eager, forceful, physical entreaties to explore the soft folds of her sex further indicated that my assessment was correct. She was warm and very wet and clearly wanted me to bring her off there; she began thrusting her hips towards me, trying to impale herself on my probing digits. I resisted, but, with my cock equally ready for some form of consummation, I knew my resolve would not last long. Full of expectation, I wiped her juices off my fingers with a tissue, turned the ignition key and gunned the motor. We left the car park at around 60kph and, weaving slightly, headed off up the road towards – where?

"The Spinney. Follow the signs for Loughborough," she instructed me while simultaneously trying to unzip my fly to pull my cock free. "There's a crossroad a little way ahead. Take the right turn towards Hathern. About a kilometre after the village there should be a sign on the right-hand side for parking. Pull in there."

Her directions were faultless. I saw the sign and pulled into what appeared to be a wild, rustic car park, overgrown in places and shaded by the branches of overhanging trees. It appeared we were not on our own, however. There were around ten or eleven other vehicles parked at the farthest end, lounging against one of which was a group of unsavoury looking men, some of who were smoking. As soon as I braked, several broke away from the group and began moving towards us. I immediately felt uneasy and also, strangely, protective.

"This might not be the best place to stop," I told her. "It looks like there's a group of fishermen over there and I don't think they are swapping angling anecdotes."

"Of course they're not." She pulled her dress over her head so that, apart from her high-heeled shoes, she was completely naked, and clambered over the seat to take up a prone position in the rear. "They're here to watch us. They want to see you fuck me."

What?

Excuse my exclamation of disbelief. I'm not a complete idiot. I knew that kind of shit went on. The more sensationalist Sunday tabloids were full of stories about so-called DPSEs (designated public sex environments) and the altogether seedier practice of 'dogging' (semantically nothing to do with exercising a canine companion but the far creepier age-old tradition of relentlessly pursuing courting couples and spying on them, in the hope of catching them having sex).

Of course, the surreptitious peeping Tom aspect had, in our age of uninterrupted access to high-definition hardcore internet pornography – complete with all its false impressions of female concupiscence and the equally false fostering of the ill-informed expectations of the viewer – long since been replaced with garrulous group voyeurism and participation with those whom they originally only sought to observe, even though they might have once fantasised about being invited to join in.

I had also seen the numerous TV documentaries, including one episode of the unimaginatively titled *A Dogger's Life*, a Channel 4 series that introduced the concept of dogging to a wider, more middle-class audience. I sat through it, experiencing an untypical range of emotions that shifted dramatically from incredulity to utter revulsion for forty of the fifty-or-so minutes the show lasted. I only managed that because of morbid curiosity. Even that eventually dissipated and I gave up, overcome with disbelief at my own stupidity for watching it in the first place.

It was nothing more than Bedlam for a new age. Having been given a window into the sordid lives and squalid practices of people who were, it seemed, intellectual dullards and moral fuckwits, the viewing public (myself included) had allowed ourselves to descend into a modern version of the lunatic voyeurism once so popular in Victorian times. It was where we, as more aspirational moralists, could watch, with ever-increasing disdain, the corruption and lassitude eating away at society, from the bottom upwards.

Daily Mail readers loved it, as it confirmed everything they had come to believe and fear about the lower classes. The programme's representation of exponents of the 'craze' was suitably antagonistic, choosing to feature the worst possible examples of human stupidity and depravity.

It featured 'Ron', a fifty-six-year-old lorry driver from Dundee, a man with the charisma (and hands) of a child murderer; 'Steve', an accountant from Staines who obviously used his personality as a social contraceptive and so had been 'forced to seek sexual gratification with nameless strangers in lay-bys and car parks'; and 'Tom', a toothless fireman from Basford in Nottingham, who was into dogging for the 'buzz' and the opportunity 'to fuck bitches stupid'.

The men were depicted – or rather depicted themselves – as opportunistic predators, a step up from rapists and a step down from swingers, the more acceptable deviants of the aspiring middle classes. The female participants came across as either immoral, insatiable nymphomaniacs or sad, confused 'victims' consumed by their own self-loathing. It was a particularly pathetic spectacle that provided both morbid fascination and repulsion in one sitting.

Remembering the show made me question once again what the hell we were doing at what was obviously a popular dogging site.

I sat rooted in my seat, unable to move, uncertain what to think, not clear about what to say. When I did open my mouth the first thing that came out was a nonsensical gurgling noise, part gasp, part moan. Eventually I managed to put a coherent sentence together.

"What are we doing here?"

Ligeia had not heard me; she was too busy watching (through the space between her open legs) the men approaching as she gently stroked her clitoris, a look of expectant anticipation on her face. More of the doggers broke away from the main group and joined those closing in on us. My heart began to beat a little faster as I scanned the faces of those nearest to the car. One reminded me of 'Ron' from Dundee, and they all looked like possible suspects in a rape, murder and buggery trial.

Interestingly – although, at the time, I was neither interested nor indeed curious – the men were all dressed very similarly. It was as though there was a kind of uniform adopted by this fraternity, an unwritten dress code that they all abided by. It consisted of dark leather lace-up army boots or those repulsive tan-coloured builders' boots that come halfway up the calf and have steel toe-caps, denim jeans, a thick ecru-coloured sweater, a green Belstaff or Barbour-style waxed cotton jacket (complete with contrasting corduroy collar) and a black woollen hat.

Most of them were unshaven, and their facial hair ranged from two-day old stubble to full rhododendron-like beards. Those that were smiling or licking their lips at the prospect of what they might see going off on my back seat illustrated that doggers appear to suffer from a range of dental hygiene problems. I repeatedly tried to push the rising feeling of apprehension away, but it returned more forcefully and with growing intensity each time.

I watched as the throng of zombie-like observers moved ever closer to the car; it resembled a scene from a George A. Romero film. They walked, loped and shambled en masse with graceless intent. I hit the automatic door lock button, suddenly aware of what might happen if they gained access to the interior and, more significantly, Ligeia.

There was an absence of any emotion, apart from lust, on the faces of the men assembled on the other side of that flimsy glass, metal and plastic barrier. It was the only thing separating us physically from them, although morally and intellectually I imagined we were poles apart; I did not share their base, animalistic compulsion. I braced myself and, with a jolt, they were upon us, leering in, steaming up the glass.

"Isn't it exciting!" Ligeia said breathlessly.

It wasn't. It was fucking frightening. I felt like I imagined victims caught up in riots must feel like moments before they are trapped by a mob and ripped forcibly from their motors and beaten to death. Outside there was a pack, and pack mentality was beginning to take over. The car began to rock gently under the weight of bodies pressed against it as they all vied to get a closer look at Ligeia finger-fucking herself. At one point, I seriously thought the back window would shatter.

"Ligeia." Attracting her attention was pointless; she was engrossed in onanistic delight. I tried again: "Ligeia!"

"Come and fuck me, Richard," she called out so that I could hear her above the increasingly loud guttural murmuring coming from outside the car.

In my head I refused, although I'm uncertain if I indicated that either physically or verbally. There was no way I was going to be able to climb over the seats into the rear of the car. My only realistic option would have been to get out, push or punch my way through the horde of horny rural gogglers and get back in via the rear passenger door. That was certainly not going to happen. Besides, my erection and my desire had completely disappeared.

Undaunted by my reluctance to comply, Ligeia continued to pleasure herself, motivating the rabble to begin calling out to her, shouting for her to let them in. It was without doubt one of the most unsettling situations I had ever found myself in, and it was not mitigated by Ligeia's next suggestion.

"Open the window for me," she gasped. "I want to feel their hands on me."

I was shocked, and this time I felt compelled to say something.

"Are you insane? They'll pull you out and either rip you to pieces or take turns to fuck you to death! No way!"

The idea apparently had the opposite effect on her as it had on me. She continued masturbating but now more furiously, her hand becoming a blur of knuckles and red fingernails. Outside, the local Neanderthals were so close as they clambered to get a better view I could see their fetid breath on the glass. Several were already wanking themselves off, standing on tiptoes so they could make their erections more visible to Ligeia. It was a nightmare, straight out of the feverish imaginings of Hieronymus Bosch.

"Please! Open it for me... just a bit... just so they can get their hands in. Please, I'm so close to coming!"

I wanted to refuse. I really wanted to deny her that

part of her pleasure because it was so alien to me. I truly could not comprehend it. But I also did not want her to have anything to reproach me for afterwards. Ours was a fragile existence; I knew that. I had become used to her, to having her around; I did not want anything to jeopardise that.

With some reluctance, I lowered the rear window a few centimetres and watched in horror as, immediately, thick stubby fingers and then grubby, hairy hands began to invade the interior, reaching out to touch Ligeia's legs, to stroke them. She was really getting off on it. Her moans of pleasure became quicker, her own hand moving faster and faster. She was seconds away from climaxing. The hands continued to paw her. I watched her neck suddenly arch as she threw her head back and, with a deafening cry, she orgasmed.

Outside there were similar noises. Grunts of approval and satisfaction, and of vile encouragement, were punctuated by numerous spurts of viscous creamy spunk that splattered against the windows. The men waited until Ligeia's spasmodic moans had subsided. Then gradually, one by one, the hands retreated, and the pearlescent emissions became semi-transparent glutinous trails moving slowly down the glass. The mob started to move away.

Shell-shocked.

That was the best way to describe how I felt in the aftermath of what I had just witnessed. I stared at Ligeia, who was still luxuriating in the afterglow of her pleasure; she was splayed out on the back seat, oblivious to me or my feelings. I sat silently staring at the crowd, who were now moving back to their original positions, lighting up cigarettes in the gathering gloom, and waiting, I assume, for the next carload of visual joy to enter the car park.

After a while, she sat up, stretched with a long satisfied sigh and slid snakelike back over the seats to retake her position in the front with me. She regarded me, imploring me to return her gaze, but I continued to stare straight ahead, fixated on a tree stump a few metres away.

"You didn't seem to enjoy that much," she stated (correctly) as she pulled her dress over her head and wriggled back into it.

I sighed, but didn't shift my gaze from the stump, which I'd suddenly noticed was covered in bright orange fungus.

"I'm afraid I was a little out if my depth. I'm not used to that kind of..." I struggled for the correct word.

"Degeneracy?"

"No." I shook my head, keen to indicate that I was not prudish. "It's just that I've never been in that situation before."

She leant over and kissed my cheek.

"You'll get used to it. It's all pretty harmless fun provided you maintain control."

Control? I wondered how that was possible.

"You don't surrender yourself; you stay in charge of the situation."

It sounded easier said than done. There must have been times when that hadn't been possible. I asked her.

"A few, yes, when I was younger and less experienced. Fortunately, they weren't critical situations. I am always aware of the inherent dangers of taking part in stuff like this; for example, there was no way I would have considered getting out of the car tonight or letting any of them in. It was alright for them to touch me, to want me, to get a hard-on thinking about doing me but another thing entirely to contemplate being screwed by any of them. Besides, I'm with you. I wanted you to fuck me. I

- 143 -

still do actually."

"So, you've never…"

She interrupted me with a fierce shake of her head.

"Never."

"But what about when you've been here before? With Derek?"

"No. He wanted me to. It was his fantasy to see me being gang-fucked on the bonnet of his Jag while he watched, but it was *his* fantasy. I never entertained it. I'm not completely stupid… or that immoral." She smiled.

I smiled back, satisfied with her answers to questions that had seriously troubled me. As I got to know her better, I learned she was probably the most honest person I had ever met and for someone so seemingly amoral she was actually a very moral person.

We drove back then, out of the countryside, back towards the normality and sanity (sanity?) of the city. I parked up outside her place and she invited me in for coffee. As euphemisms go, coffee works well for what we engaged in, which was equally hot, strong and satisfying. An hour later, I ran my hand down her smooth, slender back, kissed each of her naked buttocks as she lay on the bed and promised to call her in the morning. Then I drove home. It was eleven minutes past midnight.

Janice, thankfully, was not waiting up for me and, even more thankfully, was fast asleep as I slipped in between the sheets. Before drifting off to sleep I began formulating an imaginary scenario that would best illustrate just how monumentally dull the photography seminar had been in case she queried me about it. It proved to be unnecessary; Janice never even mentioned it.

★ ★ ★

The following morning I inspected the car and was

grateful that Janice had decided not to drive into town as she normally did on a Saturday. The passenger side was a mess. There were at least eight separate areas where the wankers from the previous evening had shot their filth over the bodywork and windows.

Some of it had dried and some of it was still forlornly clinging like gelatinous snot to the door handle and wheel arch. I tried not to retch and drove it to the nearest car wash. With some gratitude I let the swarthy team of immigrants who worked there return my vehicle to its former unblemished state. It was worth every penny of the £5 I paid them. In fact, I think I may have even tipped them.

Chapter 17

During the autumn and over the winter my pursuits ensured that I was increasingly absent from the marital home. It was either one thing or another. A chess tournament here, a literary debate there, school conferences, meetings, parents' evenings, etcetera, etcetera, *ad nauseum*. I cannot remember another period in my life where my leisure time had been overtaken so comprehensively by (ahem) social and contractual engagements.

For her part, Janice said very little. Life went on much as before. She was very accepting and never bemoaned the fact that I often had to go out at peculiar times in the evening and sometimes at weekends. To be fair, I think she enjoyed the solitude, considering that she was still benefiting from the fallout of my intensifying ardour by being screwed to the point of exhaustion (usually mine) two or three times a week. I think she would have put up with it indefinitely had she not discovered the truth behind my escalating absenteeism in the evenings. But that is another story and I am jumping ahead somewhat.

I need to explain about Paris first.

Ligeia first formally broached the subject post-coitally. She was sitting in the bed, legs spread wide to enable her to wipe up the cum that was trickling from her. She screwed up the tissue and with practised expertise threw it deftly into the waste bin by the side of the bed.

"I want us to go away somewhere," she said as she snuggled up next to me, her fingernails combing the hairs on my chest.

"Sure. Where do you fancy?" (For those who have been paying attention, her answer will not have come as any surprise, but please bear with me.)

"Somewhere romantic, where life and death exist side by side and the present waits patiently in the wings for the past to catch up. I want us to go where we can immerse ourselves in the shadows cast by a cradle of past decadence and desperate fortitude, where the spirits of artists are summoned forth by the unbridled adulation of their devotees, who only dare to dream of the beauty that they created."

I rolled over and kissed her breasts.

"Sounds wonderful. What do you have in mind? Your description could be any one of a thousand destinations."

"Uh-uh, only one place: Paris!" She was grinning.

It was the third time she had mentioned Paris. I repeated the name, with enough inflection for her to understand that I didn't exactly agree with her suggestion. I loved the idea of going away with her and being able to go around like a proper couple; I just didn't fancy Paris.

"No, seriously, it would be fantastic! We could visit the catacombs, you could photograph the cemetery at Père Lachaise, we could place flowers on Baudelaire's grave, we could go and see *L'Origine du Monde*, I could write poetry, we could drink wine, we could fuck each other to death. It would be amazing!"

Her argument had some merits, but having spent a miserable fortnight in the Loire during my early twenties, being pissed on by God and ignored by the locals, my impression of France and the French was not great. I imagined Parisians would exemplify the worst of their countrymen's characteristics in much the same way Londoners do for the British.

Could I be persuaded? It all depended on how long she was talking about.

"If we went, it would have to be during the half term or something."

"That's fine, although the price of flights rockets up as soon as school holidays begin. Can't you call in sick? We could disappear one Thursday or Friday morning, stay over the weekend and get a flight back on the Monday."

It was a consideration; my attendance record was exemplary. In nine years I had been absent (because of illness) a total of one-and-a-half days, the direct result of dental negligence after a relief orthodontist extracted a premolar and ended up causing me more harm than was warranted for such a routine procedure. On cold days my jaw still ached.

"They certainly wouldn't miss me for a couple of days. It's sounding more plausible."

"What about your wife?"

"She" – I tended not to use Janice's name when talking about her to Ligeia – "won't be a problem. I'll spin her a convincing yarn. It will be fine. There are a couple of things that might be problematic, however."

We discussed them. The first, my previous experience of the French and associated concerns, was nullified by Ligeia's insistence that we would be inseparable for the entire duration of the trip. The second was not as easily remedied.

"Don't you have any personal savings?" she asked, amazed at my apparent lack of available funds.

Having existed in a state of ignorant marital atrophy for more years than I could remember, there had never been a need to initiate separate bank accounts. I could take money out of our joint account, but it would depend on how much. If it was a large sum, Janice would, understandably, ask questions. Everything depended on the price of the trip.

"Don't worry. I'll pay for it now and you can pay me back later."

I was incensed at the suggestion, despite it making the most obvious sense. There was something about the arrangement that did not sit well with me. It made me feel inadequate. Don't misunderstand me, I had no qualms about her being able to afford to pay for me; she wouldn't have offered if she'd been unable to cover the costs. It was just that it was embarrassingly emasculating to my archaic, sexually stereotypical way of thinking.

She attempted to take my mind off the conundrum by slipping my cock between her lips and gently sucking it to turgidity. She took her time to tease me towards orgasm by using her tongue and teeth; after swallowing what I gratefully jetted into her mouth, I agreed to her proposal. Ligeia was very persuasive.

★ ★ ★

The following afternoon she called with all the details of the Paris trip. She had spent most of the morning sorting out the best times for the flights, and the airport, finding an appropriately priced hotel that was not too far out of the city, and exploring various websites so that there would be plenty to occupy us during the visit. She had settled on a hotel close to the Gare Saint-Lazare metro station. The Concorde Opéra was definitely affordable and, amazingly, breakfast was included in the price. The total cost for us both, including flights, accommodation and taxes was €1450.99.

It worked out at approximately £500 each for a four-day sex, sightseeing and photo fest, not including spending money.

"Well, are you up for it?" she inquired, unable to hide the nervous excitement in her voice.

Sure. Why not?

So we set the date, and I let her ring off to confirm the combined hotel and flight deal. We would be away from Friday 30th of March until Monday 2nd of April.

I would have to call in sick and also set adequate cover work. It left me wondering if I had been somewhat impulsive.

Not for too long.

We are, after all, I reasoned, a long time dead.

Chapter 18

One evening, Ligeia greeted me at the door with an exuberant smile, and gestured with a wide sweeping motion for me to enter. I gave her my coat and a perfunctory kiss on the cheek and walked through to the main living area, where Raphael, the friend I'd only briefly met before, sat waiting for us, drink in hand. He rose and extended his hand.

"Hello, it's Richard, isn't it?" His hand was warm, much larger than my own, and he gripped mine with a strength that was surprising. I affirmed he was correct.

"We met before, a little while ago. Downstairs. Remember?"

I remembered him, of course. He had delivered the TENS machine that, just a few weeks previously, had enabled me to capture images for my 'electro-orgasm' portfolio. Despite preliminary reservation, I subsequently considered the results to be some of the best photographs I'd ever taken. Ligeia draped herself affectionately on his shoulder and smiled dreamily at me.

"Raphael has been dying to meet you. The pair of you have a lot in common."

"Really?" I raised an eyebrow, uncertain of how I could share any similarities with this robustly physical, handsome, younger man. He smiled back at me disarmingly, nodding.

"I'm a teacher," he explained and I felt my heart sink.

The last thing I wanted to do was spend the evening swapping tedious anecdotes about policy, politics, curriculum and problem children. In the spirit of the evening I feigned interest, asking him where he taught; to be honest, though, I really could not have cared less. It transpired he wasn't even a real teacher; he was a primary school teacher, thereby immediately reaffirming that we had less in common than Ligeia believed.

"I'm going to leave you two to talk and get to know each other while I finish cooking," she said as she wandered off towards the kitchen. Raffi's also interested in photography."

Great. I really wasn't in the mood to talk shop. I needed a drink.

"He also fucks me from time to time," she added matter-of-factly.

There was nothing I could say to that.

In the silence that followed her final revelation, I had the opportunity to appraise my fellow guest. I estimated his age to be around thirty, maybe a little older. He had the chiselled looks of someone suited to a profession more rugged than teaching, especially in a primary school. I imagined that other men might be intimidated by his sculpted physical appearance and good looks. I certainly was.

"So, what do you shoot with?" he asked, displaying a set of perfect, pearl-white teeth.

I was almost afraid to reply but realised it would have been churlish not to do so just because my dental appearance was eclipsed by his, so I promoted Pentax for a minute or two and then fell silent so that he could regale me with his favoured brand of photographic equipment. No response was forthcoming. I feared we would soon drift into one-sided small talk and finally, having nothing left to say, end up staring at each other's shoes. I was determined not to let that happen; my shoes were scuffed anyway and patently less expensive than his.

"How did you meet?" I enquired.

"Online. Professional dating agency. I wasn't particularly looking for a relationship, just someone to hook up with from time to time. To be honest, I didn't think I stood much of a chance with Ligeia from her profile, but we hit it off almost immediately."

I was amazed. Looking at this confident, good-looking man, whom I considered would have virtually no problem securing admiring female glances wherever he went, I found it hard to believe he was so insecure.

"What about you? Ligeia said you two met in a graveyard. Is that right? We've done that kind of thing now and again. To be honest, it's not an ideal location in my opinion; it creeps me out. I'm much more of a Premier Inn man, if you know what I mean, but I know that kind of exhibitionist element appeals to her, so I go along with it occasionally. It certainly makes for some interesting evenings." He sipped his drink, eyeing me with what I can only describe as conspiratorial geniality. The only thing he didn't do was wink.

Determined not to appear fazed by his comment, I refused to respond directly.

"How long have you known her?"

"About a year. We met up just before she went off to do the photo shoot in the Seychelles. So... yes... about a year... give or take a month. What about you?"

How long had it been? In comparison, I'd known her hardly any time at all, and yet I felt that I had known her all my life. Or rather I felt as though I had been waiting to meet her all my life. Was it a month? Two months? Three? Did it really matter? The fact was that since I had met her my life had been turned upside-down. The days drifted into weeks and could continue indefinitely as far as

I was concerned.

I mumbled a response that seemed to please him just as Ligeia reappeared. I understood she had been busily preparing the promised meal in the kitchen but somehow had found time to slink off and slip into a vintage pale yellow and blue mini-dress. She was barefoot, like Sandie Shaw, I mused, wondering at the same time if she would have any idea who Ms Shaw was. Raphael and I, however, appreciated her transformation.

"You look stunning!" he enthused, and I agreed.

"Come and get it," she said, with more than a hint of suggestion in her voice.

★ ★ ★

Over the course of the meal I discovered that Raphael was not as big an irritation as I'd initially thought he'd be. I believe he had simply been nervous, and uncertain of how best to present himself to me, an older man and, by virtue of our professional status, obviously his intellectual superior. He was a primary school teacher, after all, and that came with a whole raft of inferiority complexes that no amount of bullshit could disperse.

The meal was sublime. It consisted of three courses that started with tempura-battered oysters, served warm in their shells with a spring onion dressing and sweet chilli dip. The main was stuffed noisette of lamb with young vegetables, baby potatoes and a Madeira wine jus. The dessert was the only letdown to what was otherwise an elegantly prepared and delicately balanced meal: a rather bland trio of shop-bought fruit sorbets served in a champagne bowl.

Conversation during and after the meal concerned itself mainly with sex in literature, or rather the way in which it was depicted. Raphael was surprisingly more knowledgeable, for a primary school teacher, than I would have given him credit for.

"You have to consider what the kids will be reading in ten to fifteen years, given that they already have access to unrestricted adult pornography via the internet. The sensationalist aspects of any novel will pale into insignificance when compared with their knowledge of sex. Books will have to become more and more degraded in order to interest a generation that are already desensitised to things like sex and violence."

I agreed in part but reminded my table companions that extreme sexual imagery was nothing new.

"That argument is pretty invalid when you consider access to extreme imagery has always been available throughout history and has done nothing to lessen our libidos over the years."

Raphael was adamant.

"Really? You think a few dirty cave paintings compares to the photographic depictions of full penetrative intercourse that some kids, perhaps as young as six or seven, are inadvertently exposed to?"

"It wasn't just cave paintings. The Greeks illustrated every conceivable sexual permutation, and so did the Romans. The history of art is littered with images like that. At the time they were produced they were considered shocking and morally corruptive. Take Courbet's *L'Origine du Monde*."

"I love that painting," Ligeia announced. "I really want to see it when we go to Paris."

"Exactly," I nodded. "It was considered to be offensive as late as the 1980s and an affront to public decency, at the same time as hardcore pornography was slipping into mainstream cinema. It's ridiculous really. Personally, I believe that looking at sex is not the same as reading about sex."

"I agree with Richard," Ligeia interjected while licking the last vestiges of her blackcurrant sorbet from her spoon. "It's completely different. I enjoy visual stimulation but it is not as emotionally engaging as reading about it. I invest more in literary representation; I tend to empathise with the characters. I often substitute specific situations from my own life and actual feelings when I read about sex. You can't do that just by looking at a photograph of a couple fucking, no matter how graphic it is."

"Okay, okay, but what I'm saying is that if kids are exposed to a higher level of explicit sex, won't they expect a higher level of explicit material in books in the future? I mean, where can it realistically go? They have to have some level of expectation; it's the nature of the beast to want more and more sensationalist shit just to satisfy their jaded palate."

"You mean how will authors be able to break new ground when writing about sex if it's all been written before?" Ligeia asked. She was answered by Raphael nodding his head energetically.

I sighed forlornly.

"Boccaccio, DeSade, Cleland, Sacher-Masoch, Miller, Millet, Nabokov, Réage, Anaïs Nin, Ballard, Joyce, Platt… I lose count of the number of authors who have used sex to carry a narrative forward. Don't forget that their work was deemed inappropriate at the time they were writing, from society's point of view anyway. You only have to look at Lawrence's brush with the law to realise that scandal is something often imposed on literature, not by society but by a small group of influential moralists."

"But there has to be some kind of moral guideline for

society to adhere to, surely. If only for the sake of the kids."

"What? So we become the moralists?" I drained my wine glass and refilled it, shaking my head. "When you were young didn't you have access to what we class as pornography back then?"

"Yes, of course."

"I didn't," Ligeia said sulkily. "It was banned in our house."

I made a note to return to her comment later, in private, before continuing.

"Do you think access to pornography affected *your* development?"

Raphael thought for a moment before answering.

"No, not at all, but there is a massive difference between what I was looking at and what kids are looking at today."

"I don't think so. What were you reading back then? Color Climax? Playbirds?"

He glanced at Ligeia and reluctantly nodded.

"In some ways they are *more* explicit than a lot of top-shelf magazines today. Playbirds, as I recall, was particularly hot on gaping gynaecological shots. I bet you also watched the occasional porn video, and these were just as hardcore as most films are today. You can't reinvent the wheel, after all, though you can change the way it is perceived."

"How come you know so much about porn?" Ligeia asked, stroking my hand. "That's not in the national curriculum, I'm sure."

"I will not flatter myself that I know more than either of you about it. I'm just a normal red-blooded male with a healthy appetite and interest in sex."

Raphael raised his glass. "I'll drink to that."

All three of us touched glasses and drank deeply before refilling. I noticed Raphael was stroking Ligeia's thigh under the table, but I said nothing.

"What was the most memorable porn film you've seen?" she asked me.

"Do you mean 'porn' or would you allow me to include erotic cinema?"

"Porn." She was adamant. "I know what mine was. I was about sixteen at the time and a group of us (all girls) had a sleepover at Freya's house. She was one of my classmates, by the way. In the middle of the night we put a video on. It was called *Susan: Peach Eater* and it belonged to Freya's Mum. We'd always suspected she was a lesbian and the film just compounded that. I think it was about fifteen minutes long, but that was long enough.

"It starts with the heroine, Susan, walking in on her boyfriend while he is fucking a girl who has unbelievably massive breasts. The sex was very graphic; all of us were shocked at first, apart from Freya, who had obviously watched it many, many times before. The dialogue was fucking terrible. Anyway, they have this huge row and she walks out and goes over to her friend's flat for support and sympathy. Needless to say, her friend is a lesbian and within a minute of comforting her has her stripped completely naked.

"It was the first time I truly understood what lesbian sex was. I used to think it was all touching and kissing; I didn't know about oral. The cunnilingus scenes blew my mind. I mean I got very, very aroused. It makes me wet just thinking about it. Afterwards, after the sleepover, I couldn't get the images out of my head. I must have fingered myself six or seven times a day back then."

"Seriously?" Raphael asked, obviously excited by her story, his hand still on her leg.

"Yes. It wasn't about the fucking; it was the intimacy of oral sex that turned me on. I would imagine Susan was licking me and literally within minutes I would orgasm. I even shaved myself once so I was more like Susan's sympathetic friend Carla."

"I presume the 'peach' in the film's title was Carla's shaven pussy?" I ventured, feeling a vague throb in my groin at the thought of Ligeia, aged sixteen, lying naked on her bed, legs spread so that she could finger her clit.

She nodded, her face a little flushed.

"What about you, Richard?"

What about me? Could I really reveal that my introduction to pornography had caused me to spontaneously ejaculate? I decided to embroider the truth slightly, if only to make me look less of a tosser in Raphael's eyes.

The porn film that was most memorable for me was another short, lasting maybe twenty minutes, called *Cream Dream*. Filmed in the heyday of West-coast exploitative pornography, it featured an array of outmoded fashion *faux pas* that included bell-bottom flares, wing-collar shirts, high-waisted trousers and sideburns. All the males were hirsute and sported drooping moustaches, and all the females were blonde, blue-eyed and big breasted.

I was similarly in my early teens when I'd watched it, and the premise seemed fairly believable to me at the time. It concerned a 'sleep therapist' called Dr Shonke, who invited subjects from a nearby high school to take part in an experiment to see if dreams could be manipulated. He chose four subjects, two girls in very short cheerleader skirts – again it seemed perfectly feasible back then – and two all-American 'jocks'. They all got to sleep in the same dormitory – introducing the promise of a little voyeurism – and had names like Jack and Chad or

Brad and Janet and Crystal.

It followed the format of all porn films of that period. Although they all went to bed in sensible attire, it wasn't long before the temperature became so unbearable that they all had to remove their clothing, which led to Dr Shonke wondering if he could fulfil one of his fantasies by manipulating the dreams of all his subjects, inducing them to sleepwalk and engage in an orgy that he could either watch or manufacture an opportunity to join in.

"I've seen that one," Raphael snorted. "It was crap."

Not to me it wasn't, at least not at the time. *Cream Dream* introduced me to the visual spectacle of the 'money shot', the deliberate withdrawal of the penis to facilitate a segue of rhythmic spurting and splashing of spermatozoa across, and occasionally into, various body parts. I found it a glorious spectacle personally. After the two female leads had had their breasts and abdomens liberally doused in cream, it was left to Dr Shonke to deliver a 'double-header'. It was during the close-up of his cock gushing over the faces of the two young girls that I experienced my first simultaneous, sympathetic ejaculation. From that moment forward I was addicted to the cum shot.

Ligeia stared at me, her nostrils flared, and then at Raphael. She had an expression of irrepressible arousal on her face.

"Jesus! I am so horny. Take me to bed right now. I want you both to fuck me."

Right.

That is exactly what she said. I just sat there for a moment, wondering what to say, wondering what to do. You have to remember that for forty-five years I had maintained a perfectly ordinary vanilla existence. Granted, I had, on occasion, allowed myself the odd sexual fantasy that would not have been considered mainstream –

although not strictly *odd*, either. Before Ligeia, though, I had never really indulged in anything stronger than a bit of experimental silk-scarf bondage, some spontaneous outdoor sex and one instance of spanking, none of which could be described as particularly avant-garde in a sexual context.

What Ligeia was suggesting was a whole new ball game (if you'll excuse the pun), although obviously not for Raphael because he was up and hastily removing his shirt before I'd even had chance to consider *what* the correct response should be. I followed suit, more slowly. Ligeia had already left the room; Raphael wasn't far behind her.

That left me alone in the living room, my shirt half unbuttoned, contemplating the melting remnants of my sorbet trio and considering whether I wanted to comply with her demands. Part of me put up massive resistance. I had never taken part in a ménage a trois – that is the correct term, isn't it? – so the etiquette was unfamiliar. Was there some etiquette to follow? What if I was unable to rise to the occasion? The prospect filled me with some dread.

The part that offered less resistance was slowly swelling in my groin. Even though it meant I would be sharing a girl I imagined would be exclusively mine for the duration of our affair with someone I had met only a couple of times, there was an excitement building inside me that was smashing any reservations I had into minuscule shards. I couldn't blame the alcohol: my glass was still half-full. I blamed my lust.

When I arrived at the bedroom door the sounds coming from within indicated that the party had started without me. Now completely naked, my cock hard and ready for whatever purpose Ligeia saw fit to put it to, I pushed open the door to find out what I was missing out on. It did nothing to dampen my resolve.

Ligeia was on her knees, hanging on to the headboard while Raphael was hammering his cock into her from behind with complete abandonment. In between thrusts I caught a brief sight of his thick, glistening shaft before he plunged it back into her. His eyes were closed, his hands on her hips guiding her back onto his cock with increasing ferocity. When she saw me, clearly delighted that I had decided to join them, she attempted to pull away from him.

"Not yet! Don't come yet! Richard's here now. Come on... come and join us."

I clambered onto the bed as Raphael slid out of her. She positioned herself between the two of us, her knees tucked up against the side of her breasts so that she presented the most succulent, welcoming target for me to pierce. I pushed my cock home to the hilt, my balls so tight against the base of my shank that her firm, fleshy lips caused them to retreat inside me with my first stroke. Her lustful moans transported me to another place.

While I thrust myself into her Raphael gently stroked his stiffness, waiting for his turn. His cock was not much longer than mine, but it was certainly thicker, the skin so taut that a fat, blue snakelike vein stood proud, pulsing gently. He had a foreskin but no frenulum, which allowed his member to extend another couple of centimetres or so. I tried not to focus on his hand gliding up and down his member.

"Stick your cock in my mouth, Richard!" Ligeia mouthed breathlessly. "Raffi, your turn, baby! Stick it in and fuck me with your big, fat cock!"

That is how it continued for a while: Raphael and me changing positions and taking turns to penetrate Ligeia while she selfishly orgasmed again and again. But it couldn't last forever. With the alternate plunging, cock sucking and the intense aural and visual stimulation, one of us was going burst. I was glad it was Raphael first.

With a guttural moan, he threw his head back, pulled his cock out of her greedy mouth and spurted over her face, repeatedly pulling his foreskin back as far it would go to ensure his rhythmic jetting continued for as long as possible. I needed no further encouragement to reach my own climax than seeing Ligeia's upturned face gratefully receiving his thick, pearlescent cum. With immense relief and a satisfied grunt, I emptied myself as deeply as I could inside her.

She brought herself to orgasm again with her fingers while I was still buried in her. She vigorously rubbed her engorged clitoris, the rapid manipulation almost a blur, until, with a gasp, she was done. It was a signal for us all to withdraw momentarily and take some time to recover before we continued. For a first experience, I had found it not unpleasant. Sadly, I was unable to rise again as quickly as Raphael did; only minutes later he began badgering Ligeia for sex again.

Still covered in a sheen of perspiration, he clambered between her legs and forced his length into her while I lay there and watched them, marvelling at how well the human form is suited for face-to-face intercourse.

Their close proximity was arousing. They provided me with a sensory overload. I could see them: their bodies intertwined and being jolted by each pelvic thrust. I could hear them: her soft sighs punctuated by his ecstatic groans. If I reached out I could touch them: I could run my hand over soft, warm satin flesh. I could smell them: Raphael's musky sweat mingled with Ligeia's liquorice-sweet perfume. I rolled over and kissed her on the lips, and I could taste them both.

It was my intention to remain there with them for as long as it was humanly possible. I was certain that I would fuck her again and I hoped the three of us would eventually drift off into a well-earned sleep that we would awaken from and remember for a long time to come.

My companions were straining now, moving ever faster, close to their own pinnacles of sexual release. Ligeia climaxed first, reaching out for me and digging her nails into my arm with exquisite purpose. Raphael followed seconds later, every muscle in his body tense for the briefest time before he shuddered and collapsed, sighing into her ear. It was beautiful.

My eyes closed and I pictured them again and again and again: a perfect image of union, of flesh in motion, of joy and ecstasy and of sweet, sweet release. It was a sublime sculpture of blood and muscle and the darkest of intentions, and it was as close to happiness as I had ever experienced. In rapture, I drifted down and down, spiralling out of control like a feather, afraid that the feeling would end. I was therefore so grateful to feel Ligeia's mouth as it closed around my stiff cock and I gave in totally; I let her own me, for however long or brief our experience might be.

When I put my hand on Ligeia's head to caress her lustrous, long hair I was surprised by how different it felt. Opening one eye I saw her, her head on the pillow next to me, watching me, her eyes filled with excitement and wide in anticipation. My situation suddenly became apparent and I glanced down to where Raphael was gently sucking my cock, his mouth moving up and down my shaft with practised ease. My heart began to hammer in my chest.

I closed my eyes and moaned uncontrollably as I shot my spunk into his mouth.

Chapter 19

It is virtually impossible nowadays for even the so-called enlightened members of modern society not to slide into subjectivity when they are viewing the lives of their fellows. It is a natural flaw in our otherwise advanced emotional intelligence, created thousands of years ago by evolutionary necessity. It is the distillation of raw, ruthless competitiveness that is in itself nothing more than a highly developed survival instinct. It is a *basic* instinct and, for that reason alone, it evokes powerful emotions in everyone it touches.

Proliferation by procreation demands conformity in order to maintain tribal and cultural identity and stability. Admittedly, within the Darwinist concept of 'survival of the fittest' there is still space for those who can't quite cut the mustard when it comes to coexisting. Within the vastness of the group, minute differences can be hidden, overlooked or ignored because there is strength in the pack, where compliance and conformity binds the whole together. Kipling once identified that aspect very eloquently.

Uniformity is a measure of the inner strength of a societal structure. It is measured by simple things like what we drink, how we speak, what we wear, how we think, how we behave and how we react, collectively, to certain situations or stimuli. These simple building blocks (norms) are the basic foundations of something larger, something that eventually establishes even greater cohesiveness: culture.

Those who actively do not conform to *all* the norms and mores of society, choose (or are forced) to exist as a subculture; they are still part of the whole but different enough to engender suspicion, fear and, in the worst cases, anger in the greater, more powerful and influential majority. There is considerable strength in the size of the pack and, understandably, it becomes much easier to pick on, pick off and attempt to destroy any weaker, marginalised subgroup.

Any threat to the harmony, compliance and constancy of the greater whole is met with immediate, initial fulminative defence; this is followed by passive or active resistance and then finally all-out attack in order to facilitate the rapid elimination of the hazard and the reestablishment of balance in society.

Delinquency, aberration, irregularity, nonconformity and eccentricity were all interchangeable in the minds of those who chose to abide by the rules and actively promote the mores of society in general. They believed that in order for civilisation to continue, to advance and to prosper, it was essential that, above everything else, a person had to fit in. Outsiders were not tolerated; they were publicly shunned and openly reviled.

Ligeia definitely did not 'fit in'. She did not adhere to the generally accepted notion of normality. Her licentious libertinism was anathema to those who believed in and strenuously safeguarded the high moral standards of society. She was the type of person vehemently denounced by the church, vilified by almost every type of religious fundamentalist group and despised by those dedicated to the promotion of standardised family values.

Her behaviour would be considered a threat to the established norms; it definitely undermined polite society and would generally be unacceptable in most cultures.

I found her attitude to sex (I can't say love) and life in general challengingly refreshing, especially considering where it all stemmed from. That was because I had the benefit of context. Had society been aware, contextually, of Ligeia's background, I feel certain they would have been more lenient, more understanding and less judgemental. But they didn't know about Max.

To be fair, I didn't know about Max initially. She'd mentioned previous male friends (boyfriends, I'd assumed) but Maxwell Willis was not a name that cropped up in any of our early conversations; it later transpired that this was for a very good reason. It was not a matter of denial but deliberate avoidance, in the way in which most of us exclude distressing events or memories that hurt or have the potential to harm us.

When she eventually brought up the subject it left me feeling angry, sickened and utterly, utterly impotent. I am certain I had never heard such a catalogue of appalling, vicious, unnecessary cruelty perpetrated against one person before or since. He was supposed to have loved her! He professed as much at least. It was obvious to me, however, that Maxwell Willis was nothing but a cunt.

She had met him while still at university; I never really did establish where exactly that had been. Her accent was southern, perhaps east coast, Southampton or Brighton possibly, although certainly devoid of the twang of a rural West Country inflection. I think I imagined once she had studied at Exeter, although that may have been me filling in blanks retrospectively.

"I was a fish out of water," she began one Sunday afternoon. Heavy rain was hammering incessantly against the window, and grey, thundery clouds were creating an oppressive darkness in her flat.

"It was my first time away from home. A bit daunting

being on my own... I didn't know a single person when I first arrived... and I don't think I ventured out of my room for the entire month... apart from the freshers' parties. I think I went to two, but they weren't really my scene. They were just venues for hordes of horny students to hook up and catch who-knows-what diseases from each other.

"Max introduced himself at one of the parties. I can't remember which one. I was very shy back then and, I have to admit it, socially inept. I smiled and tried to extricate myself without hurting his feelings. I'm not sure if I found him attractive originally; it was just that I wasn't really looking for anyone, if you know what I mean. That was the first time I met him. I didn't see him again for another month or so.

"He was an athlete, a runner. Later on I saw him around campus, jogging; occasionally he'd wave at me as he ran past. I still wasn't interested in a relationship at that point, though I'd been asked out plenty of times, mainly by the 'players', but I had no intention of becoming another one of their statistics. Over the next few weeks I saw him out and about quite often. He would always smile and wave and I began to wave back. It was nothing. Only two people who vaguely knew each other acknowledging the presence of the other.

"I succumbed to the pressure to go on a date a couple of weeks later. Jack, one of the guys on my course, asked me out... incessantly; in the end I said yes, mainly just to shut him up. He was cute, though... very boyish and quiet, and studious. He was the type of man my mother would have approved of.

"We went to the cinema that first time. As the date had gone fairly well I agreed to a second date at his place, this time for a meal, which he was planning to cook.

However, at the last moment he made some lame excuse about the cooker not working or something and asked if he could come over to mine instead. Like a fool, I agreed.

"He drugged me. He must have slipped some kind of shit in my drink and I passed out. I cannot remember anything until I came round. When I woke up I found myself in the bedroom. It was dark outside and the light was on. I was completely naked and there was some blood… he'd raped me while I was unconscious, tore me open and I was bleeding. I was shocked. He was the last person I would have expected it from, but it just goes to show how much we really know about people.

"I went to the bathroom… hobbled to the bathroom… I could hardly walk. I had no idea what he had done to me or for how long… hours probably. I realised later that he hadn't just raped me; he'd sodomised me as well. When I looked in the mirror I saw that the dirty bastard had spunked over my face. He hadn't even had the decency to wipe it off. I was sick.

"I never told anyone at the time; in fact, you are only the fourth person I have ever told. I was so ashamed… ashamed at my stupidity… ashamed that someone had not only used me like some kind of filthy sex toy but taken my virginity too. I skipped lessons for the next week or so, terrified in case I was pregnant, though fortunately I'd been spared that.

"When I went back to lectures, Jack would just leer at me, smirking from across the room. I wanted to go over and wipe that supercilious look off his fucking face, but I couldn't. I was too afraid; besides, I had left it too long. Even if I had squared up to him or reported him to the police, no one would have believed me. He, however, was Mr Popular all of a sudden.

"Jack wasn't a 'player', but he wanted to be. He

wanted to be well known and trendy. No doubt he thought that if he engaged in the same kind of shit as the other jocks did, it would somehow make him more accepted, which was a joke.

"One night, a little while later, he turned up with two or three other guys. They were all inebriated, and they were banging on the door, shouting for me to let them in. Luckily I'd had a safety chain fitted so they couldn't force their way in, but that was what they wanted. They tried. They all wanted to come in and I can only guess what would have happened had I let them.

"Then Jack persuaded me to watch a video on his phone. I agreed, thinking once I'd seen it, they would leave. It was a film of him fucking me... on *my* bed. He must have recorded it while I was knocked out. They were all laughing... all of them... and making disgusting, lewd comments. One of them pulled his joggers down and started masturbating. It was horrible. After they'd left I just cried myself to sleep.

"I was so embarrassed. I didn't know about the film but obviously there were lots of people on campus who did. It wasn't long before I couldn't go anywhere without one guy or another passing comment about the video. I felt sick. One day, a girl I had never seen before came up to me and slapped me for no reason. She called me a slag. I really wanted to die. It was the closest I have ever been to contemplating killing myself."

Her testimony was uncomfortable for *me*. I wondered how she was feeling.

"About two or three weeks later, Jack was waiting for me outside the halls of residence. He said he wanted to apologise, but I knew he wasn't sorry for what he did so I told him to fuck off. He wouldn't leave me alone after that. He followed me up the stairs to my room. He was threatening me, telling me that if I didn't agree to have sex with him, he would post the video on the internet. I was really upset and shaking so much that I dropped my keys. It was at that moment I realised how vulnerable I was. I really thought he would snatch them, drag me inside and rape me again.

"I never saw where Max came from. One minute there was just Jack and me in the hallway; the next minute, Max was there. Max swung Jack round and punched him and Jack fell down. He must have dropped his phone. The next thing I remember was Max straddling Jack and using the phone to hit him in the face. There was so much blood. I think he broke Jack's nose. I know he knocked out four of his teeth. I should have been terrified but I wasn't. I wanted Max to keep hitting him.

"Something should have warned me about Max's explosive violence at the time, but it didn't. Maybe it was because he'd stepped in and done what I should have done if I hadn't been so weak. I don't mind admitting that I experienced a weird, ecstatic, almost pleasurable feeling watching him repeatedly hit that bastard.

"When Max stood up I can't remember if Jack was conscious or not. But Max was no longer in control of his temper; he was shaking with rage and I recall he said something like 'If I ever see you hanging round here again, or bothering her, or if I get to hear about the video from *anyone*, I swear I will find you and I will fucking kill you.' I actually believed he would as well."

Outside there was a bright flash that made me jump; it was followed by a torturously long, loud clap of thunder. I apologised and asked her to continue, feeling, I imagine, much as she must have done at the time at Jack's well-overdue comeuppance.

"What happened to him?" I asked.

"He left. I think almost immediately. Nothing was ever said. Max told me he destroyed the phone and its contents and that was the end of *that* particularly horrific chapter in my life. After that, no one mentioned anything about it ever again and I started seeing Max virtually every day. He made me feel safe when he was around, and it wasn't long before he summoned up the courage to ask me out properly. I accepted, of course; I didn't hesitate. Max was my knight in shining armour and I gave myself to him willingly... totally. That was part of the problem.

"I'm not sure if I fell in love with *him* or with how he made me feel when he was around. It consumed me, though. I fell for him like a meteorite bursting through the stratosphere and wanting to explode in the earth miles and miles below. We became inseparable. As a couple, we were asked to attend various functions and parties. We went to a few because we both wanted to show each other off, to let everyone know how happy we were. And we were, except... there was one thing about our relationship that was a bit odd: sex, or rather the lack of it.

"There was no intimacy, no physicality. We would hold hands and we'd touch. We'd kiss – he was a fantastic kisser – yet we never seemed to get to where we both knew it should inevitably culminate. He never stayed over. Sometimes after he'd gone I would be so aroused I had to finish myself off before I went to sleep. I wondered if *he* was a virgin himself, perhaps a Christian. Though I did feel guilty at the time, I once even considered the possibility that he might be gay."

"But he wasn't?" I interjected.

"No." Her face suddenly became much darker, more serious. "He was trying to avoid the inevitable because of who... sorry... *what* he was and what he knew he was capable of. I had only seen the tip of the iceberg that day he attacked Jack. His temper was uncontrollable once unleashed, and he realised that. It was why he continued to resist having sex with me for as long as he could, to prevent what would be for him, irrepressible, violent sexual urges.

"But I didn't know that then. What I also didn't know was the terrible danger I would be putting myself in by attempting to uncork his bottle, so to speak."

My mobile buzzed silently in my pocket, alerting me to the fact that I had already missed a call and had, as a result of not answering, received a follow-up text. It was from Janice, enquiring where I was and what time I would be back. I replied as noncommittally as I could and turned my attention back to Ligeia. I really wanted her narrative to end well but was already acutely aware that it would not.

"Eventually we did it. I had to seduce him in the end, in my bedroom, to get him to the point where he couldn't control himself any longer. My first real... conscious... sexual experience was absolutely glorious. Spectacular. Magnificent. He was like a wild beast. He tore my clothes off and fucked me with so much passion I thought I would actually pass out from the pleasure. His orgasms were always incredibly intense... and painful I imagined at the time... and lasted much longer than my own. At first I used to love seeing the expression on his face when he came.

"Once the deed had been done, it seemed there was no holding us back. We would be at it whenever we could. He started to stay over and some nights we would literally fuck until the sun came up the following morning. I thought it was strange that he never tired, always remaining stiff, even after he'd ejaculated a few times, though I wasn't really complaining. I was deliriously happy and, I must be honest, beginning to fall madly in love with him.

"He did begin to change, though, after we started having sex. He used to be quite gentle and tender whenever he held or touched me, but he began to get a little rougher. Often I wondered if he knew his own strength. I suppose, initially, when he was getting to know me he was more careful and wary about hurting me. Over time that gentle side was replaced by a more complacent, almost callous, aspect.

"The first time he hit me was a massive shock. He'd slapped me before, you know, when we were play fighting during sex, generally when I was tied up – that was the other thing he was into, bondage – but he'd never struck me so violently. He hit me so hard I literally saw stars; he also split my lip. I told him that he'd hurt me but that only seemed to excite him more. When he fucked me it was unreal, as though I wasn't there. It really scared me, but I got used to it over time."

I was incredulous.

"What do you mean you got used to it? Are you saying you allowed it to continue?"

She nodded. Outside the thunder was getting closer.

"Well, it's not that I allowed it; I just didn't stop it. You have to remember I had nothing else to compare it to. I'd seen films, sure, but they only depicted the act, not the emotions, not the feelings that drove it.

"This was my first real relationship... my first real experience of sexual love. I know I'd lost my virginity to Jack, but I was unconscious so that didn't really count. Max was all I'd known at that point. I didn't have any friends that I could compare notes with. I honestly thought the violence was a part of sex with him. That it was… you know… a by-product of his passion.

"I suppose I became conditioned to it. The beatings during sex became more frequent and more violent. It got to the stage where I couldn't orgasm until I could taste blood in my mouth or was losing consciousness."

I swallowed hard. It was frightening listening to how calmly she spoke about it. I doubted whether her apparent lack of emotion was normal; that too had to be some kind of coping mechanism.

"I could actually cope with that… after all I didn't know any better… but it was the other stuff that I found difficult to bear. Things like his temper or his insecurity, which was not obvious to begin with, was only marginally more acceptable than his increasingly stifling possessiveness. The invites to the parties kept coming but we no longer went to them. If I tried to persuade him to go, he'd become sullen and moody or wouldn't speak to me for days.

"When my parents visited me, keen to meet Max, whom I'd spent so much time telling them about, he simply vanished for the whole weekend, not returning until my family had gone home again. I asked him where he'd been but he flatly refused to tell me. His secretive nature began to trouble me, not just in respect of his disappearance but there were other things… like the room he always kept locked at his house. I kept absolutely no secrets from him, so could not understand why he felt the need to be so furtive."

A locked room?

"That sounds very creepy. Did you ever discover what was in the room?"

She nodded.

"Eventually, though to be honest I wish I never had."

What followed was a chilling account of what sounded

like the twisted plot of a classic low-budget 1980's Italian psycho-drama/thriller by Lucio Fulci; not that I was a fan but I'd seen enough of them to understand the genre.

Max had apparently become seriously ill with a particularly aggressive form of glandular fever and, in the absence of friends or family, Ligeia remained on hand to nurse him back to recovery. It was bad. He spent three days in hospital and, on his discharge, was forced to take to his bed for a further period of recuperation. It meant that she virtually lived with him for three weeks, cooking meals for him, cleaning and generally keeping on top of things. The most important task, however, was keeping him company in between his frequent, almost narcoleptic, lapses.

It was in the quieter, boring moments while he was sleeping that she allowed her curiosity free rein and eventually strayed into the realms of fantasy. One afternoon, unable to resist her inquisitiveness any more, she plucked up the courage to investigate the mystery beyond the door. Locating the correct key on the huge bunch he normally carried around with him wherever he went was not without problem; she resigned herself to simply identifying the right one by systematic trial and error, not daring to go any further than merely noting *which* key fitted the heavy door lock.

The following day she opened the door for the first time and found a room bathed in total darkness; the windows had either been painted over or been covered by material so thick that everything within was in permanent shadow. Not even the meagre light that was allowed in from the rest of the flat could illuminate more than a few feet inside the room. She thought she could make out the vague shape of a chair in the gloom, but she couldn't be certain.

Ligeia told me that she would have ventured further that particular day but her exploration had been abruptly halted by Max calling out to her deliriously from the bedroom. She locked the door and did not attempt to enter the room for another four days. By this time, Max, still making a steady recovery, was becoming more lucid, and was sleeping less and for shorter periods. Ligeia realised that if she was to discover what it was he kept so closely guarded in the room, her window of opportunity was rapidly closing.

The evening she finally uncovered his awful secret was one that began ordinarily enough, and there had been no indication of whether, or how rapidly, that would change. Max had eaten and fallen into a light sleep. She watched over him for a while to make sure he was unlikely to stir and then, relatively certain her prying wouldn't be interrupted, continued with the investigation she'd started almost a week previously.

She allowed her eyes to grow accustomed to the inky blackness within the room, although she was still unable to discern anything beyond what she'd already seen: dark, bulky shadows within shadows. She desperately needed some light.

Not risking entry without adequate illumination, she felt blindly just inside the door for a switch; she located it easily enough but she held back from turning it on straight away. She told me that she already suspected that she would not like what she might find within those silent walls, which was why she hesitated.

"I took a deep breath, closed my eyes and flipped the switch." She exhaled noisily. It was obvious that the memory was still painful for her.

"It was a shrine." She closed her eyes and shook her head involuntarily. "I can't say how long he'd been following me, watching me, photographing me… perhaps from the very first day… certainly well before we first spoke at the freshers' party. The walls were covered, and I mean covered, with photographs of me; some I had posed for, but most were candid shots that he must have taken without me realising, with a zoom lens or something.

"There were images of me shopping in Sainsbury's, walking on campus, sitting on a bench in the arboretum, drinking coffee in Starbucks; there were even some taken of me inside my flat. He must have been watching me all the time and I had not even noticed. I mean how the fuck could he photograph me in my flat? It's on the second floor! He must have been up a tree or something!

"He also had these boxes on a desk against the back wall; small, plain brown cardboard boxes, all neatly stacked next to his laptop. Inside them there were hundreds of discs, all numbered and labelled with dates and times on. Needless to say, they were surveillance videos. He had been filming me too. I can't say I felt violated at that point but I did wonder about his level of interest in me; it was more akin to abnormal obsession than healthy adoration.

"Max had items of my clothes, all neatly folded and stored in boxes on shelves around the room. Some I recognised as ones that had gone missing since I'd been seeing him but there were others I had long since forgotten about. He must have had about twenty items of lingerie… bras… knickers … the majority of which had gone missing from my washing line. There was something else.

"Underneath the desk there was a trunk, a military-style trunk with no markings on it. It wasn't locked. He had… it contained… I think he must have rifled through my rubbish bags. They were my sanitary towels. They were all wrapped in toilet paper, the way I dispose of them. There were a hundred or more. I can't remember if I was more horrified or disgusted by the lengths to which he'd gone in establishing his shrine."

The thunder had stopped, although the rain continued to beat against the windows and sill, throwing up a mist of fine spray from the ferocity of the downpour. I tried to imagine how she was feeling as she relived those moments from her past, but it was impossible. Nothing I had experienced in my life compared to how alarming her discovery was or what was to follow.

Amongst the artefacts in the room, alongside the carefully compiled boxes of handycam footage on DVDs, the cellophane packets containing bus tickets, till receipts and meticulously straightened backing strips from the self-adhesive panels on her sanitary protection, cartons of clothes and underwear, was a large glass storage jar that was a quarter filled with used, knotted condoms that she assumed he'd worn and saved each time they'd had sex.

"I understand that it was abnormal now, that there was something seriously wrong with him... something psychologically wrong. At the time, though it grossed me out, I never thought about the darker implications of his obsessive behaviour. You have to remember I did truly love him. Have you ever loved someone *so much* that you would do anything for them, that you would forgive them for anything they did? I mean *anything*?"

I had to think... but not for long.

"No, I haven't."

She stood up and began to pace the room.

"Can you believe that I felt guilty being there, in that room? I was surrounded by the proof of his insane infatuation and all I could think was that it was my own fault for prying. Had I not gone in there I might still have been with him, unaware; I would have been oblivious to what was obviously the beginning of his descent into some kind of madness."

He found out Ligeia had been in the room, even though she was careful to leave everything exactly as she had found it. How he was aware of her trespass she was uncertain. He didn't say anything about it straight away, no doubt still weakened by his debilitating illness, although he grew gradually more suspicious of her; whenever she came around to visit, he would question her about things like where she had been, whom she'd seen or whom she'd spoken to.

When he was well they resumed their sexual relationship, although Ligeia, now aware of his devotional repository, found the thought, which quickly established itself as an invasive mental image, uncomfortable enough to begin taking the pill. Rather than being pleased that he would no longer have to endure glans desensitising latex confinement, Max erupted when he found out, accusing her of taking the pill so that she could cheat on him and fuck other guys behind his back.

Ligeia quite rightly denied the false accusations and protested her innocence. At one point she remonstrated as forcefully as she 'dared' – her use of that word indicated to me that she was acutely aware, although chose to ignore, that things were definitely *not* normal – that Max was her *only* love. But his jealousy and possessiveness had taken hold of him to the extent that, insidiously, it began to intrude on their relationship. He started to control what outfits she wore, banning her from wearing tops that were cut low, trousers that were too tight or skirts that were, in his opinion, obscenely short.

Progressively, he imposed other restrictions on her, like *where* she could go when they were not together, *when* she could wear makeup and *whom* she could speak to. Friends of the opposite sex, even her close friends and colleagues from her course, were outlawed. He insisted her male lecturers were all 'cunt-hunting lotharios' and he became incandescent with rage if she paid any man a compliment, even if it was done light heartedly.

As I have already mentioned, Ligeia was an incredibly beautiful young woman and this naturally attracted admiration from the people she came into contact with on a daily basis. Max found that the hardest to bear; he was constantly seeing men stop what they were doing to look at her, carrying out almost comical double-takes in the street or sometimes simply ogling, or occasionally leering at, her.

The full extent of his jealous intolerance became apparent during a shopping trip when he caught her smiling back at a random guy in H&M who had innocently waved at her. He seethed in silence until they were back at his flat and then he unleashed his full fury, hurling personal abuse at her in between hurtful volleys of aggressive accusation. When she threatened to leave and stay away until he had calmed down, he ran up to prevent her exit by head-butting her in the face.

"He must have knocked me out cold," she said softly. She sat down again, this time closer to me. "When I came round I was in the room, tied to a chair, facing his laptop. I was covered in blood. He'd fractured my nose. He was pacing up and down the room or circling me, round and round and round, just screaming at me the whole time.

"That was when he told me he knew I had been in his room – his study was what he actually referred to it as – and that he was very disappointed in me because I had betrayed him. I tried to reason with him, but he wouldn't listen; he just kept going on about how I'd hurt him and deliberately set out to deceive him. That was when he showed me what he called incontrovertible proof.

"I was forced to watch the film of Jack raping me. I saw it over and over again; it must have been on a loop or something. It sickened me, yet he forced me to see it, threatening to hurt me if I closed my eyes."

I held her hand, watching her eyes fill with tears that didn't fall.

"He hadn't destroyed the film at all. It had destroyed him; it was eating him up each time he watched it. In the end, any pity he had for me was replaced by anger; his anger was transformed into violence and his violence was manifested in the beatings I had to endure every time we made love. He blamed me for it all. He was such a prick."

I asked her what happened afterwards. Falteringly, she explained that he made her view the assault carried out on her until *he* was unable to watch it any further; then he untied her, bound her spread-eagled to the bed and used her until he collapsed on top of her from exhaustion. During the ordeal he had slapped her, punched her, spat in her face and throttled her to the point where she was afraid he would kill her. Almost in relief, she had experienced shameful spontaneous orgasm as he released his grip on her throat.

"That kind of thing became routine."

So began the cycle of cruelty and bitterness and hatred, spite and bile, violence and sexual gratification, followed by remorse and sorrow and finally repentance before resentment set in and the whole pattern started again. It was something she suffered for a further eighteen months, towards the end of which she had been reduced to little more than his slave, spending the last month or so a virtual prisoner in his flat.

The whole history of her shocking life with Max had

been delivered in a completely dispassionate (well, almost) and matter-of-fact manner that left me speechless. She sat on the settee next to me, her legs drawn underneath her in a graceful cat-like manner; she was calm and strangely serene. I, on the other hand, was incensed, unable to comprehend how anyone could treat another human being so shamefully.

"What happened to him? To you? How did you escape?"

She was silent for a very long time, her head bowed. I didn't repeat the question. It was obvious she had heard me, so I decided it was best not to force the issue. Eventually she sighed and apologised.

"I'm sorry, it's really upsetting me… do you mind… can I tell you another time?"

I tried not to sound disappointed. "Sure."

I pecked her cheek, a mark of my sympathy, but she wanted more and turned her head to offer me her lips. I responded to her movement with passion, pulling her in close to me so that the softness of her body moulded against me. I desired her. I wanted her unconditionally. I felt the tip of her tongue in my mouth and felt sure that if we didn't stop, our more instinctive urges would take over. I was torn between propriety and lustful intent. It was she who pulled away, a look of consternation in her eyes.

"You don't feel that I am too damaged, do you?"

I shook my head vigorously, desperate for her not see any hint of hesitancy or doubt. "Never."

"But being exposed to that level of sexual violence and imagining that it is somehow normal, at least until you know better, does leave a mark on a person's life, doesn't it?"

It was true. Of course it did. It was evident in

everything she did, in the way she celebrated life, in the manner in which she approached the whole subject of sexual intimacy and her unashamed pursuit of carnal pleasure. The real question was would I allow that to affect me? I decided that day that I would try *not* to let it and I feel I was relatively successful in regards to that aim.

That is why I could never be, even after everything that we would later go through together, judgemental about Ligeia or how she chose to live her life. If she *was* a libertine then so be it; she was a joyous libertine. I would be happy for her, for as long as she continued to be happy and for as long as that way of life pleased her. Considering her past and the emotional, psychological and physical enslavement she sustained at the hands of Max, God knows she deserved to be.

Chapter 20

<u>*Morning*</u>

The alarm that woke me from my fitful slumber a fortnight later heralded a day that had filled me with nervous anticipation for the whole of the previous week. I was in turmoil. My head was in a thousand places at once and my thoughts were a cascade that I struggled to both contain and understand. I felt as though my stomach and chest were alive with squirming, crawling things intent upon devouring me from the inside. My behaviour must have reflected my increasing insecurity and uncertainty because Janice was not the only one to comment on my odd conduct; a number of my school colleagues had mentioned it too.

Why was I filled with such trepidation? I was a man, of that I was certain, and, being a man, I was subject to the normal thoughts and feelings that any man should experience. Right? Wrong. I was desperately struggling with coming to terms with something else that, while it was generally more acceptable in our society, was alien to me with my conceptions of normality. Did the feelings that assailed me indicate that I was abnormal? Was I depraved? Was I in fact a closet homosexual?

What the fuck did 'closet homosexual' actually mean? It was a ridiculous phrase, undoubtedly popular when homosexuality *was* the love that dare not speak its name. It came from a time when such acts were considered depraved and unspeakable, and participants seen as no better than vermin, to be vilified and hounded out of polite society to the darker fringes, where only the filth existed. Is that where I would have been? Would I have deserved that? My whole being vehemently defended my desires, yet there was still this voice; it was a little way off but it was becoming louder and louder with each passing day.

Ligeia was, naturally, supportive. Being permissive by nature and having been involved in multifarious sexual activities herself, including numerous sapphic encounters, she considered my involvement with Raphael to be nothing more than a natural evolutionary step in my sexual life experience. She was more than likely correct, although it did little to calm my increasing feeling of uncertainty. To me, being brought up to understand nothing but heterosexual love, even the concept of being attracted to someone of the same sex filled me with apprehension.

Since that afternoon in Ligeia's flat I had often found myself wondering *why* I had not reacted with aversion, or indeed reacted at all, when I realised it was Raphael, and not Ligeia, who was sucking my cock. Actually, I was fascinated by this. It was true I had found him physically attractive and had become instantly aroused just watching him move as he fucked her. His body was sculpted, honed by several years of vigorous exercise or weight training. That hard musculature beneath smooth, warm satin skin was deliciously tactile. Was it possible that I was bisexual? Or had I simply allowed myself to become corrupted by Ligeia and desperate not to suffer her disapproval? Was I enflamed by her licentiousness to the point where nothing mattered any more, not even the sex of my partner?

Was I normal? What *was* normal? Could normality be

measured or gauged? If it could, against what? Someone else's normality? Who decided if *they* were normal? It was all subjective, as most things are when they involve people, because we are not the same. Similar, yes, but definitely different, individual and unique.

I had avoided over-analysing my reaction for as long as possible, but, as the day arrived when we would almost certainly indulge once again in a three-way sexual relationship, I *had* to consider the situation. There was little point, I realised, in trying to imagine what others would think about my aberrant behaviour. That was a given. Very few people within my circle of friends would have condoned such promiscuity; they might suggest that it was some form of mid-life crisis that had temporarily unbalanced me. But what about those outside of that circle? I didn't really give a toss what they thought, although Janice's possible reaction if she ever found out did trouble me.

From this, you will gather that my intentions were quite clear. I did find Raphael physically attractive and I similarly found the dichotomy of our situation sexually arousing. The truth? I wanted to explore the feelings he engendered in me and, as our situation was exclusively secure, I felt there would not be a better opportunity to experiment with them and avoid either embarrassment or hurt. In simple terms: I was ready to try a completely new experience, and decided that I would deal with any internal emotional fallout later.

* * *

We met by the main entrance of the expansive eastern cemetery. It was dark. We had chosen that particular graveyard over others because of how large it was and how easy it was to access after the gates had closed. There would be no need to crawl through fences, climb over walls or scale barriers. Obviously, the ease of access meant that night visitors like us could not guarantee being completely alone. However, all three of us were very familiar with the place so were reasonably confident we could find a spot that was secluded enough for our purposes.

Guiltily, I had the feeling that everyone I had encountered throughout that day, Janice included, had been aware of my intentions for the evening. I realised it was preposterous but such was my anxiety. I was keen to be inside the grounds, hidden by the shadows, away from the streetlight that illuminated the three of us huddled together conspiratorially as we merely greeted each other. There was the familiar wide-eyed joyous expression on Ligeia's face; as we embraced, I noticed she was literally trembling with excitement.

Raphael was much calmer. He smiled as we shook hands. I felt he was not dressed for the weather, favouring as he did a short military-style jacket (high end, obviously) and a pair of light-coloured chinos. Before I ventured out I actually contemplated putting on my tweed overcoat to ward off the evening chill. Considering we would all soon be partially or fully unclothed anyway, any reflection about the thermal quality of what we wore would be rendered academic.

The three of us walked alongside the perimeter wall, past the bank of early nineteenth-century alms houses, until we reached a small archway used by residents to access the back of their properties. Shielded from view by a tall privet hedge, the passageway led to a four-metre high redbrick wall that contained a dilapidated, rusty gate. This was where we could enter the cemetery. My heartbeat quickened.

We were eager, perhaps too eager. In our haste to unburden ourselves of the lust that had been gradually building all day, we grew bolder, throwing all caution to the wind as we tripped clumsily over half-buried flagstones and began giggling fitfully. The full darkness of the place became much more evident and we had to resort to leading each other by the hand until we reached our destination. There in the blackness we waited, listening for any sound that would indicate we were not on our own. All we heard was the silence punctuated by our own noisy breathing.

"This is perfect!" Ligeia exclaimed quietly and kissed me.

That was how it began. A gentle, tender osculation, her lips cool and soft against mine, quickly grew in intensity and urgency until we were locked together, our tongues entwined, causing my ardour to rise just as rapidly. I felt a hand stroke my stiffening cock and am not ashamed to admit I did not care whom it belonged to. When I opened my eyes, Raphael was standing next to us, his free arm around me, nuzzling the back of Ligeia's neck.

Things soon became more feverish and any trepidation I'd felt before quickly vanished. I watched as my companions kissed, thrusting themselves against each other, their hands exploring each other. I joined in as best as I could, stroking Ligeia's pubic mound through the thin fabric of her skirt. She moaned, although whether it was because of what I was doing to her, or because Raphael had exposed one of her breasts and was gently squeezing her nipple, I don't know.

They continued like that for only a few moments more until, unable to control themselves any further, they began tearing at each other's clothing, throwing the hastily removed garments in all directions. Ligeia did not even have the opportunity to step out of her briefs because Raphael tore them from her with a triumphant roar. Together they stood naked, panting, two figures almost luminous in the darkness.

I was slacking. While Raphael guided Ligeia to a nearby grave, topped with a slate flagstone, and began fucking her, I started to remove my clothes. The cold air on my body caused goose pimples to rise on my flesh. Ligeia's eyes were on me; she looked hungry, filled with longing and close to ecstasy. I watched her eyes roll back in her head and suddenly her body arched and convulsed spasmodically. Raphael continued pounding his cock into her as hard as he could.

"Off you get, Raffi. I want Richard to do me now. Otherwise I think he might go off spontaneously." She smiled and gestured for me to interrupt Raphael's thrusting, pushing against him simultaneously with her hand. He was not impressed and increased the speed of his movements, but she was insistent, eventually getting him to stop.

"But I haven't cum yet!" he complained as he pulled out of her noisily.

"Richard will sort that out for you." She smiled at me. "Won't you?"

Nothing else was said. I didn't know precisely what to say, anyway; it was all completely new for me. Raphael stood up and waited for me until we were standing so close that our erections touched. Then he kissed me on the lips. It was a strange sensation; *in my head* it was a strange sensation, although my body obviously didn't mind and eagerly responded to him. I reached down and closed my hand around his cock, gently gripping his shaft, which caused the most ecstatic reaction in him.

"Wait!" He implored me to refrain from giving him the release I knew he so desperately wanted and, turning his back to me, braced himself against a tall Corinthian-columned funereal vault a few feet away.

He leant in against the monument, his thick muscular forearms pressed against the white-veined terracotta-coloured marble, allowing me to caress his abdomen from behind. I reached around him and felt the coolness of his skin, the hardness of his stomach broken only by the wiry hair that spread upwards from his groin. His cock was ramrod-hard and it jutted upwards and out, away from his body; but I found it easily and tenderly stroked the entire length while he sighed insistently.

My body, softer than his, was pressed against him and my penis reacted to the sensation that was also causing my heart to beat wildly inside my chest. I gripped his shaft, still slick with Ligeia's juices, and pulled him gently, wanking him as my own erection jerked involuntarily against the cleft of his arse. It was similar to pulling myself except I could feel him getting more and more excited with every pass my hand made down his length. I was in control of that; I was in control of *him* and his brief submission of power was intoxicating.

His breathing became laboured as his excitement mounted, and I reached around and cupped his balls with my other hand. They were tight against the base of his cock but I could still knead them. Blood continued to course into his organ, swelling it further in my hand until, now fully engorged, it was even more solid and thicker in girth than when I'd begun. I had only seconds to react before he ejaculated. I felt the deep-seated rhythm that began pumping semen towards release and I pulled him faster and gripped him harder until he cried out, an orgasm ripping through his body.

His spunk was copious; spurting in thick streams in time with his own heartbeat, it splashed against the stonework, spattering the inscription with pearlescent emission. I held him tightly until his orgasm ebbed away; then he turned his head slightly and kissed my cheek in tender gratitude. But it was not his gratitude I wanted and he could sense this. He parted his legs a little wider and, reaching behind, assisted my cock, sliding it in until it was firmly inside his arse.

I closed my eyes and began fucking him. He could have been anyone. Despite my initial supposition, I discovered that fucking his arse felt no different from fucking Ligeia's (or even Janice's) and with renewed intention I pushed myself in almost to the hilt. His bestial groans of satisfaction were the only thing that reminded me of who I was doing. He urged me to fuck him harder, to be rougher, and through my half-open eyes I could see he was furiously masturbating as I pushed myself into him. He came again, before I did; it was the pulsating spasms inside him that started me off. I shot my load and left my cock buried inside him until my pleasure had subsided.

Ligeia urged me to join her on the grey slab where she lay. She had been fingering herself while she watched us. My eyes had become accustomed to the darkness and I could see her cunt glisten with moisture as her fingers opened her lips, moving with speed, switching between her own erection and her vagina. I pulled out of Raphael's anus and swapped partners, kneeling in front of her and burying my face between her legs. She allowed me to lap hungrily at her warm, wet sex and I pushed the tip of my tongue into her opening in response to her delighted moans of ecstasy.

Alternating my efforts with my tongue, as her fingers

had done, I brought her to the brink of orgasm before concentrating all my efforts on the gloriously stiff and swollen sheath covering her clit. Her climax was so intense she whimpered noisily into the darkness, threatening to alert anyone passing of our presence there. I had to take immediate action and clamped my hand over her mouth. After only a few short seconds she began to struggle for breath and started writhing beneath me. I looked into her eyes and saw panic there; briefly, fleetingly and perversely it stiffened my resolve to slide my cock into her cunt.

Still recovering from banging Raphael, my prick was not fully hard but pressing it against the warmth and wetness of her slit was so exciting, it allowed me to gain enough turgidity to penetrate her with one thrust. Once inside it took hardly any time before I was fully erect and as she dug her nails into my shoulders I pounded her slit. Ramming her as hard as I could against the cold slate flagstone was almost as big a turn-on as my first same-sex fuck. I spilled my second offering of sperm into Ligeia silently. Even without me heralding it with an orgasmic moan, she realised I had ejaculated and began kissing my face.

It was done. I was done. We all were, although knowing something of Ligeia's appetite I had the impression that Raphael and I would shortly be called on to service her again. Not here, though. Not in the dark. Not in the cold. I needed some warmth in order to function properly now that the moment had passed and our initial passion had been spent.

My knees felt raw from being in contact with the frigid ground.

We dressed again, quietly, and walked back to the gate in the wall.

None of us said anything for a long time. There was nothing to say. We'd expressed ourselves physically. That night Ligeia slept between Raphael and me in her oversized bed, curled up and content. I watched over her and Raphael. When I thought about the evening, I marvelled at the ease with which I had been persuaded to pleasure both of them, and I was secretly pleased that the shame and guilt I thought would consume me did not raise its ugly head. Now content myself, I drifted off into a deep and satisfying sleep.

Chapter 21

I started the journal with the best of intentions.

Paris Journal – Day One: The Hotel

The hotel where we are staying is one of those lazily indolent establishments that perhaps young, aspirational jet setters and the nouveau riche enjoy. The doors are opened by smiling, servile doormen dressed in their finest, freshly pressed livery, and they are always on hand to offer assistance, provided it is preceded by the pressing of a few coins into their white-gloved hands.

Inside, the steps lead up to a reception hall that appears unchanged in its hundred years plus of existence. Predating Art Nouveau in style, the decor is much more severe and conservative. Huge marble pillars stretch upwards towards a gargantuan fragmented mirror ceiling, from which hang two enormous crystal pendant chandeliers.

This obviously was not designed for modern web-package travellers escaping their humdrum existence via a lo-cost flight-and-hotel deal courtesy of Travel Republic; this new breed of www-tourist appears to be exceptionally well catered for amongst all the faux opulence, especially considering that it was originally intended to cater for first class passengers terminating their journey at the nearby train station, Gare Saint-Lazare. Indeed, the hotel was once called Hotel Terminus and evidence of this proud heritage can be seen everywhere throughout the lobby and reception.

There are reproductions of luggage labels, posters, advertisements for the grand hotel; bottles of champagne rescued from the cellar of the original bar before it was renovated; cutlery, corkscrews and other ephemera all bearing the HT monogram, which seems to be a consistent emblem throughout.

The concierge was well versed in sycophancy and forelock tugging, which the Japanese (who appear to make up the majority of guests in the hotel) absolutely love. While they might be keen to have their photograph taken next to anyone wearing a beret (because they look typically French) they would never consider having a photograph taken alongside someone whose job it was to ensure their stay at the hotel was as pleasant as possible.

I wonder how the Chinese (who make up eighty percent of the reception staff) feel about the over-abundance of Nipponese tourists, with their cameras and fake smiles and inexhaustible credit cards. They probably couldn't give two fucks, to be honest, provided they pay their bill at the end of their stay; and the Japs, always keen to add Paris as one of their important European holiday destinations, are happy to pay through the nose for the most mundane services, provided their sheets are clean and the mini-bar is restocked daily.

★ ★ ★

"Are you enjoying yourself?" Ligeia clung to my arm as we strolled along the crowded boulevards, taking in the sights and sounds of what was, without doubt, the most beautiful city I have ever visited.

"Yes," I replied. I may have even smiled. The only thing I wasn't happy about was the number of Japanese tourists, who seemed to be *everywhere*.

In my life I have been fortunate enough to have experienced many of the world's great capital cities and destinations, such as Rome, Prague, New York, Moscow and Tokyo. Each has its own idiosyncrasies, and its own distinct feel and flavour. Each is magnificent in its own way, although none affected me more than Paris did.

Not just me, it seemed. Some of the greatest names in the history of art and literature have been drawn like moths to the glorious radiance of the city. Some merely passed through and thereafter waxed lyrical about the opulence and splendour of Haussmann's great revival and how they would one day return to experience it once again. Others, stricken by love, poverty or necessity, never left and have provided the world with incredible, eternal testimonies that now cover walls in museums and galleries or fill the pages of countless books.

Of course, monumental talents, inspirational thinkers, artists, poets, musicians, philosophers, politicians, courtesans and lovers have been connected with Paris throughout the centuries, but it was specifically the influence of the modernisation programme, made manifest through its inhabitants and visitors, predominantly in the decades that straddled the nineteenth and twentieth centuries, that propelled the ancient fortified city into the future, one that reached out to embrace it and force it to the forefront of cultural consciousness.

There are a great many tourist traps lying in wait for the casual traveller, all of which, thanks to the grand architectural redevelopment of the remnants of the old, dilapidated Medieval Paris (initiated during the nineteenth century by Baron Georges-Eugène Haussmann), are largely accessible by foot, if you are fit enough. The Arc De Triomphe, Sacre Coeur, Notre Dame, The Grand Palais, The Louvre: the list of monuments, churches, parks and landmarks is endless, and does not even begin to cover the more secluded, secretive parts of the city we visited during our stay.

Ignoring any of them would be a mistake. For me, there was no greater or more humbling experience than walking the short distance from the Trocadero metro station to the steps of the Palais de Chaillot and up to the broad plaza to catch sight of the marvel of engineering ingenuity, La Tour Eiffel, as it was meant to be seen, in all its glory. This vast skeletal structure points defiantly into the sky, challenging Parisians and tourists alike *not* to take notice.

Any grateful surrender to long-established notions of romanticism could not have been further from my mind as I experienced Paname for the first time, however. I was not willing to put away my natural cynicism just because I was with Ligeia, although she did make it seem less daunting than trips to other foreign destinations in the past.

Being naturally suspicious and overly cautious, when we arrived at Gare du Nord I was instantly on guard if anyone ventured too close. Having seen the, admittedly sensationalist, BBC Panorama documentary about the Eurostar terminal, I was aware that it was a haven for roaming gangs of swarthy, rambunctious Romanian child pickpockets, so we quickly collected our bags and caught the first train out from the metro. It was only then that I felt myself relax a little.

We alighted at the Saint-Lazare metro station and found our hotel very easily, thanks to its grand frontage and unfurled, welcoming flags. After checking in and depositing our bags in the very swish rooms, we headed back down to the main lobby and then out into the city. Once again, my natural caution sought to temper my enjoyment slightly. It proved to be unfounded and we experienced nothing more troublesome, throughout the duration of our stay, than the obligatory capital city pavement con artist who miraculously made a solid brass wedding ring materialise out the pavement before our very eyes.

Lunch, within sight of Notre Dame and the Seine, consisted of grilled noix de Saint-Jacques and a salad with the most exquisite sesame and caramel dressing. We spent well over an hour on this, as mouthfuls were interspersed with several large glasses of chilled 1664 bier. Replete, we began our itinerary in earnest, hand-in-hand and oblivious to the curious glances we undoubtedly received from other pedestrians.

★ ★ ★

Paris Journal – Day One: Père Lachaise Cemetery

Père Lachaise Cemetery was not what I was expecting. I'd imagined it to be nothing more impressive than London's Highgate Cemetery but on a much, much larger scale. I am pleased to state that I was very wrong. It is absolutely huge and altogether more fascinating. Forget the dilapidation, the decay, and the rather overgrown and overcrowded look of the place. Ignore the cats and the nauseating acrid stench of their piss that assails your nostrils as you make your way with increasing uncertainty along the myriad avenues that criss-cross its forty-four hectares, containing over one million internees. This is a monumental necropolis. It is inspirational and deserves special mention.

I used up what remained of one SD card and exhausted half of a new one photographing the monuments there. I could have easily stayed for days.

We chose the optimum time to visit; the sun was still quite bright but sinking slowly towards the western skyline, and it cast long dark shadows behind the tombs and grandiose sepulchres. Many of the luminaries that have made Paris the city it is today can be found there and of course it is a place of pilgrimage for those who still venerate these cold, silent celebrities. It is the final resting place of composers such as Georges Bizet and Gioachino Rossini, writers like Honoré de Balzac and Oscar Wilde, and artists that include Amedeo Modigliani and the pointillist George-Pierre Seurat. Not content with swallowing up the great and good of the nineteenth century, Père Lachaise also embraces twentieth-century legends in its cold clammy arms; here lie Édith Piaf, Sarah Bernhardt, and white-faced unfunny mime artist Marcel Marceau.

According to the flimsy map we obtained at the main entrance, the cemetery was opened in 1804 and was named after King Louis XIV's confessor, Père François de La Chaise. It was not a very popular cemetery; it attracted only nine burials in the first year, owing to it being considered too far outside of the city. However, Napoleon Bonaparte's declaration in the same year that 'every citizen has the right to be buried regardless of race or religion' and some rather inventive remarketing of the graveyard ensured that, by 1830, over thirty thousand people were buried there, alongside many famous and illustrious dead celebrities.

I expected to find the place teeming with folk; thankfully, it was not. In fact, it was rather quiet, considering.

I was grateful for the absence of tourists, especially Japanese tourists, who seemed to swamp every other notable destination in the city, making it virtually impossible to photograph anything without having one of them idiotically gurning away in the background. To be fair, there was a small throng of annoying pubescent (at least I think they were pubescent) Japanese girls gathered around the grave of Jim Morrison. I doubted if any of them even knew who he was. I personally believe they, like so many other fair-weather tourists, go where their guidebooks tell them to go.

I found it quite touching that Jim Morrison's grave has become a temple of necrophilic adoration. Every year it is visited by thousands of pensionable hippies who still remember, during those episodic intervals between hallucinogenic flashbacks, the Doors front man with some fondness, as well as poets, young girls and women in love with the iconic image of the lizard king. Despite the obvious hygiene issues, there are still many who continue to plaster the monument with garish red lipstick kisses.

My favourite areas of Père Lachaise? Undoubtedly the section devoted to those who perished as a result of Nazi brutality during the Second World War, including the hundreds of French resistance fighters attempting to regain a sense of national pride for their country, so quickly relinquished by the Vichy government in 1941. That and one of the oldest parts of the cemetery, the Jewish section, although for different and much more selfish reasons.

★ ★ ★

"I hope you are not going to be taking photographs all day, Richard," Ligeia pouted petulantly.

She seldom used my name so I could tell her patience was wearing thin. It was understandable; we had been there for almost three hours, wandering up and down, stopping far too frequently as I snapped various sculptures and monuments. I later learned I had taken 1206 shots.

Ligeia had been incredibly tolerant and I was aware her mood was in danger of rapidly changing. Her body language – feet turned away from me, arms defiantly crossed against her chest – only served to reinforce my belief that the selfish pursuit of the perfect image was becoming tedious for her. Honestly, I could have continued indefinitely. I loved the place, even though the light was failing; I felt it added to the atmosphere. I took one final picture and clapped my hands with as much enthusiasm as I could muster.

"Right! Finished! Where do you want to go now?"

"Go?" She raised a quizzical eyebrow. "I don't want to go anywhere. I want to stay here with you. But just you… not your camera. I feel like we are missing out on something marvellous here… something romantic. Don't you feel the history here, beneath our feet? Don't you want to be part of that, to share yourself body and soul with the spirit of the place?"

I was pleased she didn't want to leave, although I understood perfectly that I would have to put the lens cap back on for the duration of our stay, however long that happened to be. Had I captured it all? Was I pleased with my Père Lachaise chronicle? I made a promise to review them later, when we were back at the hotel, and turned all of my attention towards my companion.

She slipped her hand into mine and together, with our fingers interlaced, we proceeded at a more leisurely pace. At the end of a particularly oppressive row of charnel houses she stopped walking and I noticed that her cheeks were streaked with tears. I feared the worst: that my preoccupation with my camera had upset her more than I'd realised. I apologised.

"What for?" she asked, turning to me so that I could see for the first time the extent of her distress. She laughed/cried when I admitted that I had not considered how boring it probably was for her trailing after a pictorial perfectionist.

"I'm not crying because of that. I love your work, honestly, and I want you to take the best pictures you can. Please don't think that I'm *that* precious. It's not that at all. It's..."

A ginger and white cat suddenly bolted across the path in front of us; we were both startled. It disappeared effortlessly, without pause, into the narrow entrance to a drainage culvert at the kerbside, something it had no doubt learned to do many times before. It was almost a blur, like a ghost. There one minute and then gone, just as quickly.

"That's exactly what I have been thinking about," she explained. "All these people. All those lives, extinguished forever. Just like..."

I tried to console her but she shook me off, half-laughing in embarrassment.

"I'll be okay in a minute. Just give me moment."

★ ★ ★

A little while later, we made our way to the first junction and then turned left before deciding to cut out the road altogether; instead, we headed through the rows of monuments that spread out and up towards the containment wall. This was the Jewish section. There was evidence of the faith of the deceased everywhere: the familial crypts, often oversized and frequently overbearing, contained various designs of stained-glass panels and almost always depicted the Star of David. We walked deeper into the maze of gravestones and plots.

If we had needed to be secluded, this section was perfect. Hardly anyone, it seemed, was keen to visit the graves of the Jews, apart from other Jews I suppose and perhaps the occasional fellow taphophile armed with a camera and/or a tape recorder. I thought the location, which was showing obvious signs of neglect and disrepair, would ensure that we had virtually no disturbance or interruption. Sadly, I was wrong about that.

We sat for a while on a long bench, the cast-iron ends of which were adorned with a municipal symbol of some description. Much of it was indistinguishable because of the layers and layers of cracked and peeling green paint that covered it. We drank in our surroundings and slowly, with an infinite degree of measured tenderness, began kissing. Her face was dappled by the sunlight peeking through the emergent leaves on the sprouting spring trees around us, inspiring me to kiss her more ardently. I was rewarded by her positive response.

As we became more passionate, our bodies demanded greater sacrifice, more exposure and increased, heightened sensation. I felt her hand on my groin and I parted my legs slightly so that she could cup my balls. My cock swelled at her touch and I squeezed her breast through the thin material of her blouse. I was desperate to feel myself inside her, to hear and feel her whimpering breath in my ear as I pushed into her eager warmth. Her tongue pushed its way into my mouth, where I received it with my own, the tips touching, running over the other, our breathing becoming faster.

We might have had sex right there except that a sudden and unusually loud noise nearby alerted us to the possibility that we might no longer be alone. Frustrated, we instantly separated, adjusted our clothing and allowed our breathing to return to normal. We could see no one, at first. All we saw was last autumn's curled, brown leaves being blown along on the pathway by the gentle breeze. However, there was a slight odour of tobacco borne on the same breeze as it moved past us. Immediately I was on guard.

"Bonjour, messieurs-dames. It is a lovely day. The promise of spring is so rewarding, is it not?"

The greeting made us both jump, as it came from the direction opposite to the one I would have expected.

The man was standing a few metres away upwind. Disturbingly, this made me consider the possibility that he was not on his own. I had definitely smelled tobacco before he'd appeared. Quickly I glanced around, but saw no one else.

He was, I guessed, based on his thick Gallic accent, French. He wore his grey hair far too long for someone in his fifties. He was paunchy and not too tall. The dirty, ill-fitting belted mackintosh that he wore had been taupe at some point in the past and was obviously two sizes too big for him. His brown brogues were scuffed. Most alarmingly, his fingers were stained with nicotine and he had filthy nails. I saw no rings on his fingers, or indeed any other jewellery.

His eyes were constantly on Ligeia. I decided to engage him, if only to break his offensively conspicuous staring. I attempted to summon forth everything I could recall about conversing in French, and even applied my best French accent.

"Oui, c'est peut-être un avant-goût de l'été á venir?"

He looked puzzled, confusion written clearly on his face.

"Oh! Excusez-moi, je pensais que vous étiez Anglais. Je me trompe, peut-être?" he replied quickly, his eyes never straying far from Ligeia's cleavage, as though he was talking to it rather than me.

Where he had appeared from I had no idea but I sincerely hoped he'd fuck off back there fairly quickly. I decided to intervene and stepped directly into his line of vision.

"No, you were not mistaken; we are English."

He stared at me momentarily, as though I had miraculously materialised before his very eyes. I am almost certain he had not registered my presence before and now stared at me with annoyance as I deliberately blocked his view of Ligeia's breasts.

"My apologies," he said in stilted English. "I am sorry for disturbing you and your daughter, but it is such a pleasant day. Perhaps too pleasant a day to be sitting here in such a depressing place?"

Daughter? Daughter!

I was about to protest when Ligeia corrected his assumption for me.

"He's not my father; he's my lover."

The Frenchman sighed and exhaled slowly, his eyes wide, and gradually began smiling in apparent sardonic approval. Given that he came from a nation that allegedly understood all about mistresses and the need for discretion in certain specific situations, I was relieved that he said nothing further on the matter. However, he did apologise and, nodding politely to both Ligeia and me, walked off back the way I presumed he had come. I stared after him, willing him to wander off the path and into a freshly dug, open grave.

"What a cheeky bastard!"

Ligeia laughed at my wounded pride.

"It was an easy mistake to make," she teased. "Young, attractive, pale, voluptuous young woman in the company of a grumpy, grizzled old fuck who is more interested in taking photographs than seeing to the needs of his highly aroused girlfriend. No wonder he thought you were my father."

I shook my head, incredulously. "How old do I look?"

She slipped her arm through mine and kissed the side of my face. "I've told you before, you don't look old at all. Not to me. But sometimes you *act* old."

It was just as well she got up off the bench and skipped out of range. I had aimed a playful slap at her arse but missed completely. Had it connected, it would have taught her a valuable lesson about the perils of tormenting her elders. She poked her tongue out at me, but she was beyond physical reach and so I captured her rudeness on camera.

It remains one of my favourite photos of our trip to Paris, and of her. She was both coquettish and beautiful, and she was mine. I decided we would stay in the cemetery until dark, when I would demonstrate just how besotted with her I was.

★ ★ ★

We found the perfect place to fuck while we waited for darkness to fall. It was a secluded area, possibly only accessible by a dilapidated set of steps that led down from the Jewish section. In the gathering gloom, our lust built until it became an inferno, fuelled by our surroundings and our increasing desire for each other. We waited until dusk had given way to early evening and, in the shadow of the old Semitic tombs that towered above us, began again where we had previously left off.

This time neither of us held back. Hidden from view in the darkened graveyard, empty save for us, we quickly lost our clothing in a hurried fumbling and desperate abandonment. It was chilly but not so cold that it interrupted our intentions. We embraced momentarily, but then I led her to a low-lying, flat-topped tomb. We were both eager to consummate our love in Paris and I entered her with ease, my first thrust punctuated by a sigh of absolute pleasure.

Spurred on by the frisson created by the *en plein air* experience, I pushed myself into her faster, more relentlessly. Her breathing became quicker and shallower, and I felt that I was but a moment away from climax. We moved together in unison but against each other's motion in order to maximise our respective pleasure. In the last seconds before I came, I felt her tense up beneath me and fall silent, but it was not because of her own impending orgasm.

I emptied myself rapturously into her warmth with a satisfied groan of pleasure and felt her nails dig into my shoulder.

"Someone's watching us... they must have seen everything," she whispered into my ear.

It is amazing how quickly one can recover when needs must. I pulled out of her, unceremoniously dribbling semen over the monument slab, and hastily located my trousers.

"Where?" I asked, frantically looking around for the police municipalé that I expected to come running towards us at any moment.

Ligeia lay exactly where I had fucked her, her legs

open, her sex on display to whoever was watching. Thankfully, she did not point.

"There… about two hundred metres away, at the top where we came down. He's just standing there watching us."

"He?"

She nodded. "I think so. In fact, I'm pretty sure."

"He couldn't have seen us surely; we are too far away."

"I don't know, but he must have heard us," she giggled.

I tried to see through the gathering murk. To be fair, I did see something, maybe someone standing very still in what looked like a pale knee-length coat. I wondered if it was the man who had spoken to Ligeia's breasts earlier on.

"What the fuck is he doing there?" I whispered, half-crouching.

Ligeia was not as coy and seemed to revel in the idea that we had been observed and that she was still the object of his attention, spreading her legs as wide as she could and fingering herself with a steady circular motion. She kept her sights set firmly on where the man (if indeed it was a man) stood.

"That's what I want," she moaned. "More of this!"

I looked back at her from my hiding place, bewildered.

More of what? Peeping Toms? Open-air masturbation?

"What are you doing?" I hissed frantically. "For fuck's sake! It could be anyone… a murderer, a pervert or even worse! It could be the police!"

That just seemed to spur her on.

I kept an eye on the form at the top of the steps and although my concentration was broken from time to time by Ligeia's moans, I was entirely certain that our voyeur *was* a man who was standing stock still with his hands braced against the rail. He appeared to be staring directly at us, or rather at Ligeia, who was in the throes of ecstasy and close to climax.

When she came she whimpered uncharacteristically, her body buckling under the intensity of her sexual spasm. I turned to look at her, at her pale, slim naked body, at her 'little death' as she slipped back against the cold stone, her breath a vapour cloud in the night air. When I turned back, the figure was gone.

★ ★ ★

We did not speak much as we made our way back to the hotel via the metro. It was one of those awkward silences, where we both knew we should have made the effort to begin some kind of conversation but in the end settled for staring blankly out of the train window at the darkness beyond. I caught sight of my reflection once or twice and had to remind myself to unknot my brow, which appeared to be set into a permanent frown. It was obvious to anyone who cared to take notice that our earlier carefree mood had changed dramatically.

I tentatively broached the subject over dinner. I made it very clear that Ligeia's frivolously oblivious behaviour earlier had been dangerous and could have landed us in serious trouble.

"Live a little," she said, with a wan, unconvincing smile.

I was not in the mood for her flippancy. I was deadly serious. She slammed her cutlery down noisily against the side of her plate, causing others nearby to look up and over at us.

"Oh God, lighten up, will you? Nothing happened. We weren't arrested. Everything is fine. I don't see the problem."

"But it *could* have. We could have been arrested, or worse. Anything could have happened. I think you… we are taking far too many risks."

Ligeia swallowed whatever it was she was chewing, suddenly serious. There was an intensity in her gaze that I had not seen before.

"Too many risks for what? For you? Does what we do… what I do… make you uncomfortable, Richard?"

I shook my head, ashamed that she would even think that. That wasn't what I'd meant at all.

"You know I enjoy sex," she stated matter-of-factly. "I know you enjoy having sex with me. You enjoyed it this afternoon, didn't you, despite all the possible risks? Nothing happened, did it? I don't know why you have to keep going on about it. Nothing happened, so let's leave it at that. Okay?"

I decided not to pursue the matter, even though I didn't entirely agree with her. I had enjoyed myself with her in the cemetery earlier, up to a degree.

She did have a point. Nothing untoward *did* happen, making whatever other misgivings I had about her 'reckless' behaviour seem superfluous. I could not deny, however, that her increasing appetite for taking risks *was* beginning to concern me, particularly when it involved me.

We continued with our meal. As I watched her, I wondered briefly if she was suffering from Artaud syndrome, then realised that such a proposition was preposterous because I had, in the same moment, completely made it up. If such a condition could exist, though, the similarities between Antonin Artaud's philosophy and certain facets of Ligeia's behaviour were remarkable.

Like Artaud, Ligeia despised God and religion, vehemently blaming both for the continuing degradation of civilisation and for representing the loss of truth in reality. She insisted religion incited delusional faith by promoting what were essentially human constructs of paradise or heaven; they were certainly not celestial.

Ligeia also constantly challenged the validity of her own belief system by stepping outside of whatever her adopted reality was at any particular moment in time. Her morality was definitely her own and was not dependant upon conventions or societal norms. She believed that her existence was based entirely on her own interpretation of her surroundings. She considered that most of the world's inhabitants were aware of the nature of reality only when she interacted with them on an instinctive level and shattered their complacent view of reality. I also wondered if, as well as being the object of focus, she was also, on some level, her own audience, much like a piece of Artaudian drama.

Chapter 22

Our second day in Paris began at 7am (8am GMT) with Ligeia waking me with an invigorating blowjob that took me almost to the point of orgasm before I turned her around and fucked her from behind, emptying myself gratefully and noisily inside her. I fucked her again in the bathroom. Then we showered and got ready for whatever else the day had to offer and descended the three floors to the opulently decorated restaurant for breakfast.

Paris may be considered a premier location for gastronomique excellence but the city restaurants know how to charge. Breakfast, lunch and dinner are all expensive, often overpriced and, sadly, not all that is on offer is first rate. This was why we both ate a very hearty *petit dejeuner* (part of the hotel deal) to sustain us for the best part of the day. We had a busy schedule planned, which would culminate in a proposed visit to the Montparnasse Cemetery in order for us to pay our respects to Charles Baudelaire.

The restaurant staff were polite but not French. They were Polish or Latvian, possibly even Russian; their command of French was concise, natural and impressive, as was the smattering of English they had picked up from tourists like Ligeia and me during their employment at the hotel. They were discreetly attentive, always ready to refill our coffee cups or bring fresh toast when requested. The waiters smiled obligingly at Ligeia and the waitresses smiled at me. We were both very pleased with the service.

After breakfast we made our way to the Opéra metro

station, a ten-minute walk away, and joined the hordes of early-morning tourists, and Parisians on their way to work, on line 8. At Concorde we changed to line 1 and finally alighted at Tuileries. We enjoyed a short, dusty walk across the garden and towards the river in the hazy, early morning sunlight. We crossed the Seine at the Pont Royal to Quai Anatole France and the Musée d'Orsay.

Naturally for such an important museum of art and sculpture there was already a long queue forming outside. We dutifully joined and spent a very pleasant thirty minutes or so embracing and kissing, much to the discomfort of those around us.

It became apparent that there was a possibility that the difference in our ages was causing some consternation. To be honest, though, our relationship had nothing to do with any of them so we ignored them and their sideways glances and disapproving comments and continued in our deliberately demonstrative osculation.

Once inside the museum we became lost in the art contained within its high vaulted rooms. Sculpture vied for supremacy over impressionist masterpieces, and we experienced a visual overload that at times became disorientating. In fact, there were times when it seemed the audacious exhibition of art might overwhelm us. At length, however, we found ourselves in front of the principal reason for our visit: Courbet's *L'Origine du Monde*.

It was inspiring.

★ ★ ★

Paris Journal – Day Two: Musée d'Orsay

The painting is much larger than one might imagine. I was very surprised by the size and also by the number of visitors who were obviously drawn to the earthy image. We were flanked by various people: hirsute intellectuals nodding sagely to one another as they discussed the artistic merit of what has become known in some circles as 'Courbet's cunt'; emotionally retarded male students idiotically nudging each other as they gazed upon something that had so far eluded them in real life; lovers (or at the very least couples who had been, or still were, intimately connected); and a group of rather plain-looking women, devoid of makeup or ornament, regarding the image in awe and discussing how redundant the penis was in comparison, using overtly indignant language.

We were uncertain how long was normal to stand before the painting, studying it, and took our cue from others around us. Ligeia, however, wanted to stay a whole lot longer to continue contemplating the canvas, so we found a discreet seat nearby, which afforded us a good vantage point without it being too obvious that the painting was our sole focus in the room.

* * *

She sat there for a long time. I began to think that she would never grow bored of gazing at *L'Origine.* I did not feel the same way about it. With such an enormous museum to explore and with masterpieces from every conceivable art movement virtually dripping from every wall I was keen to continue our visit. There was a momentary indication of hesitancy before she acquiesced and finally we moved on. Over the next forty minutes it became apparent Ligeia was becoming gradually more withdrawn, and then she fell frustratingly silent.

At a loss to know why, I attempted to engage her in conversation, but she was uncommunicative. Her mood had certainly changed. We paused by the magnificent Auguste Clésinger's orgasmic *Woman Bitten by a Snake* sculpture at the entrance to the main hall. I tried to hold my tongue, surrounded as we were by a multitude of cultural tourists, although I reasoned that most would not have understood any exchange I had with Ligeia anyway.

"What's wrong?"

She sulkily regarded the prostrate, naked white marble figure next to where we stood and shook her head silently. I was having none of it. I felt her unexpected, bizarre behaviour was in serious danger of ruining what had, for me, begun as a perfect day. I was insistent but my enquiry was met with stoic resistance.

"I want to go back to the hotel."

"Seriously?"

"Yes, seriously. I want to go now. Is that okay?"

Of course it wasn't. I wanted to say that. I wanted to tell her that her behaviour was irrational, but the truth was I was actually afraid; I was afraid she might take offence on what was only our second day in the capital and that it would turn the remaining days into a nightmare. I could not figure out what had occurred.

"What about Montparnasse? We were supposed to be visiting Baudelaire's grave this afternoon."

She simply shrugged.

"Maybe later," she said, and added softly, "I just need to go back to the hotel for a while."

Ligeia left me trailing in her wake. By the time I caught up with her she was outside the museum. Above us the sky had turned ominously black. There was a storm approaching.

★ ★ ★

<u>*Paris Journal – Day Two*</u>

The joy of being in a beautiful, unfamiliar city with an equally beautiful companion lies in the pleasure of exploring together, walking down busy streets and wide boulevards, strolling through parks, being awed by the architecture, taking in the sights and sounds, listening to the thrum of the city and being overwhelmed by the inescapable sensation of being totally...

Totally what?

The words I sought fell away from me, escaped my usually more than dexterous mind, leaving me struggling to complete the journal entry. I sat alone at the desk by the window, desperately trying to make sense of what had happened. How could we have gone from a state of euphoria to one of misery and darkness so quickly?

★ ★ ★

I decided not to continue with the journal. I couldn't think of anything worthwhile to write, apart from the fact that I was concerned the trip was turning into something less pleasurable than I had originally imagined.

Ligeia lay in bed, asleep. I hated being so far away from her.

Outside, the rain drummed against the glass, streaking it with elongated rivulets. The sky was still dark. I knew there would be no trip to Montparnasse that day.

I began to wonder if the trip was a mistake.

That evening I decided to force the issue of Ligeia's dangerously black mood at the Musée d'Orsay, if only to understand if we shared the same overwhelming impression that our relationship was spiralling into an irreversible decline.

The change in her had been so sudden and so unfamiliar that it had worried me greatly. Formulating reasons of my own for her behaviour was dangerous. My imagination was far too fertile to invent a rational explanation, so I needed to know, categorically, that *we* were okay, that I hadn't inadvertently screwed things up.

We sat sipping wine at an open-fronted café just off

the Rue Saint Honoré at the rear of the Louvre. The night was clear but still cold, so we were grateful for the long-stemmed gas-fired heater above our table, despite the noise emanating from it. Ligeia attempted to be cheerful, although the general tone was sombre and it wasn't long before she spoke.

"What's wrong?"

I was measured in my response. I was careful not to risk antagonising things further, whether my fears were imagined or not. She stared at me over the rim of her glass, waiting patiently for me to reply. I could see nothing of the darkness that had filled her eyes before, but I still ventured with a degree of trepidation.

It was strange. In the few short months since I had known Ligeia, so many parts of my life had been transformed or were in a state of metamorphosis. I had replaced an easy, long-established relationship, which had become *so* familiar that I'd become complacent to the point where even the simplest interactions felt forced or stilted, with one that was so unfamiliar yet served to excite and enrich me with each day that passed; I had used this rationale to vindicate my decision to embark on my adulterous liaison.

The simple truth was that Ligeia made me feel alive in a manner that I had not experienced for a very long time. Now, more than anything else, I was afraid of that feeling coming to an end or, what would be worse, fading away gradually bit by bit until nothing of what we were existed any more. I knew that would be an unbearable proposition. After so much light and happiness, would I be able to return to the safe mundanity of my previous *married* state? I already knew the answer to that.

I reached out for her and took hold of her hand, savouring the cool, delicate touch of her long, slender fingers. Fear threatened to consume me if I did not attempt to satisfy my curiosity. I drained my glass and asked if she was happy, cursing myself immediately afterwards for my inability to be more direct. She smiled disarmingly, although I was aware that her smile would not be sufficient for me that night.

"Rapturously so," she murmured. "Are you?"

"Yes. I'm happy." I realised I was in danger of settling into my usual mode of prevarication. "I just want *you* to be. Totally, you know?"

"That's okay then." She squeezed my thumb. "I don't think I have enjoyed any city as much, ever."

A waiter in traditional attire appeared and inquired if we wanted any more drinks. I sent him away to find a bottle of the wine we'd just sampled. Dutch courage? Almost definitely. I felt my heart beat a little faster in anticipation.

"Can I ask you something?"

She nodded.

"This morning, at the d'Orsay... what happened between us?"

"Us?" She appeared genuinely confused. "Nothing. What makes you say that?"

I attempted to drain my glass, which was already empty, and silently cursed the waiter for his tardiness. "It's just that you seemed a little distant... self-absorbed."

The wine arrived, thankfully, and I disregarded the waiter's diligent attempt to force me to test the vintage, much to his disdain. I refilled our glasses, more concerned with the importance of our continued conversation.

She pursed her lips. "Sometimes things become too much for me. It's a stupid fact of life and I have learned, over the years, to live with it. It happens from time to time, thankfully not often, though it seems to be the most ridiculous things that affect me the most."

"Like this morning?"

"Yes, I think I had a sort of sensory overload. By the time we reached the Courbet my brain was so fried I let my melancholy get the better of me. You don't have any children do you?"

Children?

I wondered where her question was going and so I humoured her.

"No. It's something I aspired to at one time, when I was younger and less selfish." I tried not to sound too wistful. "It never happened, though."

"It won't ever happen to me either. I'm no longer able to conceive."

I apologised but she brushed it aside.

"No, it was my choice. I decided that I didn't want to have children after university. I underwent a full tubal ligation when I was twenty-four. I would have preferred a full or partial elective hysterectomy, but the doctor wouldn't even consider it at my age. There has to be a very good reason these days for that kind of surgery, besides which the side effects in the worst-case scenario would have been pretty debilitating. I wasn't prepared to take the risk."

"I see, so this morning you were wondering if you had perhaps made the right decision?"

She sipped her wine and shook her head slowly.

"No, it wasn't that. I know I made the right decision and Courbet's painting reaffirmed it. It made me realise that society is fundamentally and irreparably narcissistic and that prompted me to consider why we consistently put our own needs above those of the lives we strive to create."

"You mean…"

"Children."

I may have laughed, or half-laughed, I'm not certain, but I had misjudged her temperament; she was deadly serious. When she spoke again there was more than a hint of annoyance in her eyes.

"It's not funny, Richard! It's not a comedy; it's a fucking tragedy. It's one that's been played out so many times that now it has lost its meaning. So, instead, we continue to deceive ourselves, pretending that the product of those moments of joyous intimacy is a physical manifestation of our love. In actuality, children are nothing more than the result of a profound failure to control our instincts, which, incidentally, we inappropriately label desires and then allow to gestate like some hellish parasite and misguidedly regard, thereafter, as a symbol of that union."

I was keen to get off subject as quickly as possible, before the conversation descended into something altogether more destructive. I topped up both of our glasses to the brim.

"They are our anchor to reality but we choose to ignore that. Children are the personification of the fear of our own inevitable mortality. If you think about it for a moment... we are all born, ultimately to die. All of us. It's insane... an absolute waste of time and effort on everyone's part.

"Some kids, the lucky ones, are borne out of the delusion that they somehow symbolise the bond of love between their parents, which in itself is patently ludicrous. How can we, as supposedly caring, sentient animals create someone whose life journey is unknown and subject to the fickleness of fate? How can we expose someone we profess to love to the only profound certainty, which is that they will ultimately die?

"Is that the behaviour of someone who loves? Should we create a new life, a new human being, knowing that *that* new life will be born only to experience the misery of death? If we are truly capable of love, surely we would want to spare those we love that stark reality. And we would want to safeguard *ourselves* from the effects that the death of someone we created and claimed to love would have on us. Wouldn't we?"

She was waiting for me to answer. It was obvious to me, however, that whatever I said would not alter her opinion or perceptions regarding children one iota, so I remained silent and drank.

"That was why I decided against ever having children. Whichever way it's dressed up, the truth is that the creation of new life is unfair, selfish and cruel. It serves no one, not even the parents. Our whole human condition is based on futility and that's why I want no part of it."

It seemed we were in the right city for philosophy, although I would have preferred Ligeia to have saved it for another time and place. Her dark one-sided views had the potential to ruin what had been, until our morning in the museum, a perfectly lovely short break. I was beginning to regret ordering a whole bottle of wine because her mood was definitely veering towards the maudlin. I needn't have been too concerned, though.

"Did Courbet's painting affect you so profoundly?" I asked. She nodded, a smile returning to her lips.

"A lot of art has that effect on me. Paintings, sculpture, poetry, literature, theatre, dance… I can find beauty in almost everything and that in turn fills me with a sense of the sublime. This morning, however, was too much. My head was filled with so much beauty from all the pieces we looked at that when we reached *L'Origine du Monde* and I contemplated the quality and excellence of that simple, elegant painting it touched me in a way I have seldom experienced before. Didn't you feel anything?"

"I got a touch on," I joked, attempting to lift the tone a little. "Seriously, though, it was very humbling standing in front of such a controversial picture. It did make me ask questions but not to the same extent as you."

"Such as?"

"Whether it was always intended to be a provocative image as it exists or whether it was, as has been suggested by some historians, an intimate portrait commissioned by Pasha Halil Bey that was subsequently cropped at either Courbet's or Halil's request. If the latter is true, just imagine what might happen if the rest of the image still existed. I have read that a portion of a painting, purporting to be the missing part, has been found, though opinion on its authenticity is divided. Do you think they should try to reunite them if it turned out to be genuine?"

She pulled a sour face. "It would be a mistake. The painting works because of what it depicts. It deserves to remain confrontational and enigmatic. It forces the viewer to examine their own perceptions about life and the portrayal of the naked human form, especially the female body. If we are allowed to finally identify with the model, concentrating on her expression or the radiance of her face, it will reduce the potency of the image and make the title next to meaningless."

I raised my glass to her and she reciprocated. I felt she had made a very valid point.

We discussed the speculation surrounding the sitter, allegedly Joanna Hiffernan, an Irish model and the lover of American artist James McNeill Whistler, who *had been* a friend of Courbet until – mysteriously, and giving credence to the story – immediately after the unveiling of Courbet's painting, when their relationship changed and eventually broke down irreparably. Ligeia became effervescent again, laughing and joking about the courtesan culture of late-nineteenth-century Paris, and the power of the muse and the hypnotic grip these muses had of various artists over the centuries.

Thankfully, the subject of children did not resurface.

Returning much to how we had been before the episode at the d'Orsay, we drank up and left the café. We dawdled hand-in-hand through the streets and along the boulevards, discussing the influence of Baudelaire on Courbet's work, oblivious to everyone and everything around us, and slowly made our way back to the hotel. We decided to retire early – it was only 9.30pm (8:30pm GMT) – but not to sleep.

We indulged in one of Ligeia's more mainstream fetishes. She had come prepared. I tied her to the bed using the lengths of smooth, cream-coloured satin-twist cord she'd secreted in the larger of her two cases. The design of the bed was such that it provided perfect anchor points at the wrists and ankles. By the time she was securely fastened, spread-eagled beneath me, I had a raging erection. She watched me strip naked and then I consigned her to darkness with a blindfold fashioned out of the belt of her dressing gown.

I didn't fuck her immediately, although I wanted to. I used my tongue to lubricate her, but I disallowed her the pleasure of a preliminary orgasm. Instead, I opened the mini-bar and chose a 50cl bottle of champagne, which I stripped of its foil and uncorked. I trickled some of the bubbly liquid over her body, for me to lap up. I drank the rest of it but not before exchanging a mouthful of the sparkling wine with her in a kiss. Then I inserted the neck of the bottle into her vagina.

The bottle still felt cold in my hand and I presumed

the sensation as I fucked her with it was heightened by the coolness of the glass. I began gently, despite her demands for more brutal penetration, and enjoyed watching the neck being swallowed by the space between her deliciously pink, wet lips. After several moments I stopped and teased her clitoris with the tip of my tongue until she was on the brink of ecstasy, but I again denied her sexual conclusion. I reinserted the bottle, this time into her rectum.

I was overcome by lust. Although she pleaded for me to slide my cock into her, I refused for as long as I was able; in truth, that wasn't long. Abandoning my hollow, makeshift dildo, I climbed on top of her, luxuriating in the sensation of her soft, cool, satin-smooth flesh pressed against my own and, with a single motion, entered her. Her vagina swallowed my entire length, every inch I had, too easily.

Part of me was, I knew, annoyed at the way she had behaved at the Musée d'Orsay, and I did still feel aggrieved. Part of me wanted to remind her that I had experienced a terrible sense of isolation as she slept off the despondency that *L'Origine* had caused. I wanted to punish her, but it was impossible using just my cock. As she urged me to fuck her harder, I slapped her once, sharply, across the face; her initial look of shock at my action was quickly replaced by one of lascivious need.

"Do it again!" she moaned. "Harder!"

At any other time I would have baulked at the suggestion, but now my blood was up and my ireful sensibility was far from satisfied. I did as I was instructed, striking her more brutally and enjoying her whimper of pain.

"Once more," she begged me.

As my hand connected with her face she

spontaneously orgasmed, crying out in either pain or ecstasy, or perhaps a combination of both. I pushed myself into her with renewed vigour and came after just a few frenzied strokes. I lay on top of her until the dreamlike state of euphoria had ebbed away and then untied her. Amazingly, she drifted off into a deep sleep almost immediately, a contented smile still on her lips.

I, on the other hand, did not succumb to slumber so easily and spent an hour or more going over the events of the day and what Ligeia had said about children. They were extreme views by society's standards but I think I fully understood and appreciated them. I briefly thought about writing, about resurrecting the journal I had aborted earlier that day, until sleep claimed me.

The journal was never added to during our time together in Paris and remains unfinished to this day.

Chapter 23

During breakfast on our third day, Ligeia presented me with a small packet about the size of a pack of playing cards; it was beautifully wrapped in pearlescent paper and finished off with a thin blood-red bow. She appeared very pleased with herself and simultaneously excited as she encouraged me to open it. I teased her by only half-unwrapping it and then putting it down to drink my coffee. It was obvious my action frustrated her so, out of pure devilment, I continued it for as long as I could

"Just open it!" she hissed as good-naturedly as she was able.

It *was* a pack of playing cards.

"Aren't they great? I saw them yesterday and I thought of you!"

It explained why she had been so secretive about her visit to the tabac the previous day. I turned the pale-green carton over in my hands. On one side was an illustration of a dark-haired naked woman toying with a string of beads at her throat. On the other side was a line drawing of a woman being ravished by a horned satyr, beneath which was the legend BAUDELAIRE. There was an inscription along one edge: 54 cartes raffinées consacrées au poème Les Fleurs du Mal.

"I had to borrow some paper from reception but they were okay about it. They even found the ribbon for me to tie it up with! The concierge was *so* helpful."

"Is it alright if I open them?" I asked, a little taken aback by the gift.

"Of course! That's what they're for. I thought we could take them with us today to the cemetery and, who knows, maybe they will inspire you."

It was a standard deck, but with no jokers. However, there were two extra cards that contained some details of Baudelaire's life and works in English, French, Spanish and Italian. I thought it ironic that the whole essence of such a luminary could be condensed to fill just one side of a standard-sized playing card and I wondered sullenly how much of the space the particulars of my life would fill when I died. Resisting the urge to dwell on such a depressing thought, I riffled through the cards, each of which was illustrated with images of a 'refined' sexual nature, although all featured nudity, homoerotic imagery or various other forms of copulation. In actuality, they were not bad and I smiled.

"They are fabulous!" I stretched across the table and kissed her as tenderly as I could manage on the lips. "Thank you. I will take them with me today, although" – I picked out a random card, the six of spades, showing a naked couple making love beneath a leafy arbour, and placed it in her hand – "it might not inspire me to do much work."

"Win-win for us both, then," she smiled.

My mobile buzzed annoyingly in my trouser pocket. It was a text from Janice.

    I have tried to phone! Where are you??? J x

It was unusual for Janice to call or text me at all; I chose to ignore it and replaced the phone in my pocket.

* * *

Janice sent three more texts as we travelled across the city.

The first was virtually a repeat of the first one, but the one that followed was more insistent.

> I can't reach you. Can you call me pls. J x

I felt something was wrong, but I decided not to react. It was probably nothing serious; at least I attempted to convince myself of that. Obviously, Janice did not share my view of the situation because five minutes later a further text arrived. That one caused me more concern, or rather it required some kind of response.

> You're worrying me now. Is everything OK?
> Call me. J x

As soon as I could find a safe oasis, away from the stream of people who rushed around us, I stopped and gripped Ligeia by the wrist, pulling her to one side. She stared at me with a look of bewilderment on her face, head cocked slightly to one side. The noise around us was deafening.

"Listen, I'm sorry about this but I've got to call…" – I paused and chose my next words with care – "I have to make a call. It won't take a minute. Okay?"

She nodded. "Why don't you just text her?"

It was of course the most obvious thing to do. I wondered why I hadn't thought of it myself. By texting rather than actually speaking to her, I could respond and alleviate Janice's worrying, without becoming emotionally entangled or being forced to lie about my whereabouts, which I knew with a degree of certainty I would not be able to pull off convincingly. Besides, I hardly ever called her so it would have been completely out of character for me, and the last thing I wanted to do was alert her to the fact that something wasn't quite right.

Ligeia held up both hands, palms out in a submissively

defensive gesture.

"Just a suggestion. You know your wife best. You decide."

It took less than a second for me to make the decision. My message was brief and to the point.

```
Everything fine. I'm OK. Busy. Busy. Busy.
Will call later.
See you soon. R x
```

With one press of a button the message was launched from my mobile phone in one country, travelled 675 kilometres and arrived at the mobile phone held by my wife in another country. It was a miracle of modern communication. Selfishly, I hoped it stopped her texting me.

* * *

Montparnasse Cemetery is big. While it is not as big as Père Lachaise, there is a sense of grandeur there that other cemeteries in Paris no longer possess. Montmartre is tired; even the once brightly gilded tomb sculpture of Dalida has lost its brilliance and some of the older cast-iron family vaults have fallen badly into disrepair or are in the process of rusting away. Père Lachaise is spectacular, rising and falling as it does on several levels, but it is now so old and so overcrowded that there seems to be little space left to fit anyone new.

There is a more landscaped feel to Montparnasse, with its wide central avenues and confusing, signposted, offshoots. This green, tree-filled sepulchral haven is nestled in the shadow of the Montparnasse tower and other outlying tall buildings. It is a place to wander around in a leisurely fashion; while we were there we saw plenty of people just sitting on the benches that are liberally scattered around its nineteen hectares, enjoying the fresh air. Close by is one of Paris's darker and more infamous tourist destinations: the catacombs at Place d'Enfer (Hell Square). This square is now less frighteningly named Place Denfert-Rochereau.

We found the main entrance easily and passed through the gateway, the posts of which are topped with sculpted *tempus fugit* winged hourglass motifs. Each armed with the ubiquitous bottle of water, we obtained a *Plan Du Cimetière* from the guard office to begin our exploration of the grounds. We had no plans, apart from wanting to visit the grave of Baudelaire, and so we ambled from tomb to tomb while I clicked away, filling yet another memory card with funereal images.

Ligeia navigated a casual route, and we came across the final resting places of many important names, from famous ones like Jean-Paul Sartre and Simone de Beauvoir to lesser-known but equally tragic ones like the beautiful Jean Seberg, whom I had seriously fancied when I was a teenager. The grave of Baudelaire eluded us for a while, however.

When we eventually located it, our joint disappointment was palpable. We had both expected something huge and grand, perhaps even decadent. Instead, we were greeted by a small, nondescript rectangular column tucked away from the main thoroughfare; the greatest of France's poets had been buried with his parents, as though he had died in childhood. To be fair, there were indicators that someone of note was commemorated there: floral tributes, metro tickets and sheets of A4 paper were scattered around. It was still hard to see from the path, though.

We lingered there while Ligeia read out one of her

Baudelaire-inspired poems. We were quite alone, although I am certain Ligeia would not have cared if we were not.

"This one is entitled Muse."

She folded the sheet of paper and placed it on the grave before reciting the poem from memory.

"All origin is subjective.
I reside in silent envy, in hue to match that morbid emotion
A sickly, sour distillation of phlegmatic vitriol,
Passed off as something more medicinal, something more than truth
A salve, a potion to ward off the vicious barbs of airborne cancers
Gestating, evolving, corrupting all, they infect
Their languid eyes, turned skyward from a viscous pool of oil black filth,
See nothing. Nothing.
There is only the sound,
The shriek of defiance, the screech of malevolence
The tinny whine of indolence and retribution
Hatred made manifest in hellish miniature, oblivious to elemental forces,
Immune to the elements.
How strange then that his, a sharp rebuke of God's creation,
Should make Gods of men and men into Gods with an essence
How should it be called, that tincture, that narcolepsy-inducing syrup?
It creates an impasse, it prevents and protects
Though within the same foul exhalation, destroys, utterly

Those from within to those without, staring in disgust
and horror at our failings
Forgive us! We are but mortals all!
Absolve us from such deeds imposed upon us by our
weakness!
When we roll and laugh drenched in our own sweat,
Saturated with the sweet salt sweat of others, casting
sublime thought into being
Sculpting flesh into the divine, the bizarre, the less
ordinary
From passionate embrace to creative rapture and
down,
Down, ever downwards to the depths of despair
Where only those depraved enough to skulk there
survive,
Shrivelled and twisted by obscene thought,
Or artistic majesty."

I truly wished there had been other people around to hear
how powerfully she delivered her heart up to that small,
unassuming grave. I like to think Baudelaire would have
approved.

It was shortly after that I lost her.

I'm not entirely sure how we became separated that
day. I remember going deeper into one section to check
out a tomb while Ligeia waited on the path. I couldn't
have been gone for more than four or five minutes but
when I had finished she was gone.

I didn't panic, although the memory of the weird
voyeur from Père Lachaise did flit through my mind like a
particularly disturbing dark shadow. There were a few
people around me and some in the distance, so the place
was far from deserted. Even so, I felt it important to locate
her sooner rather than later. The cemetery was large

enough to get lost in and we had made no contingency for such an eventuality. It transpired that wasn't necessary; a few moments later I spotted her.

Ligeia was up ahead, but she was no longer alone. Intrigued, but not unduly perturbed, I quickened my pace until she and the tall, slim man she was talking to were no more than a hundred metres away. He looked vaguely familiar, although I could not say where I might have seen him before. Perhaps it was his particularly generic clothing I identified rather than him. As I reached them they both turned and Ligeia, smiling, introduced her companion.

"Richard, this is Yves. He's been keeping me company while you were gone and telling me all about the cemetery. It's fascinating."

"Yes, it is," he began, extending his hand towards me. His hand was smooth and cool to the touch. "I was telling your charming companion that as well as the more obvious celebrities here in Montparnasse there are another two hundred or so artists, composers, philosophers and writers interred here. I am aware that you came specifically to visit Baudelaire's grave. It appears all three of us here share a passion for Baudelaire. But did you know that there is another monument to Baudelaire here that people often miss? His cenotaph is *superbe.*"

Yves was unmistakably French. He was dark-haired and slim but not as tall as I'd first imagined. I guessed he was about thirty years old. He was dressed in a grey frock coat over charcoal-coloured jeans and what appeared to be stack-heeled black cowboy boots. A thin chocolate-brown cigarillo dangled from his naturally pouting lips. He also sported a goatee and a superbly ostentatious waxed moustache. I would say he was handsome in a typically continental fashion, like one of those stereotypical French existentialists that are often depicted in symbolist film noir offerings of the fifties. The only thing he lacked was a hat.

Ligeia slid her arm through mine.

"Yves says he would be happy to show us."

I bet he would.

Please don't misunderstand me; he was a very presentable, personable, charming man and perhaps my suspicions about his motives were based more on my own insecurity than on anything else. I mean what possible motive *would* a good-looking guy have for taking time out of his day to escort a middle-aged foreigner and his gorgeously attractive younger companion around a graveyard? Was it out of some weird kinship forged by a shared love of transgressive poetry? Was it pure altruism, introduced to foster or further a feeling of entente cordiale between our two cultures?

Neither. I could tell from the way his eyes flashed whenever he glanced at Ligeia that his sole aim was to continue to be close to her for as long as he could manage. Was I wary of him? Yes, of course, but he wasn't much of a threat physically. Was I jealous of him? Not really, despite his suavity and natural good looks. Did I feel defensive? Absolutely. It was obvious that Yves, for all his supposed good intentions, was increasingly hopeful of some kind of flirtatious or sexual interplay between himself and Ligeia, regardless of my presence.

Perhaps I should have protested and driven the lustful young fucker away. I have often thought about that afternoon since, and I am convinced that it would have been the correct course of action. Had I followed my instincts, realised retrospectively or otherwise, and demonstrated my objection to his company, it might have created a chain reaction that would have resulted in the termination of my relationship with my Ligeia. Then none of what happened subsequently, including where I am today, would have taken place. As terrible as things became for us, I still prefer that to the notion of Ligeia walking away from me forever. It is for that reason, and that reason alone, that I did not object. I was too permissive. It was a terrible weakness in me, which fortunately she never exploited, even though she could have if she had wanted to.

"Sure, okay," I said and was rewarded with a polite, appreciative kiss on the cheek. Then, rather formally, we exchanged pleasantries and first names.

Introductions dispensed with, the three of us continued in the pale, diffused afternoon light, with me snapping away at sepulchral ornament and headstones while Ligeia, now arm-in-arm with the Frenchman, ambled along, listening intently as he gave a running commentary on each of the more interesting tombs as we passed them. On one of the wide tarmac avenues, it appeared we were being manoeuvred towards a tall monument set in a shallow grass verge. When we reached it, I discovered it was not a verge at all but a large circular traffic island, in the centre of which was a sculpture of a winged man set on a column; it was green with verdigris. The monument was surrounded by a series of well-maintained flowerbeds.

"You see here a monument by the sculptor Horace Daillion. It is called *Génie du Sommeil Éternel* or *Angel of Eternal Sleep*. Rather poignant, is it not? You see he is throwing flowers onto a grave and beneath him is the word souvenir, which means remember."

I took a few photographs. It was attractive but not as impressive as some of the other sculptures we'd seen, such as the colossal grieving man that marked one grave, the mournful harlequin that sits above Nijinsky's tomb or the magnificent deathbed memorial erected in memory of industrialist Charles Pigeon. I could see Ligeia was impressed, and not just with the angel.

"They say you can visit Montparnasse a hundred times and find something new to look at each time. Every year there are around a thousand burials here but, as you can see, it is already overcrowded." He frowned and paused to light another cigarillo.

"They say that although there are only thirty-five thousand tombs, there are over three hundred thousand people buried in Montparnasse. Père Lachaise is a slum by comparison and there are many local inhabitants who are concerned that this place, their tree-lined beautiful cemetery, will become the same, overrun by rats and predatory cats in a Satanic mouth full of jagged, rotten teeth."

She gripped his forearm.

"That is fantastic. I want to use that. Do you mind? I'm a poet."

Yves smiled and a snake of smoke escaped from his lips.

"Of course you are. Who else but a poet would be interested in Baudelaire? Yes, of course you may use my words. Once they are uttered, they no longer belong to me anyway."

Ligeia opened her shoulder bag and removed a small black Moleskine notebook and a pen. She hastily scribbled in the book then quickly glanced at me in a fashion that I had become more than familiar with. While her actions were not always obvious, the behaviour that preceded them often was. I could tell that she was fascinated by this Frenchman; by fascinated I also mean aroused, both physically and intellectually.

* * *

Charles Baudelaire was not the only celebrity in the cemetery to be feted by admirers, it seemed. Just off the island on the Avenue Transversale was another grave that was similarly bedecked in metro tickets, paper hearts, letters, garlands and other offerings, including a pink plush Care Bear. Sadly, the addition of crumpled packets of Gauloises and empty books of matches made it look more like a repository for Parisian litter that had been borne there by the wind. There was a small rectangular plaque, covered in lipstick kisses, some of which looked like they had been there a *very* long time.

Serge Gainsbourg
1928–1991

Someone had left a photograph of Serge. It had been cocooned in Sellotape, presumably to protect it from the elements. This had been ineffective, of course; nearly all of it was dry, brittle and yellow. Ironically, a plastic garden gnome, half hidden by the grasses in a plant pot that contained a miniature olive tree, looked more like the dead *chanteur* than the image in the photograph did.

"You remind me of his wife," Yves said suddenly, and then turned to me.

"Do you not think so, Richard?"

Jane Birkin? To be honest, I had not really thought about the similarity before Yves mentioned it. I had always thought Ligeia resembled Jean Shrimpton, especially when she favoured vintage clothes, but I had to admit there *was* something of Ms Birkin about her: physical similarities, certainly. The expression on Ligeia's face indicated that she was unaware *who* Gainsbourg's wife was. It was testament to my age that I was familiar with Jane Mallory Birkin OBE, ex-wife of British composer John Barry, mainly through her more recent humanitarian work.

We continued walking towards what, in the distance, resembled a sandstone column against the far cemetery wall. It was, of course, the morbid cenotaph to Baudelaire, which we discovered consisted of a representation of the poet staring out sternly from an ironic pulpit-like structure above a life-sized carving of him wrapped in a shroud. It was skilfully executed but was not as *superbe* as I had envisaged from Yves's earlier ecstatic description.

"Voilà!" Our guide extended his hand towards the monument and Ligeia ran over to it, eager to take it all in. This was the main reason we had travelled to Paris in the first place.

"Isn't it impressive?" Ligeia ran her hand over the enshrouded figure. "Photograph me, Richard!" she exclaimed playfully, almost laughing with giddy excitement. I sensed a change in her, something I'd experienced many times in the past when we were together. I tried not to let it interfere with my attempts to capture her rapturous appreciation of the moment.

Yves stayed out of the way. He leant on one arm against the wall next to the memorial, smoking, while I photographed Ligeia in various poses against the sandy-coloured carvings. She stared through the lens, through me, towards something she was obviously visualising in her head. Her eyes were bright and alive, and I knew it would only be a matter of time before she turned her attention to the Frenchman. I hoped to God that she didn't start stripping off.

By the time they started posing together it was disappointingly apparent to me that there was some kind of intense sexual chemistry between them. I cannot deny that my heart sank a little. I was hoping that I might have had her totally to myself for the entire duration of our trip. I realised that *that* was not going to happen.

A moment or so later she sidled seductively over to me and leant in against me, pressing her breasts against my hand.

"I want him to fuck me, Richard," she whispered conspiratorially in my ear.

I sighed inwardly. What could I say? Would she have listened anyway? Was it worth ruining what little time remained of our holiday denying her the very thing that made her so exciting to me? I could tell that her state of mind was irreversibly fixed. She was extremely aroused and nothing I could have said, no protestation, would have dampened her resolve. Despite everything, I almost succumbed to the notion of *inevitability*.

"Yes, okay," I answered, as dispassionately as I could manage.

"Thank you," she whispered and kissed my cheek softly. She returned to Yves's side and I continued to take photographs of them together.

Click. I watched her stroke his hard-on through his jeans and involuntarily felt my own cock begin to stiffen. Her hand accentuated the thickness of his member through the denim. Click. He threw his cigarillo stub away and unbuttoned his coat to give her greater access, eyeing me warily as he did so. I put the camera to my eye, ignored him and continued shooting. Click.

He gently stroked her hair. Click. She used her free hand to rub herself, becoming more and more excited. Click. Her mouth opened. Click. Ligeia started to unzip him, and kissed him hungrily. Click. Yves put his hand over hers and stopped her progress.

"Not here," he said, desperately looking around. "We have to be careful. Just over there is a monument to police officers who have been killed in the line of duty. It is a popular place for officers to visit who wish to pay their respects. I do not wish for any of us to be arrested."

Ligeia told me later that she had desperately *wanted* to be fucked next to, or on top of, the stone effigy of the poet. Yves was correct, however; it was too conspicuous. So she opted to let him have her within sight of the monument, shielded slightly from the main thoroughfare by a row of nondescript cast-iron family tombs. I stood guard while she bent over ready to receive him. I raised my camera and watched through the viewfinder as he unbuttoned his coat, unzipped his trousers and pulled his erection free of the confines of his jeans. Click.

Her high heels made her slender legs look even longer than they actually were. She stroked the backs of her calves, looking over her shoulder as Yves slowly teased the hem of her dress up over her hips to reveal her backside. Click. With a little difficulty he pulled the gusset of her white lacy thong to one side and manhandled his cock into her waiting orifice. Click. Click. Click. They both sighed in pleasure as he drove it home for the first time. Click. Click. I pressed the shutter and captured both of their faces. My own cock was demonstratively demanding attention.

I reminded them both not to be too noisy and he commenced shafting her. The angle was perfect for me to photograph them both at the same time, to zoom in on either of their faces or on his cock, slick with her juices as he slipped it in and out of her. Flushed slightly, her mouth frozen in a circle of pleasure, Ligeia gripped the wall of the tomb as he increased the momentum of his thrusting. His hands gripped her hips and he forced her backwards, impaling her on his penis with progressive ferocity. Despite my warning, it was not long before Ligeia began to gasp and her breathing became quicker.

The camera recorded everything. Although the act of intercourse lasted less than a minute and a half, the excitement of the act, coupled with either being watched by me or the possibility of being discovered, was such that they both orgasmed within seconds of each other. Ligeia waited until she could feel Yves emptying himself silently inside her before she moaned in climactic satisfaction. He was still thrusting, albeit weakly, his head thrown back in triumphant release in time to the ebbing rhythm of his ejaculation as I finished photographing them. I discovered later I had taken over one hundred and twenty frames of them.

In the distance, a couple were beginning the walk from the Daillion angel towards us.

With my cock throbbing, I cursed the fact that I would be unable to find the relief that both Yves and Ligeia had just enjoyed, and gestured for then to adjust their clothing. By the time the distant couple had reached the Baudelaire memorial all three of us were at the junction of Avenue de l'Est and Avenue du Boulevard, heading back towards the main gate. I was relieved that Ligeia had taken her place on my arm once more.

Yves left us at the gate after first shaking my hand, exchanging a lingering, tender kiss with Ligeia and scribbling his telephone number on a metro ticket for her.

"You are an exceptionally lucky man, Richard, to have found such a free spirit and you, mademoiselle, are also lucky to have such an exceptional man who understands you so well. If only others were as liberated from social and emotional conformity, this world would be a much better place to live in. Richard, Ligeia, I will always treasure our moments together. Adieu."

Two things went through my mind as he walked away: anarchy and bonobos.

When I was younger and experimenting with politics, I came across a number of fringe groups that were all eager to practise their own form of political expression. Generally, they were all from rich, privileged backgrounds that allowed them the freedom to bleat on about the rights of the workers, take part in pointless demonstrations and expound the theories of Marx and Engels, while benefiting from handouts from their wealthy parents. Unknown to them at the time, their radical posturing would dissolve eventually and be replaced by pure capitalism once the financially crippling reality of their post-graduate situation became apparent. They would be swallowed up by the machine that had allowed them such freedom of thought – and freedom from financial worries – in the first place. There is always an inevitable price to be paid for youthful, indignant militancy.

Before that happened, though, they would pin their Marxist, Communist credentials on their sleeves and champion any cause that they were told was 'right on'. Worse than the extreme socialists, though, were the anarchists. I am convinced that anyone who believes that anarchy might be a solution to the ills of the world really has a problem with what reality is. Again, the majority of mouthy anarchists who protested that all property is theft and that laws were made to be broken were the sons and daughters of bankers, corporate executives and aspiring middle managers. To them, anarchy was acceptable, provided it did not infringe on *their* liberties or result in *their* deprivation. Anarchism was something they applied to society but never to other anarchists.

Anarchists (and Communists) cannot, by definition, own anything, lay claim to anything or aspire to anything; they can only be an instrument of the struggle to end materialistic and consumerist oppression. They could, however, take another's property, possessions or partner. They were all fair game. The only exception to that ethos was when it was applied to *their* property, possessions or partners. It was only then that the so-called radicals realised the flaw in their plan.

However, bonobos (*pan paniscus*) or pygmy chimpanzees would be the perfect candidates for an anarchistic society, especially when it came to sharing partners for the greater good. Male, female, young, old: anything goes in bonobo society and their highly eroticised behaviour is said to be used as a greeting, a form of interpersonal appeasement, conflict resolution and post-conflict reconciliation. In short, they fuck their way through life and are generally all the better for it. Female bonobos are also excellent examples to consider when exploding the myth that *only* female humans enjoy sex because, as a species, *only they* possess clitorises. The average bonobo clit would put those of their human female counterparts to shame.

Ligeia stroked my face, interrupting my thoughts.

"Hey, are you okay? What are you thinking about?"

I did not dare reveal the truth about my contemplation, and I doubted she wanted to hear my ramblings about militant chimpanzees. Instead, I pulled her close to me by the waist and kissed her on the lips.

"I'm fine. I was just thinking that we have to leave all this behind tomorrow evening."

"I know," she frowned. "I've really enjoyed myself and I feel that I have got to know you in a way that would have been impossible back home. Yves was right; you are an exceptional man and you do understand me. It's such a shame we have to leave."

I took her hand and together we headed back towards the metro station. Her hair smelled of tobacco smoke and, for a moment, I almost considered taking up the habit myself again. At the mouth of the station someone handed me a slip of paper, which I placed in my pocket to read when we were on the train. I didn't. I forgot about it until later, my head swimming with thoughts about Ligeia and Yves.

Chapter 24

That evening, as we were packing our cases for the journey home the following evening, the events that led up to the end of my relationship with Ligeia began to unfold, literally.

I was about to stuff my jacket in the case when I decided to check the pockets. In one of them was the leaflet that had been thrust in my hand at the metro station. I unfolded it.

In the top-left corner was a picture of a miserable-looking black man. Below the photo were the words 'Cheikh Calipha: Grand Voyant Médium'. I continued reading.

Reconnu pour sa voyance et son efficacité,
spécialiste des problèmes d'amour.
Chance aux jeux. Protection contre les mauvais sorts.
Désenvoûtement. Retour immédiat de l'être aimé(e), etc.
RÉSULTATS en 3 jours. 100% garantie.
Payement aprés travail.
Reçoit sur rendezvous: 7/7 jours de 8h à 21h…

I stopped reading, screwed up the leaflet and threw it towards the waste bin. I missed and watched it roll across the floor and stop in front of the door.

"What was that?" Ligeia asked languidly. She was lying on her stomach on the bed, wearing just her lingerie, flicking idly through a copy of Marie Claire.

"Nothing, just a flyer for some bullshit fortune-teller."

She regarded me with a sideways glance, only half-committed to the conversation.

"You sound sceptical. Don't you believe in stuff like that?"

I took a swig of Peroni, letting the effervescence erupt in the roof of my mouth. "No, I don't."

She laughed. "We should go and see her... find out more about our relationship."

"Him," I corrected her. "Are you serious? Why? We don't have any problems in that department, do we?"

I made a lunge for her, aiming to slap one of her perfectly rounded arse cheeks, but she jumped up and off the bed. Before I realised what she was doing, she had retrieved the ball of paper and was straightening it out so she could read it.

"Oh." She sounded disappointed. "It's all in French."

"Yes, strange that, isn't it, with us being in France and everything?" I drained the bottle and checked the mini-bar for another but there was only a bottle of Leffe remaining.

"You speak French. Tell me what it says."

So I did, more or less.

"It's all bollocks," I added. "Honestly, it's all rubbish. It says the usual stuff. There's nothing new, nothing original. Stuff like... have your friends left you... do you want to improve your luck... have you got romantic problems? Just the usual crap."

It was a mistake. Even before I had finished, she eagerly announced that she wanted to visit the charlatan. I could tell she was deadly serious from the excited sparkle in her eyes, and I could not disguise my abject disappointment. My sincere hope was that if I agreed but then filled our itinerary for the rest of our stay in Paris, she would either forget the notion or there wouldn't be time. But, as I have mentioned several times already, I have always underestimated women, or at least their ability to get exactly what they want, whenever they choose.

The following morning would see the beginning of our last day in Paris, so I agreed. We would go after lunch. Ligeia was overjoyed. My acquiescence ensured that our nightly sexual gymnastics continued that evening, although throughout our furious coupling I did have a peculiar sense of foreboding that I could not shake. It makes me sound pathetic and uncharacteristically irrational, but I must admit it was true: I had a very bad feeling about it.

Chapter 25

The address – which the leaflet informed me was near Metro Gambetta Ligne 3 – led, predictably, to a small doorway sandwiched between two shops, one of which had long been deserted, in a particularly grubby portion of the city. The approach had been promising: the street was lined with restaurants and bars and there was a distinctly ethnic flavour to the area. I contemplated stopping and enjoying a beer or coffee before we visited the fortune-teller, but Ligeia was very keen to learn what lay in store for her (for us) and pulled me up the road impatiently by the hand until we arrived at the premises of the Calipha.

The place wasn't much to look at. The door, constructed of aluminium and reinforced glass, would at one time have afforded a view of the narrow staircase leading up to the clairvoyant's abode but was now covered with leaflets and letters of thanks, photographs and small inexpensive trinkets, offerings for readings that had apparently saved one person's life or brought others into contact with long-lost friends, family or soul mates. One photograph showed a smiling black woman proudly cradling three newborn children in a hospital bed.

We stood outside for several moments. I understood our hesitancy. As much as Ligeia wanted to know what her future held, she knew there was always going to be the possibility that it would not be what she wanted it to be. I, on the other hand, thought it was a bag of shit and was only there under sufferance and because Ligeia had been incredibly persuasive – sexually.

Eventually, though, we made the effort and, pushing against the grimy glass, made our way into the narrow vestibule and then up the cramped stairs with their undulating linoleum covering. There were strings of Christmas lights on each wall, guiding our passage upwards to the first-floor landing and a door so garishly decorated it would have given any interior decorator a heart attack. Every conceivable organic item appeared to be nailed to its bright red, yellow and green surface: dead flowers, weird seedpods, bones, the shrivelled remains of a fuck-knows-what animal (possibly a lizard), bird skulls, beads, feathers, paper-like snakeskins; there were even cigarette packets.

A sign above the door (a superfluous sign, in my opinion) proudly declared that we were standing outside 'Le Royaume Spirituel de Sa Majesté Cheikh Calipha: Grand Voyant et Médium'. With a degree of trepidation I readied myself to knock on what little surface of the door was not obscured by crap when it was suddenly thrown open. A tall black man with the whitest teeth I'd ever seen greeted us with a throaty laugh and a smile.

"Welcome. I have been expecting you! Please monsieur, mademoiselle, enter. Enter!"

Once inside, I noted that the room was much tidier than I had expected, although it was still littered with melodramatic detritus: African carvings and wall masks and other, more familiar, artefacts connected with his profession. The space was dark, illuminated sparsely with another string of fairy lights, and a persistent, cloying odour of burnt sandalwood hung in the air. He gestured for us to sit at a small round table covered in a dark red velour tablecloth, in the centre of which was a large crystal ball flanked by packs of cards, face down, and a pair of fat, flickering candles.

Ligeia was the first to take her place; I sat only after the Calipha had taken up his position on the other side of the table. He was still smiling broadly, the brilliance of his teeth spectacular. I felt intimidated by his dental hygiene.

"L'amour," he stated enigmatically, and stared into Ligeia's eyes.

He smiled again and then looked at me, switching his gaze from my face to my hands, which were resting on the table. Self-consciously, I put them in my lap, but he had already noted the pale white band of flesh on my finger. He nodded sagely before he spoke.

"Qui peut prédire si la flèche ira dans la bonne direction?" It was obvious he was not waiting for a response.

Not for the first time since we had entered his domain, I noticed there were a number of horrific scars on his face. When inflicted, these ritualistic tribal patterns must have been both deep and excruciatingly painful. They consisted of a row of six parallel lines on each cheek, fat cicatrices of dark pigmented, regenerated tissue that would defy any further healing process. Three similar vertical disfigurements dissected his fleshy lower lip. I tried not to let my morbid fascination get the better of me and averted my eyes frequently.

"Anglais?"

"Oui," Ligeia nodded.

He boomed with laughter.

"Mademoiselle, votre Française est excellent. I will talk in your tongue when I can. It will be easier, I think. I am Cheikh Calipha, a very powerful seer. This gift of seeing was bestowed upon me by my father and upon him by his father and upon him by his father etcetera, etcetera and so on for many, many hundreds of years, back through time. Our lineage has been traced back to Africa and to the plains of Egypt, where my first ancestors were liberated from the tyranny of the Pharaohs, along with the people of Judah by the great prophet Moses, etcetera, etcetera. This gift, my gift, is given by God's almighty hand and I have been charged to use it wisely and only for good. I will not allow it to be used for base things of profit or personal gain." He stared into my eyes. "You understand me? It is a sacred thing entrusted to me and me alone."

He exhaled slowly and took Ligeia by the hand. She did not resist.

"So first I have to ask you, why are you here? I thought when I first see you, it is love, but there is something else, n'est-ce pas?"

His English was good, but his African/French accent was very strong. If his roots *were* North African, it was obvious to me he was only a first generation French citizen. I struggled with some of his words because his pronunciation was so peculiar. I watched him turn Ligeia's hand over and examine her palm, tracing one of the lines with a long, pointed fingernail.

"There is a strangeness here. Here… see?" He took my hand and turned that over too. After studying both for a while, he sucked air through his teeth and shook his head. I must admit he worried me and there was a definite look of consternation, or perhaps it was concern, on his face. Finally, he spoke.

"I have come across this only one time before in my life."

He held both our hands up by the wrist so that we could both confirm what he was referring to. I couldn't see anything out of the ordinary – at least not at first. His dark brown eyes watched us both intently, as though he was searching for some kind of acknowledgement.

"Look! This is an important portent. Very auspicious. To have before me two souls that have found each other, that have been drawn together across the vastness of our world, that occupy separate bodies but share an identical fate is very, very, very rare. Impossible even, yet here you are. Here you sit! The pair of you! I too am drawn into this strangeness. My destiny now is to become intertwined with yours. Look!"

He held up his hand, palm towards us, and traced his repulsive index fingernail along the same lines on his palm, then on mine and then on Ligeia's. They appeared to be identical. That is not to say that our hands were identical, but some of the lines, specifically the life line, the head line and the fate line, *did* all look the same. Rather sceptically, I assumed that everybody's were the same but have since discovered that is *not* the case. The length, the depth, the shape and the curvature of the lines on our hands corresponded exactly.

Ligeia smiled at me, her eyes twinkling with excitement and wonder. I was less enthused, although our apparently non-unique hand markings did intrigue me. Part of me wondered what it meant, or if it meant anything at all. The Calipha was about to reveal what the markings signified but not before he upped the ante in the melodrama stakes.

He took a pinch of what appeared to be dust from a small brass bowl next to the table and flicked it into the flame of the nearest candle; a spiral of bright, crackling sparks lit up the room.

"There is great danger ahead!" His voice was loud and serious. "When destinies collide, danger is never far away. I must look very carefully at what awaits you, because what awaits you awaits me also, etcetera. Place your hands on the table, side by side, like this."

We followed his instruction. He picked up a long, partially denuded feather, dipped it into a container of inky black liquid and began drawing on our hands.

"This line is the life line. You can see that they are identical in every way. The length… everything… even the little lines which cut across it. See?"

It was difficult because our hands were now covered in an inky splurge. I nodded regardless, unimpressed.

"Everyone thinks the life line indicates the length of our lives, but it is wrong. People live their lives at different speeds and yet they can have lines of a similar length. Some live their life fast and die early, and some die only when they are very, very old. *This* line cannot tell us *when* we will die, only God may decide on that; the small comfort we have is that for all of us, inevitably, it *will* come to pass."

So far he had revealed very little of import and I was beginning to grow impatient again. Perhaps I communicated my frustration through my restless body language. The Calipha picked up on it immediately and was fierce in his reaction.

"You must learn to be patient!" he shouted at me. "You want to run but yet you cannot walk. This is not a path trod lightly. Why do you hasten to your death? Are you so eager to die?! Listen to me! You came to me to understand your fate and you treat me with the same respect you give a troublesome fly! It was fate that brought us three together and if we are to go forward from this place, we have to take notice of the signs!"

"Yes, Richard." Ligeia scolded me playfully, a mischievous look on her face, a look that rapidly vanished in the wake of the psychic's equally stinging rebuke of her.

"And you, missy! This is not a game! I am Calipha and

my words *must* be heeded. This affects you also and you would be very unwise to treat my words lightly. Now, pay attention!"

I shot her a glance, hoping it would illustrate how stupid I felt we had been in putting ourselves in such a situation. This psychic charlatan was obviously also unhinged. Wisely, she deliberately ignored me, which was just as well. Otherwise, we may well have broken into uncontrollable laughter – a natural remedy for the rapidly deteriorating situation – and be unceremoniously cast out on the street without ever hearing what bullshit he was about to come out with.

"We three *must* die."

I sighed audibly. Naturally, Ligeia looked shocked.

"As I said, it is the way of all things. All things must pass. First, though, there are portents, signs of what is to come before we come to our end."

He picked up a pile of scruffy-looking, dog-eared cards with black-and-red chequered backs and spread them out in a fan on the table before us.

"Mademoiselle, choose one."

Ligeia did as she was asked and turned it over to reveal a stark image of a vaulted-ceilinged cathedral, empty except for a row of stone columns, each illuminated by rainbow-hued sunlight bursting through a single stained-glass rose window. It was entitled Paix. He took it from her and laid it face up on the table. Then he gestured to me.

"Monsieur."

I followed suit. My card was entitled Libération. In the distance, a man was galloping away on a horse across a bridge towards the horizon. In the foreground, a length of discarded rope lay coiled up like a snake in the road. In the middle ground, dividing these two images, was a raised portcullis set in a high redbrick wall. He placed my card next to Ligeia's, then chose a card for himself.

"Pour moi, les étoiles!" He was not pleased with his choice. That much was evident from his facial expression. He again sucked air noisily through his teeth and slammed the card down unceremoniously on top of the ones we had chosen.

"Mademoiselle, it says you have had a troubled life, which has led you into great danger many times before. The past is not written clearly here because it is what *awaits* you that this card" – he stabbed her card with his forefinger – "talks to us about today. All I can tell from this is that a black shadow was cast over your life. It is like the sun was extinguished. I cannot tell why. Its light continues to be hidden from you, which is why you strive to seek it out in everything you do. It is why you long to embrace the light, for its warmth and life-giving properties. Knowing only the night for so long in your life, you live now only for the dawn. Does this make sense to you? Do you understand what I mean?"

I looked at Ligeia. Her face was drawn and serious. Slowly she nodded in affirmation. From what little I knew of her life, his assessment seemed fairly accurate, although if I was feeling particularly despondent, I could have attributed his words to me also.

"We are all creatures born out of darkness. We must one day return to that darkness, but while we live it is only fair that we enjoy some light. Don't you agree? You have been troubled, but deep down in your soul you know that it is only right to expect a moment of perfect peace and radiance. It is coming."

He paused and inhaled deeply, his face turned up towards the ceiling. He grasped Ligeia's hand.

"Ma petite gazelle, il n'y a plus de raison de chercher

la mort. La mort te dénichera bien assez tôt. Ta joie de vivre ne devrait pas être teintée d'ombres. Embrasse la vie et laisse sa lumière bénie remplir ton âme. L'amour n'est pas une torche, c'est un brasier… c'est un soleil qui illumine tous les endroits sombres, même les plus petites zones d'ombres situées dans les recoins les plus reculés des grandes cathédrales. Si tu refuses pour toujours son pouvoir, les ombres t'envelopperont et sans aucun doute te consumeront dans l'obscurité. Tu vois qu'il y a quatre colonnes qui supportent le toit de la cathédrale. Une, deux, trois et quatre: quatre opportunités. Tu ne vas pas pouvoir refuser ce grand pouvoir indéfiniment."

Even with my half-decent command of the French language, much of what he said (or what he meant) was lost on me because he spoke far too quickly. I was about to ask him to translate when he rounded on me.

"Monsieur, toi, aussi, tu as passé une grande partie de ta vie dans l'obscurité, même si celle-ci est différente de celle de mademoiselle. La tienne est l'obscurité de la maladie, celle de ton esprit. Tu as beaucoup souffert à cause d'elle, cette immense noirceur qui t'a été imposée. Elle t'a emprisonné et, cependant, tu as conscience que tu es le seul à détenir les clés pour t'en libérer. Jusqu'à maintenant, tu n'avais jamais envisagé de t'échapper. Tu vois une paix possible à l'intérieur de la cathédrale de mademoiselle, mais il y a des risques à considerer."

His preposterous, rambling verbiage was beginning to grate on me.

How dare he? Had I interpreted his meaning correctly? Sickness? Illness of the mind?

That there *was* some history of mental incapacity in the family was undeniable, but there was no direct link between that malady and me, as the Calipha was suggesting, unless he meant genetically. I was prone to depression from time to time, certainly (who in society these days isn't?) but that hardly amounted to a mental disorder.

"Tu la perdras."

I understood *that* perfectly well and naturally began to bristle with indignation before he silenced me with one hand. Then he took hold of one of mine with the other.

"C'est inévitable... incontournable. Cependant, monsieur, quand je regarde dans tes yeux, ta réaction n'est pas celle que j'attends normalement. Je sais que tu me comprends suffisamment bien contrairement à ta maîtresse et c'est une chance pour elle. En fait, la question que tu veux me poser, ce n'est pas comment? Ou pourquoi? Mais bien quand? N'est-ce pas?"

I nodded slowly, careful not to look at Ligeia.

"Alors, tu veux vraiment savoir?"

There are moments in everyone's life when the sixty seconds that constitute each minute could easily be mistaken for sixty minutes, sixty hours, sixty days, sixty weeks, sixty months or even sixty years. Generally, such time slips occur while we are pondering or reflecting on matters of crucial significance. The question posed to me by the Calipha was the same as if he had asked me if I wanted to know when I would die; obviously, it required careful deliberation. It was not that I wanted to believe any of his hokey mysticism was valid, but there always remained the chance, considering how long such divinatory practices had existed, that such insight *was* actually possible.

Given the opportunity myself, *would* I want to know when the hour of my death would be? Such knowledge had the potential to change everything because being made aware would surely cause me to alter my life accordingly, perhaps cramming more in to ensure that I experienced everything or taking normally unacceptable risks because I knew that I would not be harmed until the appointed hour. In short, the awareness of my impending mortality would, for however long was left, make me immortal. That knowledge had the potential to be very dangerous.

But knowing how long I had left with Ligeia was different, surely. The clairvoyant had *not* said she would die, merely that I would 'lose her'. He was correct; I knew that. I was unconcerned with how that would happen, only when. My head had immediately acknowledged the reality of our situation, the inevitability that our relationship would end at some point. The only information I selfishly desired was to know how much more time we had together.

Would it change our relationship? In gaining that wisdom, would we become, in the time that remained, immortal? Could I justify gaining such insight in order to have that amount of power over both of our lives, but especially hers, to create a new reality forced by necessity? One that would be noticeably different *because* I would know exactly *when* it would all go to shit? Could I be content with knowing that when it *was* over at least I could live out the rest of my time on earth with some decent memories? Isn't that all any of us have left at the end of the day anyway? Memories?

I made my decision.

"Non, monsieur, je ne souhaite pas savoir."

The Calipha smiled and patted my hand in a patronising fashion, which I found strangely comforting.

"Le temps nous marque bien plus que les rides. Je pense que tu as fait le bon choix."

Ligeia squeezed my arm, a puzzled look on her face.

"I'll tell you later," I lied. It appeared to satisfy her

curiosity.

That was the cue for the Calipha to throw another pinch of dust into the small flame that danced brightly above the candle.

"And now the truth of the situation, the reason you sought me out, mademoiselle." He placed my hand on top of hers. "He is your soul mate, and you are his. You have found each other, despite incredible obstacles, and you will always, always be together, entwined like serpents so that some who regard you will see only one creature. You two will become one…"

I tried to interrupt the contradictory Chaldaic charlatan but he silenced me with a harsh hiss.

"Be still! Be silent! You have what you came for," he said directly at me. "Now you would deny the mademoiselle the truth she seeks?"

I shook my head, embarrassed.

"Merci, monsieur."

He addressed Ligeia once more. "Alors, ma chèrie, I will continue."

Chapter 26

The things we do for love.

Pathetic.

Not pathetic being in love with her, which I now knew to be incontrovertibly true, but the way in which we change because of love. I became a different person, bound up in her and her alone, where all I thought of and all I *could* think of was Ligeia. Ligeia, my love. She possessed me, filled my mind with thoughts of her and filled my heart with longing for her to the point where nobody else and nothing else existed.

When we were apart I counted off the seconds until I could see her again. When we were together we were inseparable, and I would endure almost anything and anyone to ensure that we stayed together. Hmm, whom was I kidding? I would have endured *anything*.

Like I said, pathetic.

I was insecure in my love for her, though; I realise that. I was afraid of offending her and so losing her. I could not see the truth any longer. I lived for her and I would have done anything she asked of me, no matter how much it hurt me – some of our escapades did hurt me to the point where my heart actually became painful – but I never complained.

Pathetic.

It wasn't just the pain; some things we did scared me. There were things about Ligeia that terrified me more anything I had ever experienced before: her constant flirtation with danger, for example. Her continual desire to exceed the boundaries of what most (myself included) would consider acceptable risks was a constant source of concern. I understood *why* she felt compelled to do the things she did, but I knew there were plenty of less threatening activities she could have involved herself in.

I knew I was in love with her. It was more than infatuation, or gratitude that someone almost half my age took the time to suck my cock whenever we met up. She made me feel alive and that was something I felt, as my middle years began to take hold of me, I might never experience again.

If what I felt was not love, it was the closest thing I have ever come to experiencing that all-consuming emotion.

The day she gave me a key to her apartment, I remember sobbing with joy.

"So you can come and go as you please," she informed me.

I hugged her, crying, unable to let go for fear that I would collapse on the floor, an inconsolable heap of shit.

Pathetic.

However, I wouldn't have changed it – not a single thing, not a single moment of it – for the world.

The world, however, had other plans.

Chapter 27

Mark Zuckerberg and his friends have got a lot to answer for.

So opinion is divided on whether they were solely responsible for the concept and creation of the social networking platform. What does it matter? It is actually academic now. It's out there. With almost a billion users globally, and rising year on year, it is estimated that Facebook will have crossed the 1.5-billion mark by 2020, making it the most popular and the most widely used social media site in the world. Not bad considering it was initially set up in a university dormitory.

I have never been enamoured with social networking for a number of reasons, mainly professional. Most of my students were 'on' Facebook and through them I learned it was divisive, disruptive and dangerous. Pinning the ills of the world on an internet site seems hardly fair but, as with Zuckerberg, there has to be some level of accountability. I feel that Facebook and other sites of its ilk are partly responsible for laying the foundation for the inevitable destruction of interpersonal communication. Why talk when you can text? Why text when you can Facebook? Why use words at all when you can use an image or an emoticon?

It is a product of our times. Facebook seemingly enables people, ordinary people, to rise above their normal prosaic position in society and be elevated to the status of celebrity so that they can share their banal and meaningless lives with people they have never met and turn every insignificant event into a temporary sound bite for mass consumption. Am I interested in what someone I don't care about is listening to? Do I want to know what they watched on TV or what they had for breakfast? No. Fucking no. No.

Admittedly, Facebook has shrunk the world, connecting people across towns, cities, countries, oceans and continents, dependant obviously on access to a participation platform. Here, safe inside their SMB (social media bubble), safe within the cocoon that envelops them every time they sit in front of a PC or laptop, or pick up a mobile phone or a tablet, and shielded from the world beyond the web, they sign in. But they are not safe.

Social network sites are fantasy worlds populated by attention-seeking junkies who are incapable of separating fact from fiction, or reality from illusion. It's where liars can spin their implausible tales to an ever-hungry, gullible audience, regardless of how often those tales spin wildly out of control. They are places where every opinion becomes a fact and every fact becomes incontrovertible proof of a person's misguided and unacceptable belief system for the faceless bullies who lurk there, waiting for unsuspecting prey.

Beyond all that, however, is the greatest crime of all because, let's face it, social networkers are willing participants; no one forces them at gunpoint to sign in. This crime is that they have dumped 'Like' into our modern oral vocabulary, where it has become an extraneous verb in almost every conversation.

For all those reasons, I was not delighted when Ligeia mentioned that Raphael had been in contact with some *allegedly* like-minded Taphophilic libertines via an internet social networking site called AltRN8if (www.altrn8if.org) and they were interested in meeting us. I am not suspicious by nature but I had heard far too many horror stories to allow the suggestion to go unchallenged.

"It sounds fucking scary."

Ligeia was used to my caution but sighed impatiently.

"Look, Raphael has been very careful. He's not stupid. He's spent a long time checking these guys out. He says they're okay and if he says they're okay, they're okay by me too. I trust him. It's time you started to trust him too."

It wasn't a case of me distrusting Raphael; I just didn't have any faith in the internet.

As it turned out, my instincts were spot on for once.

★ ★ ★

We proposed that our new contacts meet us in the public car park outside the gates of the Southern General Cemetery approximately an hour before it was due to close.

Being a much larger, undulating, expanse than the General Cemetery, we decided it would be easier to lose ourselves amongst the tombs and shrubbery that separated the four main burial areas. The cemetery was not unfamiliar to Ligeia, Raphael or me, although the two others were strangers to the city. I could already foresee problems.

As usual, Ligeia became quite agitated as we made our approach to the rendezvous. She became predictably quite excitable, gossiping incessantly about the most inane things, most of which I let wash over me. I knew it was how she prepared herself for meetings with new partners. Raphael, though, sat in the back of the car, silent and stoic, which was unusual for him. Normally, he too would be competing to be heard above Ligeia's chattering. I asked him if there was anything wrong.

"No, just thinking."

I studied him more closely in the rear-view mirror. I didn't believe him.

"Really?"

He stared back at me, clearly annoyed.

"I was just wondering about the weather."

It was at that point I decided to let the matter drop.

As we pulled into the small off-road car park, there was one car already parked up: a long sleek, metallic red, vintage Jaguar that reminded me of Inspector Morse. I could see there were two male occupants, who turned their heads in our direction as we pulled alongside. From my first sight of them, I felt uneasy. They were both broad shouldered and muscular, with close-cropped hair that gave them a vaguely military appearance. Initially I wondered if they were, in fact, squaddies or, worse, undercover police officers. Once more I voiced my concerns. Ligeia was out of the car before I had finished my sentence. Gingerly, Raphael and I got out too.

The two men were being demonstratively physical, taking turns to hug Ligeia. I could tell from the look on their faces that they believed they had just won the jackpot. They greeted Raphael and me more warily, with a perfunctory handshake, and we exchanged names. They called themselves Jed (his real name was Jerry, but he preferred Jed) and Martin. Jed was dark-haired with an interesting pale scar that ran from his jaw line around the back of his ear, terminating at the back of his skull. Martin was blonde and fairly ordinary looking. I disliked both of them intensely.

There was something feral and rat-like about them, with their toothy, lecherous smiles, something feverish in the way their eyes roamed over Ligeia, darting from one erogenous zone to another, and in the way they couldn't keep still, constantly fidgeting with nervous energy. Their hands were on Ligeia all the time, pawing her, touching her, jokingly caressing her hands and arms. Cautiously I looked at Raphael and I could tell that, although it was too late to do anything about it, he was having some reservations about them too.

"Shall we go in then?" I prompted everyone, and was pleased when everyone responded obediently and made their way through the gates. We started to climb the hill towards the crematorium chapel and I explained what was going to happen.

"About 5.45pm the gatekeeper and security guard will drive along the roads around the chapel, checking that everyone is either on their way out or have left. Any stragglers will be escorted to the gates we've just come through, and then the gates will be locked and further secured with a chain and padlock. The security guard will wait just outside while the gatekeeper goes down there to the side gate," I said, pointing to a steep narrow path off to the left. "He'll lock and padlock it and then walk all the way around to the front, where the security guard will be waiting for him. Then they'll drive off."

Both Martin and Jed nodded.

"Right. So how long before we can get down to it?"

Get down to it? I really didn't care for their turn of phrase. I tried to catch Ligeia's eye but she was preoccupied with weighing up the physicality of the strangers through their clothes.

"We have to stay hidden for around twenty-five minutes. If you make any noise or if the gatekeeper is alerted by premature movement, he'll radio for the security guard to do another sweep, and it won't be as cursory. There is a good chance we'll get turfed out" – I paused and checked for any reaction before completing the sentence – "or the police will be called and we'll be taken to the station and questioned."

There was not a flicker of emotion on their faces. If they were the law, my rather ham-fisted attempt to challenge their identity was unsuccessful. Disappointed, I stopped at a crossroad in the path.

"Right, we have to split up. I need to stay around here so I can see when the gatekeeper has gone back around to the front gate. I will wait until he and the security guy have driven off and then give you a signal. Raphael will take you two to a secure location. I must warn you again, you have to stay down until I signal."

"Why can't she show us where to hide?" Martin, the lairier of the two, asked.

It was a valid question. I had no real reason for not wanting Ligeia to go with them, except that I didn't trust them. I was on the point of giving some half-arsed excuse when Ligeia interrupted, smiling charmingly.

"It's okay, Richard, I'll go and show them where to hide."

"What about the side gate?" I asked as confrontationally as I could without alerting the two men at her side. Jed had slipped an arm around Ligeia's waist.

"Surely, if you are watching the front gate, you'll see when the side gate has been locked because the gatekeeper will fuck off with the security guard, won't he?" Martin responded. His throaty voice reminded me of a football hooligan I had once heard interviewed on Radio 4.

Martin's logic was sound and he had outmanoeuvred me with hardly any effort at all. I began to feel that there was a distinct possibility that the situation was slipping out of our control and into theirs. That would have been a monumental mistake, having only just met them. Fortunately, Raphael, who must have been aware of my uneasiness, stepped in with a shrug.

"It's okay," he said. "Ligeia and I will show them where to secrete themselves."

They obviously didn't like the idea of having Raphael as an interloper, but it was decided.

"Great!" I announced. "Let's go."

★ ★ ★

Violence is not something I have ever been involved in or been overly familiar with. As a teacher, I witnessed plenty of fighting, mainly as a detached observer, watching enraged, testosterone-fuelled teenagers beat the shit out of each other for one pathetic reason or another. Once I observed Madamoiselle Lefévre, our French exchange teacher, fall victim to an unprovoked and merciless beating from one of the Year 11 students before I stepped in to pull the seething girl off the frightened, bleeding woman. I, however, have never been physically involved in any violent acts in the wider world.

That in itself is something of a wonder. We do, after all, live in a vicious world that statistics show is becoming increasingly violent. Television mirrors trends set by acts of random callousness, partly induced (some say) by the proliferation of savage computer and console games, where death, mutilation and sadism have become part of the staple diet of the younger generation. Saying that, most of our experience of violence is limited to what we watch in films and on TV, or rather what TV stations and their executives are allowed to broadcast.

So what happened next that particular evening still causes me a great deal of distress.

You are already aware that I was uncomfortable with Raphael's selection of participants for our ménage a cinq. My disquiet did not dissipate in the quiet isolation as I waited beneath a row of Leylandii trees, watching the ruddy-faced, porcine security guard and his companion drive around and then wend their way downhill towards the gates.

Ligeia had already introduced me to men like Jed and Martin before at the Spinney. In my mind, they were nothing more than horny, opportunistic sexual thugs that did not care one iota for the person in whom they were greedily burying their cocks, as long as it ultimately resulted in their own selfish pleasure. Were such men dangerous? Undoubtedly. Were Jed and Martin dangerous? I refused to consider the possibility. It was certainly a possibility, but I didn't think they posed a threat Raphael or me. Such men thrived on brutalising women; as long as I persisted in my vigilance and as long as both Raphael and I were watching her back, I was certain we could keep Ligeia safe.

The sound of the gate being slammed shut disturbed my thoughts. In the distance I could see the heavy lock being turned, and hear the rasp of a thick chain being pulled through the bars and the reassuring clunk of the padlock being closed. There was a short, muffled conversation between the two men and then slowly the bow-legged gatekeeper made his way, puffing with exertion, back up the hill towards me. He stopped at the crossroads, turned left and began the descent towards the side gate, without giving any of his surroundings a second glance.

I wondered where the others had chosen to secrete themselves and immediately cursed my tactless choice of expression. Behind me the crematorium fell into silhouette as the daylight began to fail. I could no longer make out any of the ornate leaded windows or the covered funeral reception that was used when the weather was inclement. I yearned for the return of British

Summer Time and the longer, lighter evenings, even though that would curtail our orgiastic necropolitan soirées.

Eight minutes or so later, I saw the tail lights of the security van illuminate; moments later, the gatekeeper climbed into the vehicle. With a spray of gravel, the van moved off at speed and disappeared down the road. We were finally, it seemed, alone. All that remained was for me to indicate the coast was clear and I could rejoin the others, so I stood and sent a brief text (just an 'OK') to Raphael's mobile and waited for them to appear.

Cemeteries are, by their nature, very quiet and peaceful places. This means that any noise is immediately noticeable and is generally amplified by the acoustic qualities of the open layout, so I could hear that something was kicking off long before I could see what was happening. At first there were just raised voices: I recognised only Martin's guttural tone and Ligeia's cry. Then I heard shouts of anger. Raphael called my name but then there was silence, followed by a long agonised moan. Instinctively, my heart began beating wildly, in preparation for what was almost certainly an unknown, but potentially dangerous, situation.

I called out to Raphael and was answered with another tormented cry of pain that at least gave me an idea of the direction it was coming from. Without thinking about my own safety, I began to run through the ranks of headstones towards the sound. It was getting darker. In my panic, I mistook a seraphic grave marker for a figure, perhaps Ligeia, and even though I realised it was not where the shouting, which had now turned to screaming, was coming from, I raced over towards it.

It was a costly mistake. Realising my folly and momentarily disorientated, I called out again; this time

Ligeia answered. I turned towards where her voice was coming from, only to see her running barefoot, the left side of her dress ripped open, a look of utter fear on her face.

"Quick!" she screamed. "They're killing Raffi!"

There was no time to consider anything. I simply reacted. Any notion of self-preservation was discarded as I ran towards the clearing by the tall, ghostly white Portland stone war memorial to go to Raphael's aid; Ligeia followed close behind. Raphael was on the ground, curled into a foetal position, as both Martin and Jed laced into him with a volley of vicious kicks, punctuating each blow with obscenities.

"You... fucking... queer! You... fuck... ing... cunt! Touch me... will you... you... fucking... gay... bastard!"

Raphael was covering his face with his arms but I could still hear him whimpering with each blow. I knew he would not be able to withstand much more kicking. Unaware of the danger I was putting myself in, I closed the distance between Ligeia and the two assailants and howled out for them to leave him alone.

They stopped, just long enough to assess the situation, before Jed moved away from his companion and towards me. Behind him, Martin recommenced his horrific attack.

"Have you come to help your fucking boyfriend, you fucking cunt?!" His breathing was laboured by his aggressive exertion. "Come on, you fucking queer bastard, come and get your fucking medicine! I'll fucking straighten you out!"

Raphael's moaning stopped. The kicking didn't. Ligeia screamed in a series of long, protracted sobs. Jed jabbed a finger at her.

"And you, you fucking bitch! You'd better get ready because when we've finished with these two queers, we are going give your pussy a proper-fucking-seeing-to that you are never going to forget!"

I raised my hand and showed the advancing thug what was in it.

"Tell your friend to stop what he is doing! And the two of you fuck off! Now!"

Jed did not advance any farther, but his face was still twisted in a vicious sneer. He was uncertain how to proceed. He eyed the mobile phone in my hand and laughed.

"What are you going to do? Call the police?"

Behind me, Ligeia was still crying, but at least Raphael's kicking had stopped. I shook my head, my hand still held out defiantly.

"No. I've already done that," I lied. "I guarantee they are on their way right now."

It was reassuring to see the bullishness suddenly drain from the pair. Their confidence was immediately punctured; uncertainty had set in. I made sure they understood the implications of their predicament, while, inwardly, I was ready to pass out with absolute fear.

"We'll all testify against you. They'll find your car first and then us. As soon as we hear the sirens we will begin shouting and you won't get away. You'll be arrested."

Martin was the first to turn and run.

"And you'll be charged with rape" – at that moment I did not realise that they hadn't raped Ligeia – "assault or GBH."

Jed licked his lips, eyes furtively searching the darkness for some alternative path of escape, and then chased after his friend, running away from us and down the hill towards the main gate. It was at that moment that both my legs buckled and I collapsed, shaking uncontrollably.

* * *

As a footnote to this incident, our participation in any further such clandestine encounters ceased altogether. In some ways it was a wake-up call for Ligeia that I believed was well overdue. Certainly her behaviour – in fact, the behaviour of us all – was never the same. She accepted my assertion that Jed and Martin (not their real names we later discovered but had already guessed) were representative of the type of belligerent sexual predators that lay in wait in the ether, ready to take advantage of situations such as the one we presented them with. She became more cautious after that.

Unfortunately, the police *did* become involved. The attack on Raphael left us in a quandary. He had been badly injured during the attack; as well as suffering concussion he had sustained extensive bruising to his arms and upper body and three fractured ribs. Once he had regained consciousness we all made our way to the side gate. Although getting over this gate was not as daunting a challenge as scaling the higher main gates, Raphael was still unable to do it. We phoned for an ambulance and, through necessity, had to concoct a preposterous story to explain why we were in the cemetery grounds after it had closed.

I told the police that I had been walking past the side gate when I'd heard a woman shouting for help. I ascertained from her that she had seen a man (Raphael) lying on the ground and had climbed over the gate to offer assistance. The man was unresponsive so she decided to stay with him and call for help. I then climbed over the gate and, once I had established what the situation was, telephoned for a paramedic. I told the police I did not know either the woman or the injured man. I'm certain they believed me.

Ligeia corroborated my story independently; when asked how her dress had become damaged, she explained she had torn it as she was climbing over the gate. She similarly stated that she did not know me or the injured man and had not seen anyone else in the vicinity. They accepted her version of events also.

Raphael contracted complete amnesia about the attack, as far as the police were concerned. He told them he could remember walking through the graveyard, feeling something strike him hard on the back of the head and then nothing else until he was in the ambulance. One of the officers asked whether he felt he had been a victim of a mugging, but as Raphael remained uncertain of the particulars surrounding the incident he told them simply that he was not sure.

Ligeia and I were commended by both the police and the ambulance service for our 'prompt and selfless action'. They told us the victim had been lucky we were passing by. Sometimes, they said, it was about being in the right place at the right time. Personally I think we had all been very lucky. The ending could have been so much worse. As time moved on, we didn't mention it at all.

I got to learn what had happened that night from Ligeia. She told me that as soon as they were hidden from possible view, Jed and Martin began touching her in a manner that she found uncomfortable. Raphael had tried to intervene but had been unsuccessful. As soon as they knew the side gate had been locked they attempted to force themselves on her. During their attempt to rape her they ripped her dress, and then Raphael had become the object of their fury when he had tried to pull Jed off her.

Raphael never referred to what happened. We tried to get him to talk, to exorcise the ghosts of that evening, but he became increasingly withdrawn, as though a terrible darkness had spread, not just over him but over us all. We saw him less frequently and finally he stopped meeting up with us at all. Then it was just me and Ligeia. Again.

Chapter 28

It's strange how our lives sometimes move in a direction we could never have anticipated.

I'm not a gambler. I've never had the slightest inclination to put any of my hard-earned cash in the hands of those hook-beaked croupiers or slot machine manufacturers, or those shysters running that shambolic ruination that this country endures on a weekly basis, the lottery. As a child, I imagined that a much more interesting practice was carried out behind the doors of those high-street premises called bookmakers.

In my head, it was in those uniformly anonymous, almost squalid-looking, places that armies of bespectacled pot-bellied men worked, tirelessly binding together the pictures and the pages of dozens and dozens of books before bundling them up and transporting them a few hundred yards farther along the street, where they would be unpacked and finally placed on the shelves of W. H. Smith. It was a fanciful notion and it kept me occupied for years. The reality, which I discovered when I was twelve and playing truant from school, shattered my illusions completely and simultaneously signalled the beginning of the end of my pre-adolescent naivety.

Had I been asked, at the very beginning of my relationship with Ligeia, how long I envisaged it would last, I would have been unable to tell you. However, despite the fact that I'm not a gambler or a betting man, even I knew it wouldn't last forever, regardless of any esperance I might have secretly wanted to hold on to. I'm not a pessimist; I'm a realist. The odds were stacked against us from the very start and the difference between our respective ages was only the tip of the iceberg.

For example, I was still married to Janice.

After our return from Paris I noticed things had changed at home. Janice began to be more interested in where I was going in the evenings, even more so at the weekends. Sometimes she would phone me unexpectedly, concocting some excuse or other for doing so. It wasn't long before I realised her fabrications were merely a disguise for the fact that she had grown suspicious. This led to a number of tense situations, aggressive confrontations and, on more than one occasion, full-blown arguments.

"I'm not paranoid," she would tell me. "I'm not stupid either; I know something is going on."

Largely, I maintained a stance of being vehemently dismissive of her suspicions and, eventually, the accusations. Ligeia was more concerned than I thought she would be when I told her, and she warned me to be careful. I wasn't entirely certain why she was so apprehensive. Previously, such things would never have concerned her but then I'd also noticed a change in Ligeia.

Thinking back, I believe I can pinpoint exactly when her attitude shifted. I am convinced it was on our last day in Paris, in the fortune-teller's room. That scandalously expensive African fraudster had a lot to answer for, filling her head with shit she didn't really want to hear about our 'intertwined destiny', *etcetera*. That was fucking scary. Who wants to hear that they are inescapably bound to someone forever? Really? Sometimes it is best not to know what the future holds.

We continued much the same as we had, although Janice's inquisitiveness meant that my visits and stopovers were not as frequent as they had been or as I would have liked. Our liaisons, when they happened, were still as passionate but definitely different. I was unable to identify what had altered. I just couldn't put my finger on it.

It was like… like… being with her was like standing in front of a beautifully decorated Christmas tree swathed in hundreds of twinkling, coloured fairy lights. In my head, I knew there were two hundred tiny bulbs but, unconsciously, I was aware one of them had blown. That hardly affected the overall appearance, but part of me knew something wasn't quite right.

★ ★ ★

After a particularly crap week at school – and the third exclusion that month – I coerced Ligeia into letting me cook a meal for both of us at her place. It would not be anything grand, just good-quality home cooking and plenty of alcohol. She agreed, adding that it would serve as a doubly special occasion because she was due to fly out to Prague on a minor modelling assignment the following week and she would be away for four days.

The meal I wanted to cook for her was a variation on Huntsman's chicken. A jointed rooster would be flash fried to crisp up the skin and then flambéed in brandy before being consigned to a casserole dish along with various root vegetables and grilled red and yellow peppers. The stock would consist mainly of vin d'Alsace.

I decided to shop at the local Waitrose, which was close to her apartment, because I could guarantee that it would stock all of the ingredients I required and that I would be able to source a couple of excellent accompaniments to the meal from their better-than-average selection of wines. In total, the ingredients and alcohol cost me £48.73. It's strange what things we choose to recall.

Ligeia was not supposed to be back until after 5pm, which I gauged would give me enough time to fully prepare the meal and set the table. I used my key to let myself in and stopped on the threshold, listening.

The silence that greeted me was wrong. It sounds ridiculous but the quietness of the flat seemed odd; it felt peculiar. I can't explain how, or even why, it made me feel like that. There was just something about the place that just did not feel right. I called out to Ligeia, not expecting an acknowledgement. In truth I still do not know why I did it. There was no response.

The silence was unnatural. There was nothing. Just stillness. Emptiness. I could hear nothing, not even the annoying sound of her clock. I wondered if it had stopped. For some unfathomable reason, I began to feel unsettled and, putting the shopping on the kitchen table, decided to search the rooms. I had the strangest impression that, despite the silence, I was not alone.

Ligeia was in the bedroom. It was the last place I expected to find her. I cannot remember what I said to her, or indeed if I said anything. Not that it would have mattered: she wouldn't have heard me. She was attached, or rather her neck was attached, to the metal frame of the bed head by a length of pale ivory cord. It was knotted so tight around her throat that her face had turned almost completely black.

In the quieter moments since then I have tried to recall exactly what happened, the sequence of events that followed immediately after finding her, but it is still all a blur. I do remember her tongue, a dry, distended and purple thing protruding from one side of her mouth, between her perfect white teeth. I do recollect thinking, selfishly, that I would never feel it hungrily exploring my mouth or my cock again. I recall her eyes, bulging obscenely as though ready to burst from her head, the whites of which were shot through with vibrant red and purple ruptured blood vessels.

The whole of her body was suspended as though by a hellish, inhuman umbilical cord, arms hanging uselessly beneath her. She was still on her knees, completely naked. Her beautiful, wonderful breasts hung pale and lifeless like fleshy sacs of cold fat, which of course was what they were now. I tried not to picture the joy I'd felt touching them, or the warmth of them, or the taste and sensation of her nipples in my mouth.

At this point I would like to mention that dignity, the one thing we cling to in life and that we imagine separates us from all other life on this planet, deserts us in death. It was that contradiction that appalled me the most. The romantic, sometimes noble notion of death, discussed and debated by artists, writers and poets for millennia, is reduced to nothing more than rubble by the stark realities of our expiration. I am sure that some of you are perfectly aware of that, but I was not. I was not prepared for the ignobility of her demise. Her bowels and her bladder had emptied themselves.

I screamed, I think. I know I must have gone back into the kitchen to get a knife to cut her free. That was the only way it could have turned up in the bedroom. I phoned the ambulance service, and they must have informed the police because they turned up at the same time. In all, five emergency vehicles, lights flashing but sirens silent, arrived outside the house.

Someone coaxed me away from her body and guided me into another room so that the paramedics could examine her. It wasn't really necessary; anyone could see she was dead and had been in that state for some time, but procedures have to be followed. It's the same in every profession.

Before I leave the subject altogether there is something I wanted to mention, specifically about the very last time I held Ligeia in my arms. It is weird. It was her – I know that because even with her horribly discoloured face I could recognise her... her hair... her body... her features – yet it wasn't.

The body I cradled while I waited for the emergency services to arrive was cold, stiff and unresponsive; it was no more than an abandoned vehicle, a vacant shell, the useless remnant of a life that had once touched the lives of so many others, mine included. The spark – whatever that was – that had enabled that inert mass of human cells to be so much more than the sum of its millions upon millions of individual parts had departed.

Whatever miraculous energy she had possessed was gone, transforming my once warm, vibrant, vivacious, gloriously audacious, gorgeous, beautiful, familiar, kind Ligeia into the cold, lifeless, fleshy husk I held and felt in my arms. That energy was no longer in the room, although I swear I could smell the faint odour of its discharge in the air, like the scent of spent electricity that sometimes remains after a thunderstorm.

I was questioned gently by the police at first. They wanted to know her full name, what my relationship with her had been, if she had any family. All the usual enquiries, I imagined. But then they found the knife.

The questioning became terser and more formal then, and less considerate towards my feelings. I told them simply that I'd used the blade to cut her free. It didn't appear to allay the suspicions that were rapidly forming in the questioning officer's mind. My role as a possible suspect lasted until the results of the post mortem were released, although I still felt that, generally, my version of the events surrounding the discovery of Ligeia was disbelieved. Of course, that might have just been a symptom of the depression that followed.

Janice and I separated shortly before the coroner's hearing. The whole affair was brought to Janice's attention in the aftermath of Ligeia's death, although she told me she had suspected my infidelity during the Paris trip. Apparently, in a stupefyingly uncharacteristic display of concern, Heather Mallory had telephoned during my 'sickness' to enquire how I was. I'd told my colleagues I was ill and I'd told my wife that I was away on a preparatory senior leadership course. It explained the frantic texts I received.

She filed for divorce two weeks later. I didn't contest it; there was no point. Our marriage was dying a long time before I ever met Ligeia.

The coroner returned a verdict of misadventure, which was a cruel joke of sorts because Ligeia always maintained that she was in control of everything, including her relationship with me. It was all carefully weighed up, planned, explored and calculated – except her death. According to the coroner, she had died the previous evening and had been hanging there all that night and most of the next day – until I cut her down.

My poor Ligeia: always searching, always pushing against the boundaries of existence, ever striving to exceed the limits of her experience. It appeared nothing was ultimately capable of satisfying her. She had joined an ever-widening group of unfortunate (or unlucky) ex-participants of autoerotic asphyxiation.

The police said it had been a mistake to cut her down. In retrospect, I suppose it would have made their job easier – but not mine. I would have to live with the image for the rest of my life. I didn't want to remember her that way, trussed up, suspended almost in mid-air by a slender cord. That's why I did it. I cut her down, perhaps in the hope that there was some vestige of life left in her. But it had gone. Departed. I cradled her body, aware that it was no longer her, just cold flesh, limbs and muscles stiff, face black, tongue protruding, eyes wide yet sightless.

It's odd. I never believed the Calipha. I always thought the crazy witch doctor, or whatever the fuck he was, had got it wrong when he told us that our destinies – Ligeia's and mine – were inexorably interlinked. Ligeia is gone but I am still here, and this would normally be proof positive that it is and *was* all just horseshit. Yet… maybe he was right after all and it was my interpretation of his words that was wrong.

Like most people, I guess I had always thought of our being in purely physical terms. I believed that when we depart this life, that is it. All that remains are the memories that stay with those who survive us; the only tangible things are our offspring, or whatever meagre achievement we manage to leave in our wake. As regards destiny, it was my rather uninformed opinion that it could not exist without human interaction. I mean, what good are rules if there is nothing or nobody to obey them?

It was only in the face of the insurmountable loss I suffered in the weeks and months after Ligeia's death that I came to realise that what I thought the Calipha had said wasn't what he actually meant. Only now do I understand that destiny is not a physical thing. It is not linked to our physical existence but is actually essence or ether. I know this because Ligeia and I have continued to move forward together, her destiny linked to mine. Inspired by that belief, I became absorbed in my writing.

My first novel, *Dominion*, was published six months

ago. If you haven't read it (or at least seen it on the shelves of Sainsbury's or ASDA) or read reviews praising it or slamming it, or become thoroughly sick of seeing the cover on billboards and in magazines or of hearing minor TV celebrities discussing it on daytime television then you are similarly dead. It became the UK's number one bestselling fictional whatever three weeks after it was launched. It made the US bestseller list a month later.

As I write this, there are ongoing discussions with my agent for the film rights, although it's early days. Apparently, Danny Boyle and Lars von Trier have been mentioned as possible directors of what has been described as a major Hollywood adaptation.

I have already been approached to write a sequel but where could I go with that? Instead, I have considered putting together a book of the photographs I took during our time together, not of her obviously (although I suppose one or two wouldn't hurt) but of the places that inspired us and caught us up in their wondrous majesty. I could combine my photos with some of her poems, those that were never published. It is certainly something worth thinking about.

★ ★ ★

Gone

Last night

I dreamt of other times, of halcyon days
Where love entranced me in its ways
And death was nothing more than a dream
A shadow banished by our schemes

Those days

Stretched out before me, long and luxurious
The summer sun, so warm and glorious
When I nestled in my lover's arms
So comforting, safe and free from harm

The world

Stopped dead and we alone existed
Lost to her, my soul resisted
The inevitability of time, always, ever marching on
Though I was blind, till she was gone

No more

Her eyes, her sweet and tender kiss
Upon my lips, such other things I miss:
Her naked warmth 'gainst me at night
With one embrace foul dreams took flight

A hollow

Space inside my heart, an indentation in the bed
Memories alone cannot revive the dead
Darkness now returns and time moves on
The days are short, the summer warmth has gone

The shadows

Gather in the corners of this old home
A place fit for none, though where spirits roam
And day is replaced by everlasting night
Where dreams of her are lost from sight

Trak E Sumisu

My flesh

Now so soft and thin, a parchment over bones
My hands had knuckles, now replaced by stones
Unable to grasp, unable now to hold on
Soon my days here too will be done

Kingdom come

Though I know it not, oblivious to my own fate
It was not my wish to die alone, consumed by hate
At God, merciful God who stole my love from me
And opened my eyes so I might see

At last

The world, the wheel of time revolving
My love replaced by other lovers, life evolving
And breath escapes from me, a weary sigh
Though thankfully oblivious that this is my

Last night

Epilogue

That was that.

Except it wasn't.

Exactly nine months, to the day, after Ligeia's death, I was contacted by TV celebrity psychic David Quartermaine. Apparently incensed by what he considered to be unfair and prejudicial publicity regarding the fraudulent nature of spiritualists, mediums and psychics – a direct result, he insisted, of my personal views influencing readers of my novel and a disproportionate amount of bad publicity that gathered momentum every time I had been interviewed on prime-time TV – he challenged me to take part as 'guest of honour' in an evening of what he referred to as 'genuine' spirit communication.

It was to be broadcast live on Channel 4 (after the watershed) to an estimated UK audience of between five million and eight million viewers; not a massive amount, to be sure, but *I* think it reflected the niche appeal. The intention was for Quartermaine to prove to me, and to other sceptics around the world, that communication from beyond the grave or with the spirit domain was not only possible but also completely credible. Confronted with such a fabulous opportunity to expose the idiocy of the man, I of course accepted the invitation, much to the alarm of both my agent and my publicist.

They maintained that such exposure could potentially be counterproductive to my rapidly expanding reputation as a writer. They believed that if communication was possible or if it was achieved (or maybe only *seen* to be possible), it would have disastrous consequences for *Dominion* and any of my subsequent literary works.

It was emphasised that Quartermaine – star of previously sensational smash hit TV specials such as *Memento Mori* and *Post Mortem* (whose titles were far too similar, in my opinion) – was such an established personality that the public would tune in to watch him prove the existence of the afterlife and have little sympathy for me or my views.

Bring it on, I told them, reminding them both of all those who had attempted to do the same and how it had always ended in abject failure. I explained how Harry Houdini left significant funds to ensure that every year, on the anniversary of his death, an attempt would be made to contact him in the hereafter. Because the world was shocked by the untimely death of the escapologist, some attempts were broadcast live on the American wireless service. Houdini said that if there were a way back, a way to return and communicate beyond the grave, he would find it. No such contact ever occurred.

I emphasised that I was not an expert in life after death and that my opinions were based on my own experiences. As far as I was concerned, that was more than adequate. Nothing I had encountered in my life, from Emily's prophetic utterances about Watty's demise, and the similar oracular bullshit spouted by the Calipha in Paris, to the events that manifested immediately after Ligeia's death, could destroy my faith that fuck all awaited us after we die. It was unshakeable.

I dismissed all the reservations expressed by my advisors, and a date was set. Quartermaine became more and more enthusiastic about the proposed show with each day that passed. It seemed hardly a week went by without him putting in an appearance on one show or another.

I will say one thing for the fraudster: he knew how to drum up publicity. Social media became his empire and his tweets were retweeted perpetually by his fans and loyal followers. The same did not apply to me. I was wheeled out a couple of times to proffer my own viewpoint on the rapidly approaching show and I'm glad to report that it did my book sales no harm whatsoever.

Interestingly, Quartermaine developed an increasingly vehement stance about the slur on his craft (as he called it) and the professionalism of his fellow psychics by me, whom he dismissively referred to as 'a former school teacher'. He even threatened to bring 'the wrath of the undead' down upon me if I did not withdraw some of the comments I'd made. I simply ignored him. The daily papers picked up on this and sensationalised the argument, promoting it as though it were a preamble by world-class boxers limbering up for a championship fight. It only served to ensure that Quartermaine's projected audience increased significantly, as did the advertising revenue for all the tabloids that ran with the story.

It seemed the country – at least those that actually cared – were divided into two camps: those who read the *Daily Mail* and the *Daily Express* and those who preferred the *Daily Mirror* and the *Sun*. The readers of the former newspapers had adopted me as a type of defender of their religious and moral standards, while the readership of the other papers wanted to see me humbled before the 'mystic and marvellous' Quartermaine for daring to question the unknowable. It was reported that my public humiliation by Quartermaine and his cohort of loyal believers would be a pivotal event in British television history.

Yawn.

In the days before the event I began writing the first chapters of my next book. It was to be a horror thriller, in the same vein as the worryingly burgeoning plethora of lost ancient artefact novels, although mine would be set in locations as diverse as Paris (and Père Lachaise, once again), London, nineteenth-century Yugoslavia/ Herzegovina and Venice. It was at that time untitled. Remarkably, considering the distractions going on around me, I managed to maintain incredible focus and the words (or prose) simply flowed from me. I estimated that I could stretch it to around 136,000 words and that I would almost definitely have it completed within six months.

Oh, I forgot to mention, the title of the Quartermaine special was *From Beyond the Grave* – a very melodramatic title and one that was fairly self-explanatory. That did not stop the host from taking out a full-page advertisement in all the tabloids, however, explaining what he hoped to achieve and, more importantly, why.

Those of you who remember the catastrophic episode being broadcast will no doubt recall the title music, Danse Macabre, Opus 40, by Camille Saint-Saëns, which was intended to set the scene for David Quartermaine's flamboyant entrance in a casket borne into the studio by a horse-drawn hearse. However, none of you will be aware of what transpired behind the scenes immediately before the show went on air until now.

Risking injunctions and court action, owing to the binding legislation of a non-disclosure agreement I was forced to sign by the show's producers and their lawyers, is something I really don't care too much about now. My defence is that I was led to believe that the show would be broadcast as 'an honest exploration of the true phenomena of spiritualism' and that it would not involve any special effects, trickery or contrived audience participation. With that in mind, I feel it is more important that the truth is known, regardless of how that might affect my standing in the public's perception or the reputation of David Quartermaine.

IN AGREEMENT WITH THE PUBLISHER AND THE AUTHOR, THE FOLLOWING SECTION HAS BEEN OMITTED FROM THIS EDITION OF THE PUBLICATION, PENDING THE OUTCOME OF LEGAL PROCEEDINGS.

IN AGREEMENT WITH THE PUBLISHER AND THE AUTHOR, THE FOLLOWING SECTION HAS BEEN OMITTED FROM THIS EDITION OF THE PUBLICATION, PENDING THE OUTCOME OF LEGAL PROCEEDINGS.

IN AGREEMENT WITH THE PUBLISHER AND THE AUTHOR, THE FOLLOWING SECTION HAS BEEN OMITTED FROM THIS EDITION OF THE PUBLICATION, PENDING THE OUTCOME OF LEGAL PROCEEDINGS.

And this time, that really was that.

I regret nothing. In conclusion, although the truth, that bastion of our personal morality, is often described as 'stranger than fiction' it is stranger still than our very best (and worst) imaginings. At least Ligeia can now finally rest in peace.

Requiescat in Pace.

END

CPR: Conditional Positive Regard

By Trak E Sumisu

Do as thou wilt...

Matthew Stent is an unconventional therapist, whose insight into the damaged lives of his clients has become unhealthily voyeuristic.

As he charts his life and the lives of others through a series of often brutal encounters and acerbic observations, his dubious moral compass leads him further and further from accepted normality and towards an altogether darker, unprofessional and more dangerous path.

When he becomes infatuated with Terri, the wife of his latest client, Matthew's life takes an unexpected twist that leads him on a journey to the mystic heart of England to meet the enigmatic Wiccan High Priest Tobias Greylock, and the shocking discovery that reality is more fragile than anything he could have ever imagined.

The first sensational volume of the CPR trilogy

Available from Fast-Print Publishing:
ISBN 978-178035-613-6
and selected suppliers worldwide, also available as a download from Amazon, Apple and other renowned online e-book retailers.